Making You
MINE

The Bradens & Montgomerys
(Pleasant Hill – Oak Falls)

Love in Bloom Series

Melissa Foster

ISBN-13: 978-1-948868-25-9
ISBN-10: 1-948868-25-3

Cover Design: Elizabeth Mackey Designs
Cover Photography: Sara Eirew

WORLD LITERARY PRESS
PRINTED IN THE UNITED STATES OF AMERICA

A Note to Readers

If this is your first Love in Bloom book, all of my love stories are written to stand alone, so dive right in and enjoy the fun, sexy ride! If you are an avid reader of series, you might remember meeting Aubrey Stewart in *Anything for Love* and meeting her hunky hero, Knox Bentley, in *Trails of Love*. Separately, Aubrey and Knox are two stubborn, fun, and sexy characters—but together they're *combustible*! For those of you who follow my Ladies Who Write (LWW) author group, you know we have created an entire LWW fictional world. Aubrey is one of three women who owns LWW Enterprises. She is such close friends with our beloved Montgomerys and Charlotte Sterling, I knew the Braden-Montgomery world wouldn't be complete without her and Knox's story. I hope you adore their journey as much as I enjoyed writing it.

The best way to keep up to date with new releases, sales, and exclusive content is to sign up for my newsletter or to download my free app.

www.MelissaFoster.com/news

www.MelissaFoster.com/app

About the Love in Bloom Big-Family Romance Collection

The Bradens & Montgomerys is just one of the series in the Love in Bloom big-family romance collection. Each Love in Bloom book is written to be enjoyed as a stand-alone novel or as part of the larger series, and characters from each series make appearances in future books, so you never miss an engagement, wedding, or birth. A complete list of all series titles is included at the end of this book, along with previews of upcoming publications.

Visit the Love in Bloom Reader Goodies page for downloadable checklists, family trees, and more!
www.MelissaFoster.com/RG

About the Ladies Who Write (LWW)

I am part of a fantastic group of romance authors called the Ladies Who Write (LWW), and we have created a fun, sexy world just for you! *Making You Mine* and *Anything for Love* are both set in the LWW world as well as the Braden-Montgomery world. In these books you will meet several other members of LWW, each of whom will have their own book written by me and the other authors of LWW. You'll also find LWW connections in other books I have written, such as *Embracing Her Heart*. I love connecting characters and worlds, so there will be many more LWW stories to come.

For more information on our group and to stay up to date on the release of LWW books, visit www.LadiesWhoWrite.com and sign up for our newsletter.

Chapter One

AUBREY AWOKE TO the bold, sensual scents of Oud Wood cologne and *sex*. Her fingers played over the expensive hotel sheets as she soaked in the rugged aroma of her post-charity-event hotel hookup, Knox Bentley. Eyes closed, she reveled in the weight of his strong arm around her middle and the feel of his arousal against her bottom as he spooned her.

Spooned?

Her eyes flew open. She was *not* a *spooner*. Spooning was far more intimate than sex. Spooning implied a deeper connection—the big spoon's desire to protect the little spoon. As one of the founders of Ladies Who Write Enterprises, a multimedia conglomerate, and the head of the film and television department, self-made billionaire Aubrey Stewart did *not* need protecting. Except maybe from her dangerously beautiful, too-cocky-for-his-own-good fuck buddy currently growing harder as he snuggled closer, making seductive noises that sent her pulse into a frenzy.

God…

Knox pressed his warm lips to her shoulder and rolled her onto her back, gazing heatedly into her eyes. Shivers of desire swept through her. It was ridiculous how little it took for him to get her going. A hungry sound, a whiff of his expensive cologne. Even a glimpse of that sinful look in his caramel eyes made her stomach flip-flop like a teenager's. Each of those things sparked the promise of dark pleasures, but combined they did her in every damn time.

She had a million things to accomplish this week before the winter storm that was brewing found its way up the coast, and his big, strong hand sliding down her thigh wasn't helping her get out the door any quicker.

"I have no idea what happens to me at charity events. I can't believe we did this *again*," she said breathily, trying to wiggle away before she got all caught up in him and her plans for the day went to hell.

He squeezed her thigh, keeping her just where he wanted her as a slow grin spread across his face. "I happen to you, babe. How can you resist all this?" He motioned toward his deliciously hard, naked body. "But really, we should come as no surprise." He brushed his scruff along her cheek and whispered, "We've been hooking up after charity and other business events for more than two years. Don't pretend it's only after charity events. Some people might call that dating."

"Maybe in *your* world."

She'd given up on dating long ago. Men were either intimidated by her success, too boring, or too dimwitted to keep up with her. And when it came to sex, though she'd never let Knox know it, he'd pretty much ruined her for any other man. She'd nearly lost her mind when he'd gone to Belize for business and ended up staying there for a few *months*.

"Two years? It hasn't been that long." *Has it?* She mentally filtered back to the first time they'd met, and damn...he was right. She'd met the rebellious billionaire at another charity function. Rumor had it that as the son of Griffin Bentley, a leading venture capitalist and real estate mogul, Knox had been groomed to take over his father's financial ventures from the time he was a child. He was known in elite circles for his eco-friendly business endeavors, hefty donations to children's charities—and for his determined and blatant separation from his family's businesses. Aubrey knew all about separating from a family's legacy, though hers was very different. Her middle-class roots ran deep in Port Hudson, New York, where her father coached football at Boyer University and her mother was still the *hostess with the mostest*, attending and celebrating the local high school and college sporting events and hosting after-parties even though all their children were grown. With two older brothers who were named after football stars and now played in the NFL, it was hard for her to escape being known as *the girl in the football family.*

She loved her family and she loved sports, but as a teenager she'd dreamed of blazing a path to break away and prove herself. That commonality was what had first intrigued her about Knox. Well, that and his crazy-good looks, wicked sense of humor, and after that first night, his sexual prowess…

He nipped at her jaw, bringing her mind back to the present and to his hand creeping up her thigh. "I've got to get out of here. I have resorts to check out for an upcoming movie production."

"As I recall, *Mrs. Robinson* didn't rush things along."

She scowled at him. "You're only four years younger than me. Give it up."

His fingertips brushed over the apex of her thighs, drawing a needy sigh from her lungs. "Babe, you know I don't have a problem giving it up. As I recall, I gave it up, down, and practically inside out several times last night."

Babe? That was new. She let it slide, sidetracked by the fact that she couldn't even blame last night on alcohol. She hadn't gotten hammered since college. Besides, with Knox she liked being fully present so she could experience every single incredible second of their passion.

He lowered his head, pressing his warm, soft lips to her breast. She sighed, closing her eyes as he lulled her under his spell. He was such a talented and generous lover, she allowed herself just a few more minutes of his deliciousness before giving herself over to the real world again.

"That's more like it," he said huskily.

He sucked her breast into his mouth, roughly grazing his teeth over the taut peak. She couldn't suppress a moan at the shock of pain and pleasure slicing through her. She needed to get out of that bed or she'd never get around to seeing the resorts her assistant, Becca, had scouted for her. Upstate New York could be dicey in late January, and there was a cold front moving through. Just as she closed her eyes to gather the strength and break their connection, Knox rubbed his hard shaft against her thigh, and her traitorous hips greedily rose for more.

Her phone vibrated on the bedside table, breaking the spell. She moved his hands and threw her legs over the edge of the bed with a loud sigh. He chuckled as she reached for her phone—and he reached for her. He wrapped his arms around her middle, trailing kisses along her hips and back.

"Seriously? It's Sunday, Ms. Workaholic," he said as she opened Becca's text.

"I've got several days of resort hopping ahead of me, starting today, and I can't put it off. Next Sunday's the Super Bowl. My parents are having a huge party, and I don't want to miss it."

"Hm. Sounds fun. Want some company?"

One of his hands delved between her legs, while the other cupped her breast, making it difficult for her to focus. "Knox..." Even she heard the wavering plea for more in her voice.

Ridiculous.

She forced herself to read Becca's message. *Want me to cancel today's resort meetings so you can lose yourself in that hot piece of ass and come back tomorrow sated and smiling?*

No! she texted back as Knox did his best to drive her out of her freaking mind. She never should have admitted to Becca that she'd connected with Knox, but her overly attentive assistant had noticed a difference in her, which she'd called *Post-Knox Aubrey*, in the days after they'd first hooked up. She'd had to fess up or deal with Becca's unrelenting inquisition.

Becca's response was immediate. *Can you see me rolling my eyes? Everyone knows you and Knox hooked up last night. Presley and Libby told me to cancel your appts even though they knew you'd have a fit. I deserve a raise for at least asking.*

Aubrey and Knox had never been secretive about hooking up, and her business partners and best friends, Presley Cabot, who ran the publishing arm of LWW, and Libby Warren, the director of the philanthropic division, had been at the event last night. Of course they knew about their hookup. But they also knew her well enough to realize she'd never put off work for a man.

And yes, Becca deserved a raise, all right, but not for asking about changing her schedule. She was efficient, had an impeccable work ethic, and best of all, she could handle Aubrey's tough standards with a sense of humor. Her only downfalls were that she was hot as sin, which meant every male client paid more attention to Becca than to business, *and* she knew Aubrey too well. She could tell when Aubrey had gone too long without having her *bell* chimed.

And…she knew the best remedy.

The man who was currently covering her phone with one hand and pulling her into a scorching-hot kiss with the other.

When they finally came up for air Aubrey said, "I've really got to go."

"You could give a guy a complex forgoing his cock for a phone."

"Can your cock check out resorts for me? Because that might get me very interested," she said playfully, and leaned up to press her lips to his. He really was beautiful, with thick dark hair and kind, sexy light brown eyes that could smolder so hot they could light panties on fire or emote professionalism so perfectly they could charm unheard of deals from the savviest businessmen. His manicured scruff might look too pretty on another man, but Knox was rugged enough to pull it off. His rebelliousness and killer smile were the jewels in his crown, giving him a unique edge others didn't possess.

As he lowered his lips to hers, she put her hand on his chest and said, "Shower. We have to multitask."

He chuckled as they headed for the shower. While the water heated up, she told him about each of the resorts she was checking out between Virginia and New York over the next few days.

"Don't you have minions to do that legwork for you?"

"Usually," she said as she stuck her hand into the shower and tested the temperature, thinking, not for the first time, that Knox was the only man she'd ever showered with. Well, besides that one guy in college, but that hardly counted. They were both drunk and fully clothed. At least at first. "But this is for my very best friend in the whole world, erotic-romance author Charlotte Sterling. She's an LWW girl, too, and she wrote a book inspired by her and her fiancé's courtship called *Anything for Love*. We're making it into a movie for our new Me Time channel. I want to check the potential filming locations out for myself and make sure they're perfect."

They stepped into the shower. His arms came around her, his slick body hard and enticing at once.

"The Charlotte you grew up with who lost her entire family while you were in college?"

She froze. "How do you know that?" After losing her parents in a plane crash and then losing her last surviving relative, the grandfather she adored, Charlotte had holed up in the family's estate, which had once been run as an inn. She'd found solace in writing and had remained at the inn ever since, but Aubrey couldn't remember ever telling Knox about her.

"Babe, there's not much I don't know about you. You talk a lot after sex."

"Since when do you call me *babe*, and I do *not* talk a lot after sex."

"Since *now*, and you do. How else would I know you and Charlotte bonded with Presley and Libby over your mutual love of writing in college? Or that you all hated the drama of sororities and started an LWW *sisterhood*, which is really just a fancy name for *sorority*?" He grabbed her ass, bringing her even closer as warm water rained down over them. "And that LWW now owns the sorority house where your *sisterhood* began. I swear you LWW girls are everywhere."

"Yes, we own the house, and it still runs as a sisterhood, not a *sorority*, thank you very much. Girls who are interested in writing in any medium—bloggers, authors, screenplay writers—can pledge. We're going to take over the world one day. But I'm not a talker, which means you've stalked me." She cupped his balls and said, "Spill it, or lose them."

He pushed his fingers between her legs, instantly finding the magical spot that sent her up on her toes. "Now, why would you want to do that? You love what my body does for you." He kissed her neck. "You *are* chatty. In your post-orgasmic haze your lips get a little loose. Besides, I like to know who I'm sleeping with. Is that a crime? And I'm pretty sure *your* Charlotte is engaged to my business partner's brother."

She closed her eyes for a second as he teased her breathless. "I forgot Graham Braden was the other B in B&B Enterprises."

"Just don't ask us which B comes first. It might cause a brawl."

"Guys are so competitive." She opened her eyes and said, "So you knew my Char was your friend Beau's fiancée?"

"I knew they were engaged, and I *thought* she was your Charlotte. You know," he said as he nibbled on her neck, "I'm familiar with the Sterling House, the property where they met and fell in love, and none of the resorts you mentioned are rural enough to measure up."

She poked his chest and said, "I think I know what's best for my clients."

"We'll see." His hands glided down her hips, and he kissed her again. "I'm meeting Graham and his wife, Morgyn, later this month in New York City for dinner. You should come with me."

"Like a double date? No thanks. Let's just get back to you touching me."

"I'm not sure how much I like this dirty-little-secret thing we've turned into."

"It's worked so far." She smiled and took a step back as she said, "I could shower alone." Thank God for birth control, because they'd have to buy stock in condoms if they went that route.

He frowned, but in the next breath his hand moved down her slick belly, over the belly button ring she'd gotten on a dare in college, and he drew her close again. "Must be stressful for Beau, having an erotic romance writer as a fiancée. Nothing like trying to measure up to fictional sex. I wonder if she fakes it."

"*Please.* Beau is the real deal. A woman may be able to fake a few orgasms, but there is no faking the look of an orgasm-induced coma."

"Is that a challenge?" He flashed an arrogant smile as his thumb began teasing over her most sensitive area. "But don't kid yourself, sweetheart." He rained kisses down her neck. "You do talk a lot after sex. I know all about your Cheetos fixation and love of eighties movies, that business deal gone bad with the asshole producer, and that you had a massive crush on Tom Selleck when you were a teenager."

Her eyes fluttered closed. She didn't care what he knew, as long as he continued his masterful ministrations. He slid down her body, caressing and tasting, tugging on her belly button ring with his teeth, teasing it with his tongue. Her entire body felt like one raw nerve, and when he finally put his mouth exactly where she needed it, she leaned back against the tile wall, giving in to her desires.

"That's my girl. Now, stop worrying about what you told me and let me show you what else I know about you."

And he did...*several* times.

AFTER THE BEST damn shower since New Year's Day—when he and Aubrey had last woken up together following an insatiable night spent tangled up in each other's arms—Knox stood before the bathroom mirror in his slacks and open black button-down, wondering how in the hell he could be sated but not satisfied. He watched Aubrey in the mirror as she brushed her teeth. Her black pencil skirt hugged her curves, and the lace bra she wore begged to be ripped off. Long golden tendrils hung loose and a little wavy over her shoulders. He could still feel the silky strands between his fingers and brushing over his chest. There was a time when he'd been sated *and* satisfied the mornings after he and Aubrey had been together. He'd been fine with their no-strings-attached hookups. But over the past several months, he'd been thinking about her more often, wondering who she was with and what she was doing in between their hookups, what the parts of her life that he hadn't experienced with her were like. Hell, he'd even begun texting her between hookups, wanting to keep their connection going long after they left their hotel rooms.

She rinsed her mouth and leaned one hip on the sink. "Why do you look like you're trying to puzzle out world peace?"

He hauled her against him. Her amber eyes flamed with heat, but she instantly grew rigid, placing a hand on his chest.

"Down, big guy. I've got a schedule to keep."

She was the fiercest businesswoman he'd ever known, and he respected the hell out of her. The trouble was, she was also the most sensual, passionate creature on earth, and he couldn't get her out of his mind. Not even when he'd gone to Belize with

Graham last fall to kick off an investment project. But Graham had brought Morgyn along, and they'd tied the knot while they were there. They were so happy and in love, it only made Knox think of what he wanted with Aubrey even more. He'd remained overseas long after Graham had returned home, hoping to shake the unfamiliar emotions, but nothing had dimmed his desire to be with her. They clicked as friends, lovers, and in business. They were a perfect match, and she'd not only gotten under his skin, she'd also burrowed into his heart, something no woman had ever accomplished. Not for lack of trying on their part. He liked his traveling, no-strings-attached lifestyle, though Aubrey was changing that. He enjoyed every minute they spent together, and it went far deeper than sex. But she was like the deal he couldn't make, the most precious jewel even his billions couldn't buy.

"Let's go on a real date," he suggested. If she'd just slow down enough, she'd realize how good they could be together, too.

She pushed out of his arms, avoiding eye contact as she dug around in her makeup bag. "What is it with you? First it's *babe* this and *babe* that, and now you're asking me out? Do you want me to make you my grandmother's *love cookies*, too?"

"Hey, sounds good to me."

She rolled her eyes. "That's one recipe I'll never make. They're supposed to be made only for your one true love and all that nonsense. I don't have time for drama in my life, Knox, and neither do you. It's why we get along so well."

She opened her lipstick and leaned closer to the mirror as she applied it. Why the hell did he enjoy watching her do that? And *why* couldn't he stop wondering how many other men had stood where he was? He gritted his teeth and buttoned his shirt, trying not to ask the question that would make him seem pathetic.

"What?" She looked at him out of the corner of her eyes.

"You tell me." He rolled his shoulders back and ran his hand through his hair. When she said nothing, he tried a softer approach and put his arms gently around her, drawing her closer again. "We're great together, Aubrey. Why not take it out of the bedroom? Give it the weight it deserves. No drama, just dinner."

She sighed. "We had dinner at the event last night."

"Yeah, with about two hundred other people. I mean just the two of us."

"Knox…"

He pressed his lips to hers, the hell with her freshly applied lipstick. If he couldn't talk sense into her, he'd remind her how good they were together in other ways. She returned the kiss but was still holding back. He took the kiss deeper until she went soft in his arms. And then he intensified it even more, grabbing her ass and holding her against his hardness. Her fingers dug into his shirt the way he'd come to adore when she wanted more.

He lifted her onto the counter and slid his hands along her thighs, taking hold of her panties. "Tell me to stop, Aub, and I will."

She panted, her eyelids at half-mast, lipstick smeared over her plump lips. "I hate you right now for making me late." She lifted up, allowing him to take her panties off.

He wedged himself between her legs and said, "Sure you do." He brushed his thumb under her lower lip, wiping off the smeared lipstick, and then he kissed her again, slow and sensual. As their lips parted, he trapped her lower lip between his teeth, giving it a taunting tug. He knew his lips were smeared with lipstick too, but he didn't care. The greedy look in her eyes was what he craved.

She started unbuttoning his shirt, and he pressed his hand over hers, stopping her. Her brows knitted.

"We're good together," he said again. "Say yes to one date."

Her brows rose in amusement. "Knox Bentley, are you saying no to sex unless you get a date?"

Damn. Was he? "Just say yes, Aubrey."

"No," she said with a seriously *hot* look in her eyes. "I won't be blackmailed."

"I think you know me better than that." He took a step back, and she hooked her finger into the waistband of his slacks, pulling him closer. "Change your mind?"

"No." She pushed her hand down the front of his pants, palming his erection. "I'm hoping to change yours."

"Fuck, Aubrey. You know I want you."

"That's what I like to hear. Now, how about you show me how much before I run out of time."

He dropped his pants and said, "How long are you going to hide behind that excuse?"

"About ten more minutes, if I'm lucky."

She slipped off the counter, wrapping her legs around his waist, her body swallowing him to the root. Their mouths crashed together, hips thrusting and grinding. She pushed her hands into his hair, pulling just hard enough to cause a sting of pain, shooting heat to his core. He drove into her faster, harder, as they ate at each other's mouths. Her legs tightened around him, and he slowed his efforts the way he knew drove her wild. Using his shoulders for leverage, she moved with him, clinging and moaning into their kisses as he took her to the brink of oblivion and held her there.

She tore her mouth away long enough to plead, "Come with me—"

She didn't have to ask twice. He sent them both soaring, and his name sailed from her lips like a chant. "Knox, Knox, *Knox*—"

Music to his ears.

When she collapsed in his arms, her heart thundering against his as she rested her cheek on his shoulder, she said, "God, we're good at that."

"We're good at everything, Aubrey. One day you'll see what's right in front of you."

She lifted her head with a coy smile and said, "Don't you mean *inside* me?"

"No, babe." He brushed her hair from her eyes and said, "I've got a hell of a lot more to offer than amazing sex."

Chapter Two

AUBREY WAS SITTING at her desk late Friday afternoon, scouring resort websites, when Presley and Libby sauntered into her office. Libby carried a bottle of wine, and Presley carried three glasses. The three of them were different in many ways, but they'd clicked from the first moment they'd met, and their bond was strong as steel. Just the sight of them made the tightness in Aubrey's chest relax. She'd spent every minute since leaving Knox Sunday morning visiting resorts and trying to charm resort owners, to no avail.

"Thank God the cavalry has arrived," she said as Presley set the glasses on her desk. "I swear I'm ready to ask Charlotte to change her mind about filming the movie at her resort, and I know that's the last thing she wants to do."

Presley lowered herself gracefully into one of two plush leather chairs in front of Aubrey's desk and crossed her long legs, holding up her glass. "Fill 'er up, Libs."

With her vibrant burgundy hair and love of everything designer, Presley always looked like a million bucks. She was a shrewd professional, but beneath her posh exterior was a sensitive woman who had spent years battling her weight, until after college graduation, when she'd dedicated herself to becoming healthier. Aubrey, Libby, and their friend and personal trainer, Trinity, had been with her every step of the way. Presley had always been beautiful, but strength looked amazing on her, and it carried over into every aspect of her life. In addition to Charlotte, Presley was Aubrey's go-to friend for no-bullshit answers. Presley didn't coddle. She gave it to her like it was—the good, the bad, and the ugly. Aubrey was happy for her friend's newfound love, Nolan Banks, who adored everything about her and treated her like gold.

"My pleasure." Libby, the demurest of their trio, was the caretaker. She'd lost her brother to spina bifida and honored him by running the Wish Network, one of the state's most successful charities. She was the sensible, strong, silent type, and when she spoke, everyone listened.

Libby tucked her wavy brown hair behind her ear, turning a soft gaze to Aubrey, and said, "I checked with Treat Braden, one of our largest donors. You met him at the Christmas party with his wife, Max. He owns several resorts."

"Yes, I remember. I asked if he'd played basketball because he was so tall."

"That's him," Libby said. "He said you can use any of his resorts; just say the word. But he didn't seem to have any that were as secluded as you'd like. He's putting out a few feelers for you, though."

"Thanks, Libby. It's a hard location to find, but it's even harder to find a place that's willing to close down during filming." She took a sip of her wine. "Why couldn't Char have fallen in love at a busy inn instead of one that no longer functioned as a resort?"

Charlotte had lived in her family's inn ever since losing her grandfather—her last living relative—right after college graduation. Before Beau came into her life, Charlotte had rarely left her office, spending all her time crafting her novels. They were getting married in June and had begun renovations with plans to reopen the inn. Charlotte seemed happier than ever, but she didn't want to have the movie filmed at the place she called home. She didn't want that type of attention, and frankly, Aubrey didn't blame her.

Libby settled into a chair and said, "Too bad we don't have the budget to build a set for the inn, like you're planning for Snow White's cottage."

Like Charlotte, her great-grandmother had loved fairy tales. Charlotte's great-grandfather had replicated Snow White's cottage on the grounds of the inn, and her great-grandparents had lived there. Beau was renovating that cottage for him and Charlotte to live in. Aubrey knew it would be impossible to find anything remotely similar to the unique cottage, which was why they were building their own for the movie.

"Where would we build an *inn?*" Aubrey asked. "Besides, this is for Char. It needs to be *perfect*. I'm just going to keep plugging away until I nail it down." She had to work fast. They needed to pin down the location and secure the filming dates within the next ninety days or they risked losing their lead actors. *No pressure or anything.*

"I knew it would be a massive undertaking. Have you tried sweet-talking one of the resort owners?" Libby suggested.

Presley scoffed, eyeing Aubrey with amusement over the rim of her glass.

"Like I'd ever lower myself to *that?* Hell no, Libs."

"I've gone through all my connections," Presley said. "Nolan said he'd ask Carter to see if he knew anyone." Carter was Nolan's very competitive brother. He and Nolan had both worked in finance, with high-profile clients, prior to following their passions and opening a pub and brewery in Port Hudson.

"That's mighty big of him, asking Carter for help," Aubrey said. "Then again, the man would do anything for you."

Becca rushed into the office like a whirlwind, carrying a giant bouquet of Cheetos and peach roses. She set it on Aubrey's desk and placed her hands on her hips, surveying their drinks. She embraced her hourglass figure—and fashion from every era. Today she was rocking a seventies minidress with swirls of purple, yellow, orange, white, and aqua. She wore white knee-high boots, and her long blond hair was ironed pin straight and pulled back with a matching colorful headband. From her ears dangled enormous gold peace signs. She was also a graduate of Boyer, and though she was younger than Aubrey and her friends, she'd been an LWW sister, too.

"Sorry to interrupt, but this just arrived. Drink up, ladies, because there's more to this little delivery ensemble." Becca turned and sashayed out of the office.

"What the heck is *that*?" Aubrey stood and fished out the card.

"Looks like someone knows you pretty well," Presley said. "Libs?"

Libby held her hand up. "Don't look at me."

Aubrey silently read the card. *All the resorts sucked, huh? Figured you needed this today. Knox.* "I'm going to kill Becca."

"Who's it from?" Libby came to her side and read the card. "Oh, Mr. Bentley sure does know you."

"Becca Nunnally, get your pretty little ass in here," Aubrey hollered.

Becca hurried in carrying two six-packs of Stewart's Orange 'n Cream soda, Aubrey's favorite. She set them on the desk and said, "Sorry. These came, too, and one more thing." She stepped out of the office and returned carrying a gift-wrapped box tied with a pretty gold bow and handed it to Aubrey. "Now, you were about to yell at me?"

Presley and Libby laughed.

Aubrey narrowed her eyes. "Exactly how does Knox Bentley know the resorts didn't work out?"

"Was that a secret?" Becca gasped. "I'm *so* sorry, Aubrey. I swear that man could charm the panties off a nun. He called while you were at that meeting yesterday afternoon, right after you *vented* about the resorts to me. I gave you his message when you got back. I believe you crumpled it up and tossed it in my trash can. Anyway, he asked how you were and how the search was going for the resort. He mentioned the places you were visiting like you had already discussed them with him."

"Oh boy, Aubs. That's very boyfriendish. This man is *not* going to take no for an answer." Presley reached for a bag of Cheetos, and Aubrey slapped her hand.

"Hands off. I need them now more than ever. I thought I was firm enough with him that he understood where I stand on the whole dating thing."

"If you're done reprimanding me, I have to run to my boxing class. Okay?" Becca backed toward the door and added, "For what it's worth, I really like the guy. Like all of Taylor's clients, he thought she was a guy when he hired her, and when he found out she was a woman last month at the New Year's Eve party and that her online male personas were for her protection, he didn't get mad like some of her bosses have. I like a guy who rolls with the punches." Becca's sister, Taylor, cared for their ailing father and worked as a virtual assistant for several busy executives.

Becca flipped her hair over her shoulder and said, "*Ciao*, ladies!"

Aubrey's phone vibrated on her desk as Libby said, "Open the present. You have to admit, Aubrey, he *does* know you. Most guys would send red roses."

She saw a text pop up from Knox and turned her phone upside down. "I hate red roses."

"No kidding," Presley said. "Which is why there's a massive bouquet of Cheetos and peach roses on your desk. You know, maybe you should give him a chance."

Aubrey sighed as she opened the gift box and lifted out a handwritten note taped to a smaller box. She read it aloud. "'Because I like watching you put it on.'" She lifted her eyes and said, "I'm not sure I want to open this in public."

"My ass." Presley jumped up and grabbed the box.

"Presley Cabot!" Libby shook her head.

"You're no fun." She handed the box back to Aubrey.

Aubrey laughed and opened the box slowly, surprised to find a black and gold lipstick container.

"Oh my gosh." Presley snagged the gift and inspected it. "Yup. Tom Ford's Original Sin. You've got yourself a *classy* dirty boy."

"Give me that." Aubrey grabbed the lipstick and set it on the desk. She lifted another note from the box and read it. "'Because putting on lipstick usually leads to taking these off.'" She shot a look at her friends. "This ought to be good." She whipped off the lid, and her body tingled at the sight of a black lace thong and matching bra nestled within the tissue paper.

"Wow. Those are gorgeous," Libby said. "May I?"

Aubrey shrugged and held out the box for Libby to feel the material.

"That's Agent Provocateur," Presley said as she admired the lingerie. "It's made with French lace. Gorgeous. The man has—"

"Invaded my personal space *and* my privacy." Aubrey snapped the lid back on the box, trying to ignore her racy thoughts of Knox tearing them off her.

"And I'm about to invade it even more."

They all spun around at the sound of Knox's deep, sexy voice. There he stood, six-plus feet of gorgeousness, clad in a black leather jacket, jeans, and black boots that probably cost more than Aubrey's desk. A charming smile lifted his lips as he said, "Hello, ladies."

"Hi," Presley and Libby said in unison, both of them all agog over him.

"Knox." The breathless sound of attraction in her voice annoyed the shit out of Aubrey. She squared her shoulders and said, "What are you doing here?"

"I knew you wouldn't sleep until you found the right location for the movie," he said as he closed the distance between them, his gaze never wavering from hers. "I happen to know the perfect place. I texted to tell you I was on my way upstairs." He eyed her phone with a shake of his head. "Pack your bags, babe. We're taking a little road trip."

"Wha…? I can't take a road trip." If he kept looking at her like he wanted to devour her, she wasn't going to be able to form another sentence. *Why* did he have this power over her? She shifted her eyes to the desk and said, "Thank you for the gifts, but can't you see I'm busy? We're in a meeting."

His gorgeous eyes swept over their wineglasses. "I can see that."

"How did you even know I was at the office?" She glanced at her desk, loaded up with his thoughtful—and presumptuous—gifts. Libby was right. Most guys would just send flowers, but Knox knew just how to rev her up. She couldn't deny the way her body had reacted at the thought of his hot hands tearing that slinky lingerie off her.

"Loose lips, remember? You always have drinks with the girls on Friday evenings." He cleared his throat and said, "I mean, you always hold *meetings* with Presley and Libby on Fridays."

"Busted," Presley said. "Well, I have to take off and meet my man, so she's free from my tethers."

Aubrey glared at her.

"Me too," Libby said cheerily. "Not to meet my man, but I have a…We have…I have a *thing* to take care of."

Libby sucked at lying. Damn her for choosing to do it now.

"Nice to see you both," Knox said as Presley grabbed the wine and their glasses.

After they left, Knox stepped closer, settling his hands on Aubrey's hips, and said, "Nice to see you, beautiful." He dipped his head and pressed his lips to hers.

Aubrey did not kiss him back, earning a frown.

"Aw, ease up, Aubrey. How can you be mad?"

"You sent me *gifts*." *And it totally threw me off-balance.*

"Most women would simply say thank you."

"We don't have a gift-giving relationship, and we don't have a surprise-visit relationship, either. We don't have a relationship. Period." She turned out of his arms and walked around her desk, hating to be so harsh, but she needed to remain focused on work.

He followed, bringing his sinful scent with him. The sexy bastard.

"We have a relationship, Aubrey, even if, until now, it has

been more casual. But it's time to change that."

She turned toward him and crossed her arms, needing the barrier between them, because her insides were going all mushy at his romantic efforts. "I told you I don't have time for drama in my life. I have a business to run and continue to build, and this"—she waved at the gifts—"is drama to the max."

He smiled. "This is *affection*."

"Affection my ass." She knew it was a bitchy thing to say and that he was trying to show her another side of himself, but already this little show of his had sidetracked her from the job she was supposed to be doing—searching for a resort for Charlotte's movie so they didn't lose the A-list actors they'd secured.

"I adore your ass," he said seductively. He leaned closer, brushing his lips beside her ear, and whispered, "And all the *affectionate* things you allow me to do to it."

"Knox" slipped out weakly. This was *her* domain, where *she* was in control. It was so foreign to her to be weak-kneed in her office that she quickly stepped back, speaking firmly as she said, "*Knox*, this is how drama starts. First it's gifts, then dinners. Then it's 'Move in with me,' then, 'You work too much,' or 'You're always traveling,' and we grow to resent each other. Then I find you in bed with another woman, and…See? Drama!"

His face blanched. "Aubrey, has some asshole done that to you?"

"Good God, no. But I work in media. It happens all the time."

He threw his head back with a hearty laugh. "In movies maybe, but most of the guys I know aren't assholes. And your life isn't a movie. If some guy hasn't scorned you, why are you still bucking the idea of us?"

"I didn't work this hard to get where I am just so I could become a baby maker or a woman whose career comes second to a man's. I *like* who I am alone, Knox. I like my life with no one telling me what to do or that I need to change."

His jaw tightened, and his eyes grew even more determined.

She shifted her eyes away, catching sight of a picture of her with her brothers after Joe's Super Bowl win, reminding her of all the reasons she'd fought so hard to become the successful businesswoman she was. "Think of me as a lone wolf."

"Wow. You've got me all figured out, all right," he said. "The old ball and chain who wants you barefoot and pregnant. The guy who wants to keep you from becoming the best person you could be, because you know, I get off on that shit."

He walked over to the windowsill and picked up a picture of her with Presley and Libby. They were standing outside the LWW building, beneath the LWW Enterprises sign, smiling proudly. It was taken the day they opened the doors to LWW. She couldn't think of a single prouder moment than that one, when their dreams had come to fruition. It had taken hard work and dedication to get where they were, to repay the loans and build their stellar reputations in several cutthroat, male-dominated industries. No way was she going to get sidetracked now.

He held up the picture and said, "I hate to tell you this, babe, but you're already part of a pack. And a damn fine one at that." He set the frame on the sill, rolled his shoulders back, and said, "With your lone-wolf image shattered, how about we just agree to disagree? Go pack your shit, and we'll get out of here so you can see how perfect the Monroe House is for the movie location."

Business. This she could handle.

"I appreciate your efforts, and you have impeccable taste," she admitted. "The Monroe House was my first choice. But I've already spoken to Vincent Monroe, the director of public affairs, and he shut me down completely. He said they no longer allow the media onto their grounds."

"Vincent," he said under his breath. That cocky grin slid back into place. "I've got an in with the owners. Pack your bags, babe, because I can make this happen."

"Seriously?" She knew Knox had connections all over the world and she shouldn't be surprised he knew the owners of the elite resort, but she wanted it so badly, she could hardly believe her luck.

"No. I'm going to take you out to a remote inn and keep you captive as my sex slave for the weekend, and I figured lying to you was the best way to get you there. *Of course* seriously. Come on, Stewart. Let's go."

The resort was two and a half hours away. Plus she'd need time to meet the owners, who would probably be gone by the time they got there. Her hopes deflated. She'd almost believed he was trying to help.

"Knox, I'm sure the owners will be gone by the time we arrive. Maybe you should reach out to them first," she suggested.

"They live there, and I've already told them we're coming."

"They *live* there?" Okay, so maybe he was trying to help, but Vincent had been very clear with her. "Why bother if they'll just say no?"

He crossed his arms and sat on the edge of her desk. "You really have very little faith in me. That's surprising, considering you trust me with every inch of your body. This type of negotiation is best handled in person, and I know these people. They need to be finessed. We have a breakfast meeting early tomorrow morning, and I didn't think you would want to risk getting caught in traffic and being late or missing the meeting." He pushed to his feet and said, "Or you can take your chances. Maybe you'll find a second-rate place. It's up to you."

She was already getting excited about the possibility of securing the Monroe House. That location would blow this movie out of the water. It was the equivalent of a Sterling House doppelgänger, the perfect setting. "Separate rooms?"

"Why on earth would you want that when you *know* we'll just end up in one?"

He had her there. Maybe they could accomplish this as a *team*. "Do you really think you can change their minds?"

"I never lose a negotiation."

"God, you're cocky." And she loved it.

"Do you mean *cocky*, as in my"—his gaze dropped to the impressive package bulging behind his zipper—"or *cocky* as in arrogant? Because I can see how either would fit here."

She stifled a laugh, knowing she was in big trouble, because his personality was what she craved even more than their incredibly hot sex. She picked up the bouquet of Cheetos and roses and thrust it into his hands. "Those are coming with us. I'll grab the soda."

He reached for the box of lingerie and the lipstick. "Let's not forget the good stuff."

AUBREY'S HOUSE WAS nothing like Knox had imagined,

which would have been something classy and understated, like her. Surely not a stately stone mansion that had to be well over ten thousand square feet, with enough glass to feel like he was outdoors and a grand view of the Hudson River. Mocha hardwood floors shone throughout the expansive and pristine living room, which led out to a slate patio and a built-in pool. Bright white Scandinavian-style furniture with sleek lines and extra-deep cushions were accented by luxuriously crafted black glass end tables. Plush area rugs boasted vibrant gray, white, and black abstracts. The walls held black-and-white museum-worthy pictures, crystal-and-gold chandeliers hung from elaborate ceilings, and arched entryways with intricately carved moldings led to adjoining rooms.

Aubrey tossed her purse on an expensive-looking table by the door with a sigh and said, "It'll take me only a minute to gather a few things."

"Your house is incredible, and a little surprising." As one of the world's wealthiest women, Aubrey deserved such a house, even if it showed Knox an unexpected side of her. The river view was the only thing he didn't find surprising. He'd imagined Aubrey to be a water lover. It was easy to picture her lying out in a bikini, her long legs stretched out before her as she read a script or strategized her next big move for the company. It wasn't a far reach to imagine her frolicking in the ocean on some faraway beach, riding waves, or even sailing. Sure, outside of the free-spirited lovemaker she was in bed, she tried to come across as all business, but there was no mistaking the mischievous glimmer behind those amber eyes. It was the first thing that had attracted him to her, second only to the way she'd sidled up to him as they'd left the charity event the night they first met two years ago and said, *I'm in the capital suite,* flashing that confident, stunning smile that had piqued his interest even before his cock got the message about her sexy invitation. Aubrey was a woman who knew exactly what she wanted in life, and she didn't hesitate to go after it—just like *him*.

She waved a hand dismissively. "I couldn't let my brothers have the biggest houses, could I?"

"A little friendly competition?" he asked with a laugh, following her through the living room to a grand staircase. "What do your brothers do when they're not playing football?"

"Get on my nerves, mostly." She glanced over her shoulder and said, "Make yourself at home *down here*."

"What? I don't get to see your bedroom?" he asked with more than a hint of innuendo.

"Ha! You're lucky I let you in here. I don't make a habit of bringing men into my personal space."

"Ah, I get it." He took a few steps back. "You don't trust yourself with all this." He gestured at his body. "I don't blame you. It's a lot to resist." He winked and walked away chuckling as she stalked upstairs.

Knox wandered around the luxurious first floor. The house was impeccably clean, every surface shining. The kitchen was bigger than any he'd ever seen, outfitted with several ovens, custom cabinetry—all white like the rest of the house. He flipped open a cabinet, eyeing the neatly stacked china. Her house looked unlived in, which reminded him of the home in which he'd grown up. His gut clenched with memories of his stifled childhood, when proper etiquette and black-tie dinners took precedence over everything else. Could he have completely misjudged who Aubrey was at her core?

He meandered through a handsome library outfitted in rich

mahogany to a room that looked like an art gallery, and down the hall he found another large room outfitted with leather chairs, a gorgeous pool table, and an expansive, fully stocked bar. With each elaborately decorated room, his gut clenched tighter.

At the end of the hall he came to a set of intricately carved doors. If he were a real gentleman, he'd turn around and leave those doors closed. But his curiosity was far stronger than his desire to be chivalrous, and he pulled them open, revealing a gigantic—and treacherously messy—media room.

He flicked the light switch, and a ring of neon purple lights illuminated a black arched ceiling with tiny inset lights, like a planetarium. He couldn't stifle his grin. This was *nothing* like the theater room in his childhood home. Oversized couches were littered with Cheetos bags, candy wrappers, and soda bottles. Books and magazines were strewn across the floor and coffee table, along with a half-empty bowl of popcorn and a handful of remotes. Piled on the couch cushions were a quilt and several New York Jets and Giants blankets, the teams her brothers played for. A bedroom pillow was squished against the arm of the couch, as if Aubrey frequently slept there.

Well, well, sweetheart. Looks like I didn't read you wrong after all. You're just secretly comfortable. He wondered who she entertained that she had to keep the rest of her house in such immaculate condition.

And then he wondered about her bedroom...

Was she her messy, comfortable self in there?

He plunked himself down on the couch only to jump up when something poked him in the back. He snagged a book sticking out from between the cushions. *Wicked Envy* by Sawyer Bennett. He leafed through the dog-eared pages and found several erotic scenes underlined. "My girl likes to study. *Nice…*"

He set the book down and hit play on the remote that looked most like it would work the television. The overhead ring of purple dimmed, and tiny purple dots appeared on the walls. *Funky. I like it.* He tried another remote, and the projector came to life.

Knox picked up the bowl of popcorn, tossed a handful in his mouth, wincing at how stale it was, and settled back to watch *Some Kind of Wonderful.* Man, he'd forgotten how cheesy the movie was. *The hair! The clothes!* He chuckled to himself.

"Dude," he said to the screen a few minutes later. "Can't you see she's crazy about you?"

"*What* are you doing?" Aubrey walked in looking hot in a pair of skinny jeans, knee-high boots with fur around the tops, and an off-the-shoulder sweater. She frantically began picking up her mess.

"You said to make myself at home, *Wattsy*," he said with a snicker. Her wide eyes told him she knew he was referring to the best friend who was helping the nerdy boy get a date with the popular girl in the movie she'd left in the projector.

He turned off the movie and pushed to his feet to set down the popcorn bowl. He spotted another paperback on the floor, picked it up, and waved it at her. "I find these *very* interesting. Let's see…*Beg Me* by Jennifer Probst. Let me guess. Erotic romance? Underlined passages?"

She groaned and lunged for the book. He pulled it out of reach and swept his other arm around her waist. "No wonder you're so good in the sack."

"It's my *job*," she said, straining for the book.

He arched a brow.

"*Reading*, not being good in bed!" She wrenched free of his grip and grabbed the book. "Oh man. This was a good one. Almost as good as Charlotte's Wicked Boys After Dark series."

"I'll show you *wicked*." He reached for her again and she dodged him, laughing as she bent to retrieve candy wrappers from the floor. He couldn't resist smacking her ass.

"Stop! I'm usually not this messy."

"Uh-huh. The rest of the house made me wonder if I'd mistakenly wanted to date Felix Unger. I'm relieved to see you're more like Oscar Madison."

"Haha." She tossed the book on the couch and carried the candy wrappers to the trash can. "I have to keep the rest of house clean for when I host holidays."

"You mean like Christmas?"

"No. I mean like the second Monday of the month. Of course Christmas. Do you want to go, or do you want to harass me?"

"I like this. I'm learning a lot about you. For instance"—he followed her out of the room and down the hall—"you keep your house immaculate for eleven months out of the year so you'll be prepared for *one* holiday."

She glared at him. "I don't *use* the rest of the house. I'm one person. What am I going to do, entertain myself and sit properly in the living room? Give me a break."

He carried her bag out to the car, and when they settled into their seats, she said, "See? I'm not a good candidate for your baby-making mama, so you can take me off your dating list."

"First of all, I'm not looking for a wife or a baby maker. And you couldn't be more wrong, Wattsy. Learning about the real you makes you even more intriguing." He stole a glance at her as he drove toward the highway. "You can't tell me you don't think about me when we're not together."

She grabbed a bag of Cheetos from the bouquet in the back seat, tore it open, and quickly stuffed a handful into her mouth, staring wide-eyed out the windshield.

Chapter Three

"YOU'LL NEVER GUESS where I am," Aubrey said into the speakerphone to Charlotte the next morning as she finished dressing for her breakfast meeting with the Monroes. She still couldn't believe they had agreed to meet with her and Knox. She was beyond nervous and excited. Before her friend could respond, she blurted out, "The *Monroe* House! And we might have a shot at securing it for your movie!"

"What?" Charlotte squealed. "Are you pulling my leg? You said they turned you down flat."

"They did, but Knox knows the owners, and he thinks we might have a shot. Char, this was my *top* pick. It's as spacious and luxurious as your family's estate, and it's in the Adirondacks, about an hour from town. I'm telling you, it's absolutely perfect! Fingers and toes crossed today, okay? I'd say legs, too, but Beau might shoot me."

Charlotte laughed, and then her voice grew serious. "Wait. I just realized you said *Knox*. I thought the two of you were just acquaintances with benefits. Are you doing business together now? Or getting serious in a relationship? You know he's Graham's business partner, right? The Bradens *love* him."

"We are *not* getting serious. It's purely a business thing."

She eyed the Cheetos bouquet on the dresser and the unlocked but *closed* door that adjoined hers and Knox's suites. She'd been surprised when he'd gotten her a separate suite after all his pushy declarations. She'd thought it was just a ploy and that he'd join her in the night. She'd even worn the sexy lingerie he'd given her, but he'd never come through the door. He hadn't even poked his head into her room to flirt. She didn't know if she was disappointed or relieved that he'd respected her wishes enough to let her be in control.

"Well, now that I've met him, I'd *really* like to nudge you over that colleague hump to something more. I like him, Aubs. He's funny and cute, and from what Beau says, he's a really honest, good man. Not without flaws, of course. Apparently he's one of those guys who'll make waves when he wants something, when others might walk way."

"Yeah, tell me about it." Aubrey slipped her feet into a pair of taupe heels and took one last look in the mirror. "I'm going with my navy Chanel pantsuit. I think it says smart and business minded, and I look hot in the slacks. What do you think? The Monroes are known for being ultra conservative. Think I need to wear a skirt?"

"It's not the fifties. You'll look great in anything, and besides, clothes don't matter. The minute you open your mouth, your personality and intelligence will tell them everything they need to know. I've got to run. Beau made omelets, and I need to go show him what I'm *really* hungry for. I swear you should just start calling me *nymph girl* because when I'm with him, he's all I want. Let me know how it goes!"

"Love you. Enjoy." *Nymph girl. Seems like an ample name for me around Knox, too.* It was a good feeling, even if a little terrifying. Her thoughts turned to Charlotte and Beau, and she filled with happiness. Holing up in the defunct inn had been fantastic for building Charlotte's career, but nonetheless Aubrey had worried endlessly about her living all alone in the Colorado Mountains. She was glad Charlotte had Beau with her now and that she'd found a man worthy of her good nature and love.

Love…

It was times like these, thinking about Charlotte and Beau or Presley and Nolan, that Aubrey waxed romantic about what life might be like if she were the type of person who wanted a relationship. Her parents had a marvelous marriage, full of love and, to this day, also full of fun. But her mother had built her life around her father's career, supporting him in every way. She blended into his world like an extension of the man he was, sharing his love of sports and cheering him on as much as she cheered on his team. Aubrey had no problem with the support and the cheering on, but her world was different from her mother's. She had yet to meet a man who would take a backseat to *that*—to be there to support *her*, cheer *her* on without resenting the time it took to be the head of a corporation the size of LWW Enterprises. She knew how entitled that sounded and how unfair it would be to expect that of anyone when she wasn't willing to step back and play second fiddle to a man's career. But above all else, she was a realist, and she wouldn't allow herself to pretend, even for a minute, that she could be something she couldn't.

A knock at the door pulled her back to reality.

She shook her head to clear her thoughts, pocketed the room card, and went to answer the door. Knox stood before her, his thick hair brushed back from his clean-shaven face. She couldn't remember the last time she'd seen him without perfectly manicured scruff, and holy mother of hotness, the man cleaned up so well. She wanted to rub her cheek over his, just to feel the only part of him she'd never before touched. *Virgin cheeks*, she mused, stifling a laugh. Her gaze slid lower, to his crisp white shirt, dark jeans, and what she knew were his favorite biker boots, which he wore when he rode his motorcycle. There was nothing hotter than Knox Bentley pulling up to a charity picnic on his shiny black Ducati.

But this wasn't a picnic. This was a very important meeting with conservative businesspeople, and he was going to blow it.

"Wow. After a night of erotic fantasies about the woman behind the door, you are a sight for sore eyes." Knox leaned in and kissed her cheek. "Morning, beautiful. Sleep okay?"

"Yes, but, Knox…jeans? Really? These are the *Monroes*. They come from old money. Don't you think you should dress for the occasion?"

"I already told you, I have an in with them. They know me. They know how I dress."

She sighed. "I hope you're right. I don't want to blow the only chance we have." She couldn't resist reaching up and stroking the smooth skin along his rugged jawline. "You look great like this…"

"Yeah?" He leaned in again, bringing his face closer to hers, and said, "I can't wait to see if you enjoy my smooth cheeks on your thighs more than the scratch of my whiskers."

As if she weren't nervous enough, her body celebrated his naughty temptation like the Fourth of July. Now she had to meet with the owners of the inn with *that* on her mind?

"Let's see how our meeting goes," she challenged. She was dying to ask him why he hadn't come visit her last night, but she'd been the one to demand separate rooms, so she let it go. "We should go so we're not late."

They followed the midnight-blue carpet to the central staircase. The Monroe House was more elegant than Charlotte's estate, but some of that could be toned down when filming by removing certain elements, like the elaborate lanterns that anchored the staircase and the grand piano she'd seen in the lobby. But the rich wood and the serenity of the remote inn was ideal.

As they neared the staircase, she felt like she'd swallowed a nest of butterflies. Negotiating a business deal was nothing new to her. She shouldn't be this nervous. But after being turned down flat by Vincent Monroe, she couldn't help it. It wasn't her practice to beg or to use her connections to undermine a final decision. But she wanted this movie to be perfect for Charlotte, so she tucked that pride away and hoped for the best.

As they made their way down the staircase, Knox put a hand on her back and said, "Remember, this will take finesse. Let me handle bringing up the project."

"Okay." She glanced at the reception area. A woman behind the reception desk was on the phone and another was speaking to a man across from the desk. Nearby, several well-dressed men and women stood close together, deep in conversation. She wondered if they were the Monroes.

"Nervous?" he asked thoughtfully.

"How'd you know? Do I look nervous?"

He stopped on the landing and said, "Not in a way anyone else will see. You look like the gorgeous, confident executive you are. But I notice a difference."

She cocked her head in question.

"I feel it here." He pressed his hand more firmly on her upper back. "Your heart is beating fast. Unless that's just from being close to me?"

She sighed.

"We've got this, Aubrey. We make a great team, in and out of the bedroom. We'll need to do a little finessing, as I said, but we're both good at that."

"How do you know what we are outside the bedroom?"

"Guess you're not too nervous to hear what I said. That's a good thing." He smiled and said, "We've attended enough of the same business functions for me to see how you operate. You're impressive, but I think you know that already. We're both ruthless negotiators and we know how to read people. When to give"—his eyes grew darker—"and when to *take*."

"Knox! You can't do that when we're in the meeting," she said in a hushed tone.

"Do what?" He stepped a little closer.

"That!" she whispered. "The whole *I want you in my bed* thing you do to me, and probably to every other woman you know."

She turned to head down the stairs, and his hand circled her arm, bringing her back to him. His eyes were narrow and hard, colder than she'd ever seen, but his grip was light, possessive but not aggressive, eliciting a devastating combination of emotions.

"You think I pick up women everywhere I go?"

"I'd be a fool not to," she whispered. "Look, Knox, I don't believe in fooling myself. The way we came together the first time, and every time since, it tells me something."

"Really? Then maybe I've been looking at this all wrong. Should it be telling *me* something about you, too?"

"No," she said firmly. "I mean, I'm not a person with sexual hang-ups, but—"

"That's one of the things I like about you," he said heatedly, but the question she hadn't answered lingered in his eyes.

"As I do about you," she said honestly. "I've been with my share of men, but I don't make a practice of hooking up after business events."

"You didn't hesitate to seek me out," he pointed out.

"And you didn't hesitate to accept." She narrowed her eyes, her heart racing. "Maybe I lost my mind that night." *And still haven't found it.* "I don't regret it, but please stop trying to make it into something it's not."

"You know damn well you didn't lose your mind, Aubrey. Our connection was—*is*—inescapable. There's no one else I want in my bed. And yeah, it took me a while to figure that out, but what about you? Is this your way of saying you're sleeping around?"

"Knox!" A tall, impossibly thin brunette ran up the stairs in sky-high heels and dark designer slacks. She launched herself into his arms and kissed his cheeks so hard she left lipstick prints. Her dark hair was pinned up in a casually sexy partial topknot, with long wispy bangs. The back hung loose and shiny. Her skin was pale, her makeup expertly applied, and her big brown eyes were heavily lined. She was *stunning*, even if painfully thin. Her arms fell from around Knox's neck, and one hand remained on his chest. "It's been way too long since I've seen you. You look amazing."

Great. I came with you to see another lover? What the ever-loving fuck?

Knox dragged his gaze down the pretty pixie's body, his arm circling her tiny waist. "So do you. Are you doing okay? Everything good?"

"Oh my goodness, yes! But I hate not seeing you for so long. You haven't come out since before you went to Belize last fall. You can't leave me for that long, even if we chat on the phone. I have Knox withdrawals."

Give me a fucking break. Aubrey stood up a little taller, ready to tell Knox she was going to have the front desk locate Vincent Monroe so she could get this over with and head out of there, when Knox took hold of her hand and said, "Paige, this is Aubrey Stewart. Aubrey, this is Paige."

"Gosh, this is such a pleasure!" Paige ignored Aubrey's out-stretched hand and wrapped her lithe arms around her in a warm embrace. "I am in awe of the empire you've built. You've given women everywhere something to aspire to. I wish I had half your business sense, but Knox and Landon got all the business skills in the family."

Family? Oh shit...

"Nonsense," Knox said. "Paige is an amazing model but an even more talented events coordinator and artist."

Aubrey was still trying to pick her jaw up off the floor at her misconceived assumption. She'd known Knox had siblings, but they'd never talked in detail about them, only in generalities. Now, not only did she see the resemblance in Paige's warm cocoa eyes, but the way Paige was looking at Knox was probably very similar to the way Aubrey looked at her brothers. Though she didn't gush the way Paige did, she admired her brothers' successes and the men they'd become.

"I am passionate about parties and painting," Paige said. "They're much more interesting than modeling, and I am an impeccable planner. Come on, let's head over to the restaurant."

"You work here?" Aubrey asked as they followed her down the stairs.

"Yes. Knox, have you spoken to Landon lately?"

"We've exchanged a few texts."

"Well, beware. I swear he's been a grouch ever since Carlos

Ruiz stayed here a few months ago. Actors stay here all the time, and Carlos has vacationed here a number of times, but I'm sure you heard about the media circus that took place during his last visit. Landon has been on edge ever since. I guess I don't blame him, since it created all sorts of privacy concerns for our clients."

"Oh, I think I remember that," Aubrey said as they crossed the lobby toward the restaurant. "It was in all the tabloids, Hollywood's eternal bachelor engaged to…that model. What's her name?"

"Brenda Marlow," Paige said as they entered the restaurant. "They called off the engagement a month later. You should have seen Landon when *that* happened. Some reporters came nosing around, and he shut them down hard. Landon does *not* like drama."

"A man after my own heart," Aubrey said with a smirk aimed at Knox.

"You might have to grow a penis for that one," Knox said, earning a laugh from Paige. "My brother is into guys. Sorry, Aubs, your gender isn't going to give you any pull during this meeting."

They were meeting with his *brother*? She thought they were meeting with Vincent Monroe. If Knox didn't know the owners and this was some crazy ploy in his dating scheme, she was going to kill him.

"Oh, are you two *dating*?" Paige asked excitedly.

"No," Aubrey said at the same time Knox said, "Yes."

Paige's brows drew together in confusion. "Okay. I won't go *there* again."

"Why is it so quiet in here?" Knox asked. "Isn't it usually busier this time of year?"

"Yes. Ever since the new ski resort opened we've been much slower. But things will pick up," Paige said hopefully. "There's Landon."

Paige pointed across the room to a tall, handsome man rising from a table near the windows. He was talking into a cell phone, and he was definitely *alone*. Aubrey bit back her frustration and smiled as Landon lifted his chin in their direction. He looked similar to Knox, tall and broad, with hair a few shades lighter than Paige's, which was a softer brown than Knox's, but he held himself more rigidly than Knox, and his eyes were warier. His sharp gray suit was precisely tailored, and his cuff links shimmered against the light from the chandelier, a stark contrast to Knox's jeans and boots.

Landon was ending his phone call when they arrived at the table. He slid his phone into his pocket, a practiced smile forming as his gaze moved quickly over Knox, whose jaw tightened, and he offered his hand to Aubrey. "Landon Bentley," he said in a deep, smooth voice, softer than Knox's but every bit as potent. "You must be the illustrious Aubrey Stewart. You have quite an impressive reputation. It's a pleasure to meet you."

KNOX COULD TELL from the set of his brother's jaw that Landon's shorts were in a twist even more than usual.

"Thank you. I didn't realize Knox's siblings were part of Monroe Enterprises." Aubrey gave Knox an inquisitive look.

"Monroe is our mother's maiden name," Landon explained. "We all own a piece of this resort, and others. Including Knox and our cousins Vincent, Elsie, and Carlisle Monroe, though only Vincent works here."

He and Landon had had their differences over the years because of Knox's decision to extricate himself from the family businesses and highbrow lifestyle, but Landon seemed to have an extra edge today. He was sure his brother had added that little tidbit about Knox's ownership of the property—from birth, not earned or by desire—just to ruffle his feathers. He'd all but relinquished his decision-making authority. And he would formally relinquish it if his family would accept it. Knox and each of his siblings also had embarrassingly large trust funds, but other than using his as initial investment capital, Knox hadn't touched it. He'd also never used his Bentley name or connections to gain favors. Until today. A fact Landon was clearly homing in on. Knox had made the call to Paige and set up the meeting only because he knew how important Charlotte was to Aubrey. Aubrey may not realize how much she'd shared with him over the past two years, but he'd remembered every word—and even more importantly, the moments she'd gone silent. *We've been there for each other for everything from our first crushes and losing our virginity, to the loss of her parents and...*She'd remained quiet for so long, Knox had felt the presence of secrets she hadn't wanted to share. When she'd continued speaking, she'd said, *Just when we'd found our footing again, she lost her grandfather. I would do anything for Charlotte.* The fact that she hadn't mentioned any of her own crises hadn't been lost on him. Charlotte Sterling might be like the sister Aubrey never had, but Knox was sure there was more to that story, too. He'd do whatever it took to ensure Charlotte's movie was just as perfect as Aubrey hoped it would be. Including pulling the Bentley card.

"Does he?" Aubrey said with a bite in her voice, bringing Knox's mind back to the conversation. "I guess I should have dug a little deeper when I was doing my research."

"How about we stop sharing family secrets now." Knox pulled his brother into a manly embrace and said, "Paybacks are hell, bro," earning a familiar scoff.

Knox pulled a chair out for Aubrey and one for Paige, and then he took a seat beside Aubrey. "I'm glad you could make time for us on such short notice."

Landon held his gaze and said, "There's always time for family, little brother."

The veiled spear hit with pinpoint accuracy, like a hot needle beneath Knox's fingernail.

"Will Vincent be joining us?" Aubrey asked.

"No," Paige answered. "Unfortunately, our cousin had to go out of town this weekend for meetings at another property. I know he would have enjoyed meeting you."

A waitress came to take their orders and fill their coffee. After she walked away, Landon spread his napkin on his lap and looked curiously at Knox. "I'm interested in hearing about the project you'd like to discuss, but given that this is the first time in a decade that you've brought a beautiful woman to meet the family, should I be preparing a best-man speech? Rent a tux?"

Aubrey choked on her coffee.

Knox patted her back and handed her a napkin, glaring at Landon. Landon's eyes filled with a sincere apology.

"No," Knox and Aubrey said in unison. Aubrey cleared her throat, regaining her composure.

"Are you okay?" Paige asked.

"Yes, thank you," Aubrey said, though irritation lingered in her eyes. "And no, there is no need for a tux. Knox and I are colleagues."

"We're more than that," Knox said boldly. "But we're keeping that on the downlow at the moment."

If looks could kill, Aubrey would have slain him right there and then, which his brother was taking all too much pleasure in. He'd never been good at hiding his emotions, and he wasn't a game player, but for Aubrey's sake he reluctantly told himself to temper his outward displays of affection. At least until she gave in to the truth of her feelings.

Paige smiled at Aubrey and said, "That particular older brother can be a little pushy, but I get it. On the *downlow*." She pretended to zip her lips.

"Thank you," Aubrey relented tightly.

Not the best way to start a meeting, but hey, at least now they knew where his feelings lay. Knowing Landon had issues with their recent media circus gave Knox a leg up, a strategy to try to avoid his brother's concerns.

"Now that that's been cleared up..." Landon paused as the waitress brought their breakfasts. "Thank you, Sarah. It looks marvelous."

The waitress smiled, and after asking if she could bring them anything else, she stepped away. They made small talk as they ate. Knox noticed Landon watching Paige eat even more closely than he was. It had been two years since Paige had left modeling to deal with her eating disorder and more than a year since her doctors—and Paige—had proclaimed her to be *in a good place*. They'd kept her struggles under wraps, per their parents' requests, which was something neither Knox nor Paige had been happy about. But they both found ways to help others struggling with eating disorders. They texted and spoke on the phone often, not just so he could keep tabs on her health, but because they were the closest of the three siblings. He knew she was doing well, but like Landon, he would never stop worrying. They'd learned that eating disorders didn't go away; they were simply *managed*—until they weren't.

When they were finished eating Paige said, "I'm excited to hear about the project you wanted to discuss. Knox was very mysterious about it on the phone."

Knox glanced at Aubrey, fighting the urge to reach for her hand and give it a squeeze to let her know he had her back. "As you know, Aubrey is one of the founders of LWW Enterprises. She also heads up the media department, handling film and television. She's launched a new television movie channel called Me Time, and a movie she's producing is based on a book written by one of her closest friends, Charlotte Sterling."

Paige's eyes lit up. "I *love* her erotic romances! I read about the upcoming movie version of *Anything for Love*, and I cannot wait to see it. The book was incredible. The love between her characters was so real, like two hearts beating off the page."

"She's really talented," Aubrey said. "I know with the right location the movie will be just as powerful. We've already signed Duncan Raz for the male lead."

Landon's eyes narrowed, as if he knew where the conversation was headed and wasn't the least bit pleased about it.

"No way!" Paige leaned closer to Aubrey and lowered her voice to say, "He's even hotter than Zac Efron. I've had the *biggest* crush on Duncan Raz since he starred in the movie *Country Hearts*. He is so yummy with those big blue eyes. *Mm.*"

"I can introduce you," Aubrey offered. "He's Char's fiancé's childhood friend, and a really nice guy."

Paige gasped with excitement.

"How about we table the dating game," Landon said firmly.

"I think we should get back to the project you wanted to discuss. Clearly that's why Knox has come to visit."

"We'll talk later," Paige said to Aubrey.

Knox let his brother's barb go and said, "As I mentioned, the movie Aubrey is producing will be made for television, not the big screen, and it's set in an inn very similar to this one. Aubrey would like to secure the Monroe House for filming."

His brother's hands slipped beneath the table, and Knox knew they were fisting. Landon had never publicly shown aggression, and he was a master of the feigned look of interest that remained on his face.

"It would require closing the inn to the public during filming," Knox continued. "Aubrey's willing to work with us on timing." He glanced at Aubrey, who nodded confirmation despite not having discussed that. He knew she'd stop at nothing to get the space. "Given the issues you've had with the media, LWW will make arrangements for extra security *and*, to the best of their abilities, keep the news of filming private. It would mean a lot to me if you would consider this."

"Wow, really?" Paige's gaze moved between Aubrey and Knox. "That would be exciting, and it comes at an opportune time, since we're losing bookings to the new ski resort. I'm sure we can find a way to keep the media out. They do it all the time for modeling shoots and movies."

"This isn't a decision we can make here and now," Landon said evenly. "There's a lot to consider, with the closing of the inn, prearranged bookings…But we'll take it under consideration."

"Landon, think of all the exposure we'd gain after the movie is out," Paige urged. "We'll be fully booked for years."

"Decades," Aubrey said. "People still flock to the inn where they filmed *Dirty Dancing*."

Landon was quiet as they finished eating.

"I appreciate your consideration," Aubrey said. "If you agree to allow us to use the inn, I will personally arrange for extra security, as Knox mentioned. We estimate that filming the part of the story that takes place at the inn will take three to four weeks, and in case you have concerns about the type of movie we're producing, it isn't an erotic romance, and it isn't violent or offensive in any way. It's a tasteful and beautiful love story about two brokenhearted people who were never able to fully heal on their own finding happiness and healing together. I'd be happy to share the script with you."

"Thank you, Aubrey," Landon replied. "That won't be necessary."

"We also haven't talked compensation yet, but I'm certain we can come up with a figure you're happy with. And I hope you'll find your way to a conclusion that will be mutually beneficial to the long-term success of the Monroe House as well as the movie. Thank you both for your time this morning and for your consideration."

"I'm so glad we got to meet you," Paige said. "And I think the movie would be good for the inn, but the final decision is really Landon's, as he and Vincent handle the overarching media and public relations for the inn."

"And Vincent?" Aubrey asked. "Should we plan a time to meet with him as well?"

"No. I'll relay this information to him, but the final decision is mine. It's been a pleasure meeting you, Aubrey." Landon set his napkin on the table and checked his watch, clearly done with the conversation. "We'll take it under consideration and get back to you. Now, if you'll excuse me."

He pushed to his feet, and Knox rose, too, putting a hand on Aubrey's shoulder. He didn't want her between him and Landon. "I'd like to meet with you for a few minutes to discuss some family business."

Paige looked up from her seat and said, "Does that mean I can steal Aubrey for a little while? We can get to know each other while you two chat." She grabbed Aubrey's hand as she rose to her feet, bringing Aubrey up beside her. "I'll give you a *behind-the-scenes* tour of the inn."

"That sounds wonderful." Aubrey shook Landon's hand. "Thank you again for meeting with us. It's really nice to meet Knox's family. He seems like such a lone wolf sometimes."

Knox slipped an arm around her waist, wondering if she realized she'd called him the same thing she'd called herself in her office, and said, "I've got room in my den…"

Aubrey glared at him.

Landon laughed. "No wonder there's no need for a tux. Real couth, little brother."

"You got all the couth. I got the witty charm and good looks."

"Apparently I got the only normal genes in the family. Come on." Paige pulled Aubrey away from the men. "I'll bring her back later, don't worry."

"There's a storm brewing," Landon called after them. "Don't be too long."

Knox wasn't sure if he was talking about between them or the cold front blowing through.

Chapter Four

"WHERE ARE WE headed?" Knox asked as he followed Landon out of the restaurant.

"To my office. How's it going for you, Knox? I mean beyond your affinity for a particular blond businesswoman. Mom and Dad missed seeing you over the holidays. We all did."

"Yeah, I know. Sorry about that. Business is going well. We're building a sustainable community just outside of Seattle, and the surrounding neighborhoods are really rallying in support of it."

"I heard about that. Congratulations." Landon glanced at him and said, "I know you said you had to stay in Belize for project oversight, but we both know it was completed well before the holidays. And I haven't seen any announcements about new overseas ventures for B&B Enterprises."

"Right. There was some follow-up to be taken care of. And Sage Remington and I were making plans for our next joint project." Sage was an artist and the owner of Hydration Through Creation, which specialized in funding wells for newly developing nations through the sale of artwork. Knox and Graham had partnered with Sage to build tiny houses for a community in Belize. Knox had returned to the States on New

Year's Eve with the intention of visiting his family, but the minute he'd landed stateside, his heart had had other ideas. He'd made a beeline for the Ladies Who Write New Year's Eve party, knowing Aubrey would be there. They'd spent two ravenous nights in a luxurious hotel wrapped in each other's arms, watching old movies and snacking on their favorite junk food. And though Aubrey didn't seem to want to give their relationship any weight, they'd talked a lot and caught each other up on the months they'd missed. She'd turned down his invitation to take their relationship to the next level then, too. When they'd left the hotel that foggy morning, he'd been more determined than ever to change her mind. If he'd realized one thing while he was in Belize, it was that she was the only one for him. There would be no getting over Aubrey Stewart, and if she ever put her stubbornness aside, she'd know he was the one for her, too.

"I heard you were around for New Year's," Landon said as they entered the executive wing and made their way toward his office.

Damn. He hadn't counted on Landon following his every move. Of course, he probably should have. They may have a strained relationship, but Landon had always acted like Knox was his responsibility.

"I know you were at LWW's New Year's party in Port Hudson, Knox. It's not that far from here. You could have come by. Mom and Dad aren't getting any younger, and Paige needs the connection with you."

Once in Landon's office, Knox closed the door and said, "I was in touch with Paige while I was away, and Mom and Dad knew I was tied up. They seemed okay with it."

"Because they've accepted the fact that you're above attending their parties." Landon waved to one of the chairs in front of his desk and lowered himself into the other.

"Not *above*, dude. I just don't like the pretense of needing to flaunt what we have or celebrate every holiday like it's one for the record books." His parents' holiday parties were never about just family. They were all for show, to pretend they were the happy, rich family without issues. Spending the holidays in Belize with people who knew how to cherish family and treated him like one of their own had given him a huge dose of what he'd craved his whole life. He wanted that, and the truth was, he wanted it with Aubrey.

"What's eating at you, Landon? Why are you playing hard-ball with Aubrey? So you had a media crisis. There are worse things to suffer in this lifetime."

Landon shifted his eyes away, but not before Knox saw pain swimming in them. His gut sank. "Bro…? Is something going on with Mom and Dad that I don't know about?"

Landon lifted his chin, and when he met Knox's worried gaze, the pained expression was gone, replaced with the practiced pleasantry that annoyed Knox so much. He'd give anything for Landon to loosen up, show his emotions, and be clearer about what he felt. Hell, he'd be okay with Landon hollering at him, or decking him for that matter, but this hidden agenda thing just pissed him off.

"No. They're fine."

Knox pushed to his feet and paced. "Then what am I sens-ing here? What's got you more uptight than usual? Because I know you can handle a little media bullshit."

"I'm worried about Paige." He rose to his feet and walked to the window. "It won't be good for her to get swept up in that world again. You know how impressionable she is. She needs us to watch out for her."

"Unless you've seen something I haven't heard about, she's doing great. She didn't push her food around on her plate or gorge at breakfast. She's interacting well with the people at Project ME. She's productive there, helping others, setting up fundraisers, and she loves the work she's doing here at the inn and her artwork." Project Mindful Eating was a nonprofit Knox had founded that supported individuals and families affected by eating disorders, providing access to treatment, counseling, and education.

"And apparently she's also into Duncan Raz." Landon shook his head. "A guy like that, with all those women chasing after him, could send her right back to square one."

"So this is about Paige falling for some actor who probably has more women than he can shake a stick at? No problem. I'll stay during filming and run interference. Whatever it takes."

"You show up here once every few months and suddenly you're willing to stick around? You must really be into Aubrey."

"I am. She's important to me, but not at the expense of Paige. I think Paige is doing fine, but if you're concerned, I'll take full responsibility while the filming takes place."

"No," Landon said flatly, crossing his arms. "It's not a good idea."

"Because you don't trust me to handle it, or because you think Paige is so weak-minded that nothing will stop her from giving herself over to this guy?"

Landon leveled him with an unwavering stare.

Knox closed the distance between them. "I'm the one who helped her get treatment and got Mom and Dad into therapy. I set up the foundation for her to focus on, so she could help others and see the value in remaining healthy. I'm the one who visited her while she was in treatment nearly every day. She lived with *me* when she left the care facility, Landon. I have *never* let her down. And Paige? Paige is not a little girl who needs us to monitor her every emotion. She's a grown woman, and yeah, she's twenty-four and that's young, but she's smart as hell and you know it. She knows the signs that lead to trouble. She lost her best friend to that fucking disease. Do you really think I'd leave her emotional health up to chance? What's this really about? Do *you* have a thing for Raz?"

"Fuck off." Landon stepped away, and Knox grabbed his arm, staring into his eyes. The pain was back, and it cut Knox like a knife. Landon had been openly gay from the time he was a teenager. But he'd never flaunted his relationships, leaving the rest of them to guess what he was up to and who he was seeing. He'd had a long-term relationship in college, and Knox had no idea why it had ended, but he'd looked as broken then as he did right now. It was a look Knox would never forget.

"Talk to me. For once in your life, let me in, Landon. I know you, and this isn't about not trusting Paige to handle herself."

"You don't know me." He wrenched out of Knox's grip and stalked away.

"Bullshit. And if I don't, then clue me in. Don't use our sister as an excuse for your decisions. Did that asshole Ruiz or his entourage piss you off? Did he harass you? Did someone else? Did he hit on you?" His voice escalated with each question as his frustration mounted. Landon's nostrils flared, and he knew he'd struck a nerve.

"Fuck off." Landon stalked across the room, his back to Knox.

"Great repertoire you've got going there, bro. Did the media threaten the inn in some way? What the hell is going on?"

Landon gritted his teeth, seething. "Let it go, Knox."

"No. I care about Aubrey, and she cares about Charlotte, which makes this important to me. I deserve to know why you give a damn about something like this. Some prick hits on you and you go off the deep end? I don't believe it. You've been hit on by a million guys. What happened, Landon? Did *you* hit on *him* and he turned you down? Because that's sucky, but it's not—"

"I was in love with Carlos!" Landon snapped, red faced, nostrils flaring. "Jesus, you just can't leave well enough alone, can you? You're such a fucking bulldog."

Knox was stunned into silence. Landon paced like a caged tiger, muscles flexing against his suitcoat. Knox tried to find his voice. "Landon..."

Landon glowered.

"I'm genuinely sorry, man. Did he know?"

Landon continued glaring at him.

"But he was getting *engaged*. He's bisexual? I'm not being an ass. I'm just trying to understand what happened. I'm racking my brain, and I can't remember ever hearing about Carlos Ruiz with a guy."

"He wasn't *out*. I was an idiot. He'd vacationed here eight months before that media nightmare, and we got together. We saw each other often after he left, but we kept it quiet." He sank into the leather couch across the room and buried his face in his hands.

"Your trips to L.A. and Sacramento." It was all falling into place. "His dirty little secret. I'd like to kill the motherfucker. What were you thinking? You've been out forever."

Landon looked up at the ceiling and said, "I wasn't thinking." He leaned his elbows on his thighs and cocked his face toward Knox. "I was so into him, I didn't care that he was closeted. It was stupid and reckless." He scoffed. "Something you would do."

"I'm sorry, bro." Knox sat beside him, his heart aching for Landon. "So, what went down? How'd he end up engaged?"

"He found out the media had pictures of us. We were so damn careful, never doing anything in public. But one night we were having a few drinks on the lawn, and I couldn't help it; I reached for him, and he didn't fight it. They got pictures of us kissing, hands all over each other."

"Aw, fuck."

"I forgot, or maybe subconsciously I thought he'd come around and see we could be together publicly. I don't know. I've asked myself a million times if I did it on purpose. But I swear, Knox, all I remember was how great it felt to make out with him out in the open, even if it was dark and I didn't think anyone could see us."

He put a hand on Landon's shoulder and said, "I get it. You don't have to explain. Love's a powerful driver."

Landon nodded. "Do you love her? Aubrey?"

"Hell, I don't know. I know I care more about her than I ever have about any woman, and it's different with Aubrey. It's like we're the same stubborn person. I can't get enough of her, and I know that's never going to change."

"I know that feeling. Careful, because she nearly choked at my wedding comment."

"She nearly choked at the word *date*."

They both laughed.

"I never saw any pictures of you and Carlos," Knox said. "Did you pay off the paparazzi or something?"

"Hell no," he said adamantly. "He did. He paid them to run the engagement pictures instead. It was all a farce to save his Hollywood reputation. He said he'd never get romantic roles if he was openly gay."

"He *told* you he paid them off?"

Landon nodded.

"Guy's got big balls."

"That's when I ended it. The media came sniffing around again after that, and thank God I didn't have the pictures of us that they had. I was so hurt and angry, I probably would have paid the guy to run them." He laughed and said, "Not really."

"No shit. That's not your style." Knox sat back, glad Landon was letting him into his life and wishing he'd been there when it had all gone down. "Are you really worried about Paige and Raz?"

Landon shrugged.

"You have my word about Paige, but I have faith in her strength. I think she's too invested in being happy to let herself get lost in some guy."

"Maybe you're right. She doesn't know about any of this, and neither does anyone else. I'd like to keep it that way."

"Of course. We'll just let them think you have a hair up your ass about paparazzi. You going to be okay?"

"Eventually..."

"I might be a stubborn ass, but I love you," Knox said honestly. "You know that, right? I'm here for you. And when I'm not physically here, I'm a phone call away. Got it?"

"Sure. Thanks."

"You know what happened between you and Carlos has nothing to do with Aubrey using the inn for the movie, right?"

He nodded. "But I still don't want a movie filmed here.

Movie stars and media...It's all a bad memory. Isn't there anywhere else she can go?"

"She's been looking for a long time. On the way here she said she was trying not to get excited but that she had her heart set on this place. You don't think you're making this too personal instead of thinking about what it could do for the inn? It sounds to me like you need a good publicity push now that the ski resort opened."

"Aren't *you* making it too personal?"

Knox exhaled loudly. He wasn't willing to give up. His brother was a smart man. Eventually he'd come around and realize it would be good for the inn, for Aubrey, and even though Knox wasn't always his favorite person, Knox knew Landon loved him. He hoped seeing how much this would mean to him would also help change his mind.

"Maybe we're both wrong," Knox admitted. "But I'm a stubborn dick driven by emotions that are bigger than me, so I'm going to suggest that we both give it some time before writing it off and see how we feel in a couple weeks."

Landon shook his head. "You coming to Mom and Dad's Gratitude Ball in two weeks? I'm sure you got the save the date *and* the invitation."

"Not a chance, and yes, I RSVP'd. So, a couple weeks, then?"

"You always have to push the limits."

Knox rose to his feet and smiled as he said, "And you always have to live within them."

Landon moved to stand, and Knox said, "Relax. I can let myself out. Couple weeks? Then we'll circle back, talk it over?"

"We can circle back, but you know what my decision is going to be."

"We'll see about that." Knox pulled open the door and said, "They don't call me the closer for nothing."

"If you close deals as well as you nail down a commitment from your girlfriend, I'm in the clear."

His brother's snickers followed Knox out the door.

PAIGE GAVE AUBREY a tour of the inn, and with every spacious room they explored, Aubrey became even more certain that the Monroe House was the right location for the movie. The inn had staircases with intricate iron balusters instead of elevators, exquisitely carved moldings throughout, and attention given to the smallest of details, like monogramed soap dishes, romantic canopy beds, and antique furniture in the suites. The inn also boasted several elegant terraces, just like the Sterling House.

As they crossed the hardwood floors in one of the ballrooms, Paige said, "I know books and movies differ, but remember that scene in the book where the heroine made that romantic sheet fort under the stars? The *dreamscape*? Will that be in the movie?"

Aubrey remembered that scene well. It was one of her favorites. Charlotte had told her that she'd created a dreamscape for Beau, and it had been a changing point in their relationship. "Yes," she said. "Char would be devastated if it was cut."

"I'm glad to hear that. We have the perfect grouping of trees for it."

She pointed out the terrace doors over acres of crisp manicured landscape beneath the winter-white sky. Flurries danced in the frigid air, dusting the ground.

"See where the property dips just beyond that cluster of bushes? It evens out just down that hill, and there's a clearing with a big oak tree and several other trees with low branches. Knox hung a swing from the oak when they were kids, and *boy* did he get in trouble. He snuck out and did it during one of my parents' parties, came back with bloody hands, his nice clothes dirty and torn up from climbing the tree. He was a mess, but he smiled like he'd just done the greatest thing in the world. And to me he had. My parents were renovating the wine cellar at the time, and he'd stolen some expensive wood, cut it up—cut his hand in the process. There was blood everywhere. But he made the swing, and then he sat out here on the terrace during the party until he saw me walk by. He said he felt like he'd sat there forever but was afraid to go inside looking like he did because I wouldn't get a chance to see the swing. He motioned for me to come out, and then he took me down there." Her gaze softened, and the sweetest smile appeared on her lips. "I loved that swing so much. Still do. I go down there to get away sometimes. And that was so typical of Knoxy, to risk getting in trouble for me."

"*Knoxy?*" Aubrey warmed at the endearment and went all soft and gooey inside knowing he'd done something so special for Paige.

"Oh gosh, I know," Paige said softly. "Don't you dare tell him I let that name slip. He only lets me call him that when no one else is around."

Paige was so enthusiastic. Aubrey guessed her to be twenty-three or -four to Aubrey's thirty. She remembered what she'd been like at that age, bold and bubbling with excitement at every new thought and adventure. She was still bold and excited over new endeavors, but she'd been hardened by the cutthroat business world. She'd felt the changes taking place over the years, but never had it been more noticeable than it was as they toured the inn and Paige's love for the property, and her family, came out in droves through her effervescent sharing of their history. The world hadn't yet slayed Paige with cynicism, and Aubrey realized Knox came across just as optimistic and trusting. He might have blazed his own path away from his family businesses, but he obviously cared deeply for them.

"My lips are sealed," Aubrey reassured her. "Were you two always so close?"

"For the most part. We went to the same prep schools, but he's older than me, so we had different lives. But he always made time for me, searched me out to make sure I was okay and wasn't getting into trouble."

"Bet that was fun, trying to date with him around."

Paige fiddled with the ends of her dark hair, her smile fading a bit. "I didn't date, but not because of Knox. Or Landon for that matter. Landon was off to college by then, but he still kept tabs on me. I missed family, being home. So I never thought of my brothers' attention as a bad thing. Besides, while my friends were into boys as teenagers, I was a late bloomer. I was just glad to have girlfriends who included me in their lives as if I were their family."

There was sadness in her voice, and just as Aubrey opened her mouth to ask about it, Paige lifted her chin, exhaled loudly, and smiled as she said, "The truth is, dating wasn't part of my life until I became a model, and even then, there wasn't romance as I had envisioned there would be. My life was crazy all the time, between traveling and keeping up with my parents' events. My mother, ever the matchmaker, was always setting me up with these prominent, wealthy men—all too stuck-up for me. And then there were the model groupies—the guys who thought they could bang us because we sometimes modeled lingerie. I swear true romance doesn't exist in the modeling world."

Paige sighed and said, "I lived and breathed the business, and I thought I was *on top of the world*. Thank God for Knox. You know how pushy he can be. He's been my savior more than once. So…?" She leaned closer, touching Aubrey's arm like she was sharing a secret. "What's *really* going on with you guys? He's never brought a woman home. Not even a business associate."

Paige was so open and warm, it was easy to share with her, and though Aubrey quickly weighed the pros and cons of revealing any of her heart, the truth came tumbling out. "We're close, have been for a couple years. He's special." He really was, she admitted to herself. *Oh God, here I go again, waxing romantic.* Nipping that slippage in the bud, she said, "But we're not dating, though he'd like to be. I've just got so much on my plate right now with the new movie channel and the rest of the business. I don't want to get caught up in anything that might thwart my attention from where it needs to be."

"I totally get that," Paige said as they headed out of the ballroom. "Relationships take effort, and being with Knox, well, that's like *strap on a seat belt and get ready for a wild ride!*"

Thinking of how wild Knox was in bed, Aubrey felt her eyes widen and quickly tried to wipe the grin off her face.

"What?" Paige asked innocently. "I know my brother, and he's *drama* personified. He's relentless."

She thought about the gifts he'd sent and the fact that she was standing in the Monroe House, exactly where he'd wanted her to be. "You can say that again."

"He's just so darn passionate about every project he takes on—don't think you're a project, because that's not what I mean. The fact that he's here asking for a favor shows just how far he's willing to go for you because my brother does not ask us for anything. *Ever*. He's the giver when it comes to me and Landon, but he's never a taker."

Aubrey swallowed hard. Why hadn't she realized that earlier? She knew how hard he'd worked to separate himself from his family businesses. "I appreciate Knox going out on a limb for me, but please don't feel like you have to agree to it just because he's family."

"Are you kidding? I want to do this because it's exciting. And...*Duncan Raz*! I'd have to be a crazy woman not to want to meet that tall glass of champagne. But I'm not the one he has to convince."

She glanced down the hall and smiled. Aubrey followed her gaze and saw Knox standing and talking with a gentleman.

"Before he steals you away, can I just say something? I really like you, Aubrey, and you know I love Knox. I wish you wouldn't close the door between being *close* and *dating* too fast. He's a really good guy, and yes, he's passionate and not quiet about his opinions. But you've done so much with your career. You're obviously dedicated and want to continue building LWW, which is so admirable. I'm in awe of you. But please be careful. I know you seem happy with your life as it is, but being that focused on work can hinder people in ways they don't realize. A person can actually be unhappy when they think they're at their happiest. I'm not saying that you are. I'm just saying maybe there's room in your life for a little *more* happiness."

"You sound like you have experience with that," Aubrey

said softly.

"Don't we all?"

Aubrey watched Knox striding toward them, his gaze shifting from Paige to her. His friendly smile morphed to one of desire, and Aubrey felt her cheeks heat up.

Paige nudged her and whispered, "That blush is happiness, too. Just a different kind."

Chapter Five

"YOU COULD HAVE clued me in about you and your family owning this place," Aubrey said to Knox on their way to her suite a little while later. "That's more than having an *in* with the owners."

"An *in* is an *in*," he said with a bite to his tone.

"Are you okay? I didn't mean I don't appreciate it."

"I'm fine," he said a little softer. "Family stuff, that's all."

"Because of me wanting the inn?"

Knox smiled and said, "No."

"Did you think I wouldn't come with you if I knew you were a part owner?"

"Would you have?" he asked as she used the keycard to open the door.

"I don't know. I want the inn for Char's sake, but I know how hard you worked to distance yourself from your family's business enterprises. Why did you offer to try to change their minds?"

He followed her into the suite and said, "Because Char's important to you."

"Still..." She tossed her keycard on the dresser, trying to ignore how deeply that touched her. She rooted around in her suitcase for jeans and a sweater to wear on the way home. "Thank you, Knox. I appreciate you going to bat for me. That was very generous. I like Landon and Paige. They seem nice and like they miss seeing you. Is it true that you haven't seen them since before you went to Belize? Don't you miss them?"

His arms circled her waist as he said, "Shh. We've got this gorgeous suite all to ourselves." He eyed the bed. "We could make good use of this bed before we leave."

He kissed her neck. His tongue slid along her skin, bringing rise to goose bumps. He continued tasting and taunting, and Aubrey mentally debated a quick tryst before their drive home.

"I love how sweet you taste," he said as he groped her ass, holding her tight against him.

"Knox," she said wantonly, and closed her eyes, reminding herself to be careful. He was too easy to get lost in, and now she was even more curious about the rest of his life. She was usually so good at compartmentalizing their togetherness. But everything he was doing—asking his family for a favor, getting her a suite of her own, taunting her with his wicked mouth—made her want to step outside the compartment and explore.

"Hm?" *Kiss, kiss. Lick.*

"I don't trade sexual favors for business favors," she said half-heartedly.

He drew back, brows knitted, eyes serious. "That's what you think this is?"

"No," she said honestly. "I'm just trying to keep my head on straight. You haven't even told me how it went with Landon."

"It's going to take some time and finesse, but he's thinking about it." A smile rose in his eyes and he said, "Don't worry, beautiful. I've got this. Landon and I go way back."

"Like to *birth*," she teased. "It seemed like things aren't great between you two."

"Actually, this is pretty good for us. We're about as tight as two brothers who grew up wanting different things could be. I'd kill for him, and he'd call out the guards to kill for me."

She laughed. "He looks pretty fit. I bet he could kick some serious ass."

"He could, but he never would. He's too refined for that."

"Well, I like him. And not that it's my business, but time with family is important. Even when you have differences." She patted his chest and said, "I should change so we can get out of here before the storm hits. I still have some shopping to do before my mom's Super Bowl party tomorrow."

"Want to take me as your date?"

"If you saw me watching the Super Bowl with my family, you'd change your mind about dating me. It's not pretty. Oh! I just remembered. Paige said you built her a swing when you were younger and that it would be the perfect place for a scene in the movie. I'd love to see that before we take off if there's time."

"There's always time," he said as she carried her clothes toward the bathroom. "I've seen you naked. You can change here."

"If I take off my clothes in front of you, the only hard wood I'll see is in your pants."

AUBREY SHOVED HER hands in her coat pockets as they walked across the lawn toward the woods. Even with her hat and gloves on, she was freezing. She rounded her shoulders against the bitter cold, and Knox put an arm around her, drawing her against his side.

"Thanks," she said. "Aren't you cold?"

"Nope. When I'm near you, I'm hot all over."

She laughed. "Your sister was right. You are relentless. Why me, Knox? Why now?"

He stopped walking and turned, gathering her against him again. He did that a lot, she realized. But the look in his eyes was one she hadn't seen before, so honest and open it made her feel a little vulnerable, which made no sense at all. *He* should feel vulnerable, but he looked completely confident.

"You're a brilliant businesswoman, a goddess in the bedroom, and I've peeked behind your walls, Aubrey. I've gotten glimpses of the real you. All those times you don't remember talking with me into the wee hours of the morning? They showed me who you really are. The messy-media-room you. I don't know your entire story yet, but I want to. I like who you are, and we're similar in many ways. I even enjoy the way you refuse to go down easy for me."

"The thrill of the chase will wear off," she warned.

"When that happens, the real thrill begins. If there's one thing I learned from growing up with a silver spoon in my mouth, it's that the best things in life don't come easily." He pressed his lips to hers and then he said, "And you, Wattsy, will never be easy."

With his arm around her, they headed down the hill and into the woods. She'd expected him to make a joke, or laugh off her questions, but his honesty made her walls come down a little more.

"Why now?" she asked. "After all this time, why are you so determined to get me to go out with you now?"

"I could lie and say it's because this is what people do after they've been sleeping together for so long. But it's more than that. I saw things in Belize that opened my eyes. I met people who had nothing, but in reality, they had everything because of who they shared it with. They weren't asking for more or ruing what they didn't have, and I realized the only time I feel that way is when I'm with you."

She stopped cold, the magnitude of his confession burgeoning around her. She needed space. She needed to *run*. But he held her too tight.

"Scared shitless?" he asked.

"Kind of," she admitted. It had always been so easy to be herself when they were together. He was her *escape* from the pressures around her, but there was no denying that somewhere over the last two years he'd become more than that. *Much more.*

"Good," he said. "That means you are on the same page as me, like it or not. I knew it New Year's Eve, when we were so desperate for each other that everything else failed to exist. Remember the sparks that flew when you saw me walk into the party? Because I sure as hell do. We barely made it to the hotel room—and then we couldn't tear ourselves away from each other the next day. I'll never forget that, Wattsy."

Her heart was pounding just thinking about the way they'd torn at each other's clothes, devoured each other's bodies like they'd never get enough. And they hadn't gotten enough. Forty-eight hours later, when they'd finally left the hotel, she'd sent a 911 text to Presley and Libby. But when they'd arrived at her house, she couldn't tell them how she felt, because it was *too* big, *too* frightening. She'd dodged Knox's texts after that, until she'd thought she could handle even that small connection without feeling like she was splayed open and his for the taking.

And then they'd seen each other at the event last Saturday night and her desires had grown even stronger. She'd fought against them, but as he'd approached, her resolve had lessened. And when he'd whispered all the dirty things he'd wanted to do to her, she'd surrendered, telling herself it was *just one night.*

"Knox! My boy!"

The excited shout startled Aubrey as a thick-bodied man burst through the trees, bundled up in a black parka and knit cap, arms open wide. He had a white beard and mustache. His cheeks and the tip of his bulbous nose were pink from the cold. He squinted from behind wire-framed glasses, laughing heartily as Knox embraced him.

"Paige mentioned you were coming," he said. "You look good. *Happy.*"

"Thank you, Leon. So do you." Knox put a hand on Aubrey's back, guiding her closer to him. "Leon Rice, this is my very good friend Aubrey Stewart. Leon has been the groundskeeper here forever. He knows all my secrets."

"It's a pleasure to meet you," Aubrey said, offering her hand.

Leon took her hand between both of his and said, "The pleasure is all mine, my dear. And don't let him fool you. Knox couldn't keep a secret if his life depended on it."

"Hey, come on, now," Knox said. "What are you doing out here in the woods?"

"Just securing the swing before the big storm hits. I like to leave it functional for Paige when the weather permits."

"I'm sure she appreciates it. I was just taking Aubrey to see the big oak and the swing."

"She's a beauty," Leon said. "But it's the swing that brings this area to life. It's still Paige's favorite thinking spot. Are you staying for a while? Joyce would love to see you. She stocked up on Goobers and Wonder Bread." He leaned in and said, "Don't tell your mother. You'll get my wife in trouble."

Knox laughed. "I know better. We'll stop in and see her before we take off." He turned to Aubrey and said, "Joyce is our second mother. She cooks for our family."

Leon shook his head. "Cooks, coddles, and misses you like the devil while you're gone. Never seen a woman take so much pleasure in stocking up on Goobers."

"Goobers?" Aubrey raised her brows. "I thought your favorite junk food was Reese's Peanut Butter Cups."

"A very *close* friend, indeed," Leon said with a warm smile. "Looks like you know his *not-so-secret* secrets." He turned his attention to Knox, eyes serious, and asked, "Have you seen Landon?"

"Yeah. I had a nice visit with him."

"He seem okay to you? I'm worried about him," Leon said. "He's been a bit off lately. Uptight."

Knox's expression turned solemn. "He's got a lot going on, but he'll be okay."

"Alrighty, then. I trust you'd know better than me. I should get back up to the house. I still need to take care of a few things before the wind picks up." He turned his palm up toward the sky and said, "Flurries are starting." He patted Knox on the back and said, "Missed you, kiddo." He winked at Aubrey. "Nice to meet you. Enjoy the afternoon, and you two kids drive safely, you hear?"

Aubrey liked the jubilant man. He obviously cared deeply for Knox and his siblings.

"Don't worry. We will." Knox reached for Aubrey's hand.

"I love him!" she gushed "But *Goobers*?"

"You were right. Reese's are my go-to junk food. But Smucker's Goober peanut butter and grape jelly, spread thick on Wonder Bread? Besides you, that's my secret pleasure."

"Oh man, I love that stuff. Why can't you tell your mom about it?"

He made a noise in his throat, a cross between a laugh and a scoff, and said, "Because the Bentleys are too good for preservatives and common foods."

"Are your parents that rigid?"

"I think you mean 'well bred.' Most of us do as we're taught, carry on the ways of our parents." He guided her toward a beautiful oak tree. A swing hung from a thick limb, secured to the trunk with a rope.

"Sorry, yes. *Well bred.* I guess you and I never got that memo," she said, thinking of their junk-food fest. She looked at the enormous oak and surrounding trees. Paige was right. In the spring or summer the leaves and surrounding foliage would be ripe with color, perfect for the dreamscape scene. But it was the swing that drew her forward. She ran her fingers over the wooden seat and the ropes that tethered it to the massive trunk. She imagined Knox as a young boy, climbing the tree, the rope wrapped around him as he shimmied out on the limb to secure it for his sister. "How old were you when you made this for Paige?"

"I don't know. Ten maybe."

"Why did you do it the night of one of your parents' parties? To piss them off?" She knew he'd always been rebellious, and she was curious about how he'd pushed his parents' buttons.

"We lived at school, and when we were home, most of our time was spent following our parents around the world for our father's business or sitting quietly by while they hosted dinners or parties. You know most of being from old money is keeping up appearances, supporting those with like stations in life, and of course, making more money." He pushed a hand through his hair, which was now speckled with snowflakes. "All Paige ever wanted was to play dress-up and hide-and-seek, have a swing set, and be a typical little girl. But between traveling, attending functions, and our parents' charitable obligations, there was no time for normalcy." He shrugged. "She spent years trying to be perfect in every way, and it nearly killed her."

Aubrey's heart sank. "How?"

"She never had to work, and she still doesn't. But she wanted to prove herself and do something she loved. She got into modeling, and because of it she developed an eating disorder. She's always been thin, but along with modeling came insurmountable pressure. Drugs and alcohol were prevalent. It was a toxic environment."

"You said she wanted to do something she loved. Do you think she loved modeling? Or was she trying to fulfill her young-girl fantasies of playing dress-up? Either way, it's awful to go through life feeling invisible. She's so sweet. I can't imagine what she's gone through."

"It was bigger than playing dress-up," he said. "Feeling invisible is pretty spot-on. She craved attention, being part of a group that would see her for *her*, not part of all this. But in the process, she lost her best friend, Adele, whom she'd known since she was a kid. Adele's family owns the Bagnor Modeling Agency."

"Oh gosh. Adele Bagnor was her best friend? I read about her having a heart attack on the runway."

He nodded. "Paige loved her so much. I thought we'd lose

her, too. I had tried to get Paige out of that environment and get her help, but she wouldn't leave Addy. She called me when Addy collapsed. I flew out there, determined to drag her back to New York with me, but I didn't have to. She was a mess and was finally ready to seek help." Sadness washed over his face. "She told me Addy taught her how to purge and how to starve herself. I had no idea she was doing it, but it all started to make sense."

"How horrible." Aubrey wrapped her arms around her middle, thinking of how Presley had done just the opposite, eating her feelings before finally taking control of her health.

"Paige might appear frail," Knox said, "but she's strong and determined. She was just lost. Once she made up her mind to get healthy and deal with all of her issues, we got her into a treatment facility. When she left there she came to live with me. And now she's in a good place. She volunteers at another facility helping others who are suffering through the same disease."

"Wow. I had no idea she'd gone through so much. She seems so happy."

"She *is* happy. She's *alive*, and she knows she might not have been if she hadn't gotten help. She also has twenty-four-seven access to me and Landon, real friends she's made at the inn and through an online book club she's involved with. She travels pretty often to see the friends she's made in her club. She needed that normalcy. And she really is fantastic at event planning, but you should see her artwork. It's her secret gift. Painting was part of her therapy, and she pours her emotions into it."

"And your parents? Where did they fit into her therapy? Seems like they might have been at the root of her problems."

"They stepped up for Paige. They were there for her during

her recovery. They went through counseling with her, and they've been there for her ever since. It nearly killed them. Honestly, it was the first time I saw them as *parents*. They've softened a lot since then."

"A silver lining to an otherwise awful story." The more Knox shared, the closer Aubrey felt to him, and she was surprised how much she liked it. "I'm glad Paige is okay now."

"Eating disorders don't go away, Aubrey. It'll be an ongoing part of her life that needs managing like an alcoholic or a drug addict. But we talk often, and now Landon and I know what signs to look for. We both got educated. I only wish we'd done it sooner."

"My father always says there's no crying over fumbles; just make sure you don't make the same mistakes twice." To lighten the mood she said, "Given all you've just said, I take it you and Landon never wrestled around in the grass or ran around like wild banshees?"

"Landon?" He smiled. "Hell, even as a kid my brother would rather negotiate than argue or get physical. I was wild enough for both of us, usually convincing some of our parents' friends' kids to come along with me."

"The troublemaker." She stepped closer, gazing up at him and seeing him through new eyes. He wasn't just a cocky guy who loved great sex and had a fun sense of humor. He was a caring, deeply connected *brother* and friend. "That doesn't surprise me, but it does make me sad. It sounds like you and your siblings missed out on a lot."

He shrugged again. "Trust me, I didn't miss out on that much. I didn't forgo fun. I just got grief from my parents when I had it."

"I'm getting a pretty good idea of why you put distance

between you and them."

A flash of something dark—regret maybe?—flashed in his eyes. "I love my family, Aubrey. I just don't belong in this world."

"But you still attend events elsewhere, and you are in this world just by the nature of your worth."

He shook his head. "No. I mean *this* particular world. I couldn't run a business with my father or attend functions feeling like the protégé he only wanted to show off. I'm not about those things. You know that."

"I do," she said. "But I didn't know you grew up here at the inn."

"I grew up in the schools I told you about." He put a hand on her back, guiding her through the clearing to a path in the woods. "I spent time at the inn for functions, and I knew the staff, who were always so happy to see me that I would go in and hang out with them instead of my parents. I used to follow Leon around the yard pestering him."

"He must not have minded, because he obviously adores you."

"As I do him." The path ended at an estate surrounded by endless lawn and gardens. "But this is where we slept. Our childhood home."

Where we slept. It was sad to hear him refer to his childhood home that way, but she was glad she understood *why* he did. She couldn't help but gawk at the sprawling stone estate that put her ridiculously large house to shame. There were so many wings to the mansion, it looked like it could sleep all of Port Hudson, her small hometown. There was a pool, tennis courts, and several other houses on the property.

"Are there more siblings I don't know about?"

"Nope. Just the three of us. Appearances, babe. That's what the Monroe and Bentley families are all about. At least my parents' generation. Paige and Landon aren't like that."

"But they live here and work with your parents?"

"Yes, but Landon and Vincent run the show at the inn. I'm sorry if Vincent was rude to you on the phone. I think he was just following Landon's orders about unwanted events that might cause a stir with the media. Landon works with my father on other projects, but he's a pleaser. We're very different."

"I saw that, except I think you guys also have a few things in common. But wow, Knox. You grew up with a tennis court? I thought I had it made with a trampoline *and* a tree fort."

"I'd rather have had the trampoline and tree fort. I guess I shouldn't mention the indoor pool, sauna, six-thousand-square-foot pool house, guesthouses, eight-car garage, or the house-keepers. And of course no mansion is complete without a wine cellar."

"Okay, yeah, you probably shouldn't mention any of that. It's a bit intimidating. I feel like I should have kept on my Chanel and Christian Louboutins."

He pulled her closer as they traipsed across the lawn and said, "You look hot in anything, but I prefer you in this. Actually, that's not true. I prefer you *naked*, but you'd freeze your sexy little ass off."

"You've got sex on the brain."

"We could sneak in to one of the guesthouses…"

"You have no shame. Is it true that you stole wood for the swing from the wine cellar?"

"Yup. I also almost lost my virginity in the wine cellar." He arched a brow. "Leon cockblocked me, and then he gave me a lecture about how to treat a woman."

"Oh my God. That must have been embarrassing."

"Nah. I was barely fifteen, and he was right. The girl was seventeen and staying at the inn. I'd only just met her, but she was flaunting everything and I was a kid with a raging hard-on every time the wind blew."

She gazed up at him, blinking away the snowflakes peppering her lashes. "So you've always had a thing for older women."

He just grinned, so cocky. *So Knox.*

Snowflakes floated around them, giving the moment a magical feel. Aubrey had so many feelings and thoughts about all that he'd shared with her, but the overriding one was that she didn't want to drive a wedge of space or time between them. She wanted to do something just for Knox, to give him something no one else had made an effort to do. She couldn't change his childhood, but maybe she could make part of one of his childhood dreams come true.

She took his hand and said, "How about you give me a tour of that wine cellar?"

Chapter Six

KNOX LED AUBREY down the stone steps from the yard and into the wine cellar beneath his childhood home. The familiar rich scent of cold stone brought memories of following his father down to get a bottle of wine and the lessons that came with each expedition. He and his father had shared rare moments of warmth, but for the most part his father had used their time together to prepare Knox for his life as a Bentley. Lectures on the value of a dual-zoned, temperature-controlled wine cellar and tamper-proof, biometric security systems were part and parcel to his education. But the lessons his father thrust upon him the most revolved around investment strategies and negotiation tactics. As far back as he could remember, his father had groomed him toward financial endeavors. He'd done a fine job, because Knox was an investment prodigy. He'd begun investing when he was in high school, and he'd made his first million before he'd graduated from MIT.

"I've seen some impressive wine cellars, but this takes the cake," Aubrey said, running her hand over the back of one of two leather couches.

The walls and floor were stone, the ceiling a mosaic of Italian tiles. Built-in floor-to-ceiling wine racks showcased more bottles of expensive wine than one family could ever drink, and glass partitions protected large refrigerated areas. The cellar boasted a series of tasting and workrooms, crystal chandeliers, and the lounge where they now stood, which had two staircases—one that led outside and one that led into the house.

Aubrey sauntered around the couch, pulling off her gloves as she went. "So this is where you thought you'd lose your virginity?"

She dropped her gloves to the floor and shrugged off her coat, letting that fall to the floor, too. Her knit hat came next, tossed behind her as she closed the distance between them, looking sexy as fuck. Knox unzipped his coat and took off his gloves, his body sizzling with desire. She had a way of turning him on in seconds—one look, one touch, one scorching kiss...

"How would that have gone?" she asked as she pushed her hands beneath his coat and over his shoulders, sending it to the floor.

"At fifteen? I'd imagine I'd barely have gotten it in before I lost it."

She laughed and pulled off his hat. He loved her laugh and how she let her guard down so easily when they were alone.

"You sure fixed that problem," she said huskily, "didn't you?"

She pushed his chest, and he plunked down on the couch, catching her hand in his.

She straddled his lap and began unbuttoning his shirt. "I hate that you were cockblocked and had your horny teenage dreams squashed."

He fucking loved that she cared enough to put herself out there for him. He framed her face with his hands and captured her mouth in a ravenous kiss, pouring all of the unearthed emotions into their connection. When he tried to shift her onto her back, she fought for dominance. Relenting was not a hardship. He eased his efforts, allowing her to take control. She deepened the kiss, taking as much as she gave as she ground against him. She tore away long enough to say, "I love kissing you," and then her mouth found his again, forceful and hungry.

He knew how much she loved kissing, how she lost herself in it every time they were together. He could kiss her for hours, and sometimes they did just that after making love. She moaned and mewled, fisting her hands in his hair and driving him out of his mind. He buried his hands in *her* hair as her mouth slipped away, and she kissed his cheeks, his jaw, and worked her way down his neck to his chest. She unbuttoned the rest of his shirt and roughly pushed it open. Heat and desire glimmered in her eyes as she kissed her way down his body. She slicked her tongue over his abs and moved off his lap, kneeling before him as she ripped open the button of his jeans. He made quick work of pushing them down to his ankles.

"Commando," she said hungrily. "My favorite playground."

She had no idea how much of her heart she revealed with her comments, but Knox didn't miss a thing, and with Aubrey, he never had. She dragged her tongue from base to tip, lingering at the crown. His head fell back and he closed his eyes as her hand circled his cock, and she lowered her mouth over every inch of him. She worked him tight and sucked him hard, knowing exactly how to bring him to the edge of release.

"Holy fuck," he said through gritted teeth.

His hips rocked in time to her efforts. Just when he was about to lose it, she drew back slowly and said, "Don't come. I want to do it here with you to fulfill that fantasy."

She lowered her face between his legs, sucking one of his

balls into her mouth, still working him with her hand. His eyes slammed shut as he fought to stave off his orgasm.

"Christ, babe. If you want to fuck me, you'd better get to it, because you are *way* too good at this."

She lifted her gaze, full of wicked intent, and lowered her mouth to his inner thigh to place a feathery kiss. And then she sank her teeth into his flesh.

"Jesus, fuck." His hips bolted off the couch and she took him into her mouth again. She knew all his favorite things. "Baby, baby, baby," he panted out, gripping the base of his cock, trying not to come. But her mouth was heaven, and her hands and teeth were magic.

Fuck. This.

He grabbed her and crashed his mouth to hers as he rose to his feet, bringing her up with him. He tore off her sweater and bra and stripped down her jeans and panties.

"Boots!" she panted out.

He chucked his shirt and boots and stepped from his jeans as she tore off her own. They were naked, save for their socks, but he wasn't about to slow down for that. He lifted her into his arms and lowered her onto his shaft. They both moaned with the intensity of their connection. She dug her nails into his shoulders as they ground and thrust. But it wasn't enough. He needed to be closer and ungracefully lowered them to the couch, earning a sweet and sexy giggle. Man, he loved that, too. He drove into her harder, faster, and she met every thrust of his with an angle of her hips, a sinful noise, or a plea for more. She clutched his ass when she got close to climaxing, and he knew just what to do, slowing his pace so he stroked over the secret spot that made her whole body flex.

"Yes, yes, *yes!*" she cried out, bucking wildly as he followed her over the most exquisite edge, chanting her name like a prayer.

They clung to each other, panting through the very last aftershock, their bodies slick with perspiration despite the cool temperature. Her head fell back and her eyes fluttered open. She was so unguarded, so beautifully open, he swore his heart skipped a beat.

They lay together for a long while as their breathing calmed, and then they lay there longer, tangled up on the couch like one was not complete without the other.

"That was so much better than teenage sex," he said. Then he kissed her smiling lips. "Did I ever tell you about the time I was cockblocked in my parents' car?"

She laughed.

"What? I figured we could live out all of my old fantasies."

"How about we live out mine instead?"

"Now we're talking. Spill it, baby. I will make every juicy detail come true."

She bit her lower lip, trying to halt an unstoppable smile. He kissed her lip free and she touched his cheek, studying his face like a map. Her expression turned serious, and she said, "I'm sorry you had a stressful childhood."

"It's all good, babe. Your dad's advice was solid. The past is the past." He pressed his lips to hers and said, "Now, about those fantasies...?"

Her expression remained serious. "Right now I'm fantasizing about your fancy parents having a bathroom in the wine cellar."

He touched his forehead to her shoulder, breathing her in. "Why do you fight what's between us? Joke it off?"

"I'm lying naked with you inside me. That's not exactly

fighting," she said softly.

He gazed into her eyes. They were softer now, trusting and open once again. There were so many things he wanted to say—*Let me all the way in. Don't be afraid of us*—but instead he said, "I love your body, but it's your heart I want."

Her eyes narrowed a little, as if she were thinking. A small smile lifted her lips and she said, "Knoxy, you are my favorite pushy man."

"*Knoxy?* Goddamn *Paige...*" He climbed off her and pulled her to her feet, gathering her in his arms. "I'm your *favorite* playground, your *favorite* pushy guy. Are you trying to tell me there are others? Because there's only been you since last year."

Her eyes widened.

"It's true, Aubrey. Is that so hard to believe?" When she didn't respond, but continued looking at him like a deer caught in headlights, he ground out, "Shit. You're seeing other guys and don't want to stop." He pointed to a hallway and reached for his shirt. "The bathroom's down there."

She gathered her clothes, clutched them against her chest, and headed for the bathroom.

Knox washed up after she was done, telling himself he was a fool for thinking she wasn't seeing other guys. He'd disappeared for months. A woman like Aubrey was probably propositioned all the time. Why wouldn't she accept? He looked in the bathroom mirror and said, "You stupid fuck. This is karma. Payback for all the shit you did as a kid."

He threw open the door and found Aubrey sitting on the floor, her knees pulled up to her chest, her arms circling them. She lifted her chin, her amber eyes full of worry, her golden hair framing her beautiful face.

He dropped to one knee. "What's wrong?"

"You," she said flatly.

"Whoa. Okay. I get it, Aubrey. You don't have to feel bad for having a personal life."

"I don't."

He pushed to his feet, and she reached up and used the waist of his jeans to pull herself to her feet.

"Let's get out of here before the snow hits," he suggested. He needed space between them so he could wrap his head around the reality he didn't want to accept.

She shook her head. "I meant I don't have that type of personal life. I haven't been with anyone else for a long time. I just didn't want you to know that because it gives you more fuel for your *date-me* fire."

It took a few seconds for him to fully process what she'd said. "Holy shit, Aubrey. You're a brat—you know that?" He backed her up against the wall.

"That's definitely not going to win me over," she said teasingly, but he could tell she was still getting used to the idea of starting to accept her feelings for him.

"Do you have any idea what type of torture you just put me through?"

"Do you know what kind of torture it is feeling this way about you?" she snapped. "About a guy whose middle name is *Drama*? I've worked so hard, and this is scary stuff, admitting that to you. I can't afford to be sidetracked from my career, especially now that I have a new channel to get off the ground."

The affection in her eyes belied the vehemence of her words. "Since when are you afraid of *anything*? Including a little drama?" He pressed closer. "You know what I think? I think you need to be punished for making me think I was so off base."

Her eyes darkened, and as he lowered his lips toward hers,

she said, "We'll never beat the storm if I let you near my body again." She wiggled out of his arms and took off running for the stairs.

KNOX GRABBED THEIR coats and took the steps two at a time, catching Aubrey around the waist before she reached the top. She squealed, crashing against his chest with an *oomph*. She tried to scowl, but his laughter only made her laugh even harder.

"You cannot escape me, Aubrey Stewart."

She struggled against him as voices filtered in through the door at the top of the stairs. She froze, only then realizing she'd run up a different set of stairs than the ones they'd come down. "Who's that?"

He looked at the door as a muffled male voice sounded. "Sounds like Leon and my father."

"Your *father*?" she whispered harshly. "We had sex in his wine cellar and he was right upstairs?" She swatted his chest.

"Hey! I didn't know he was here," he whispered. "I figured my parents were out since Landon didn't mention them being home."

"Let's go out the other way. This is embarrassing."

She started down the stairs just as the door opened at the top, and Knox grabbed her hand.

Leon peered down at them from the top of the stairs. Snow dusted the shoulders of his coat and hat. Beside him stood an aristocratic-looking man dressed in an expensive suit and tie, with thick salt-and-pepper hair, black-framed glasses, and a broad shoulder line as rigid as the set of his jaw. His eyes were as sharp as Knox's were playful—though at the moment there was nothing playful about Knox's expression. But in his father's wise eyes she saw a hint of his son, and when his lips lifted into a slight smile, she caught another glimpse of Knox in him.

Leon winked at them, grinning like a coconspirator. "I was just telling your father that you were giving Aubrey a tour of the house."

Guess he hadn't wanted to cockblock Knox this time…

Knox pulled Aubrey up to the step beside him. "Thanks, Leon. Hi, Dad. Aubrey, this is my father, Griffin Bentley. Dad, this is Aubrey Stewart. Aubrey and I had a meeting with Landon and Paige earlier, and I thought I'd show her around."

In her head she heard him say, *And fuck her brains out in your wine cellar.* She forced those thoughts—and her embarrassment—aside and extended her hand to his father as Leon quietly slipped away. "It's a pleasure to meet you, Mr. Bentley. Your properties are gorgeous."

"Thank you," he said as they joined him and closed the cellar door.

Griffin's eyes warmed as he looked at Knox, both of them stepping into an awkward embrace. Before that moment, Aubrey could never have imagined Knox looking awkward doing anything.

"You look good, son. Paige mentioned you had a project you wanted to discuss with her and Landon," Griffin said. "I assume things went well?"

"Yes," Knox answered. "I didn't realize you were here. I would have come through the house."

"Well, you know now," he said evenly. "Perhaps you can stay for a visit? It's been too long."

"Do I hear *Knox*?" A female voice traveled down the hall before a tall, slim brunette appeared through an arched entryway. Her hands flew up in surprise. "I'd know my boy's voice anywhere." She hurried toward them, her high heels clicking on the marble floor as she motioned for Knox to come toward her. She embraced him warmly, air-kissing each of his cheeks. Then she held on to his arms, her happy gaze rolling over his face. "You look good, sweetheart. I've missed you."

"Missed you too, Mom." Knox reached for Aubrey's hand and said, "Mom, this is—"

"Aubrey Stewart," his mother said warmly. "Oh, honey, Aubrey needs no introduction. She's only one of the best role models for women today. Why, the ladies at the club and I were just talking about all that you and your partners have accomplished with the Ladies Who Write." She took Aubrey's hand and held it as she said, "It is an honor to meet you. My name is Elizabeth, and I hope you will consider joining us for a family dinner this evening."

"Thank you so much for the invitation," Aubrey said. She was pretty sure his parents wouldn't understand her need to attend a Super Bowl party, so she said, "But we're driving back to Port Hudson today. I have a lot of work to catch up on tomorrow."

Elizabeth's brow furrowed. "Oh, goodness. Haven't you seen the weather? We've gotten six inches of snow. They're calling for upward of six more before nightfall, and it's supposed to continue snowing through tomorrow evening. The mountain roads will be treacherous. I'm afraid you're stuck here. But we can make the best of it, have a nice dinner, get to know one another. I can have Joyce whip up something wonderful for us and invite Paige and Landon."

Aubrey must have looked as shocked as she felt, because Knox's hand landed protectively on her lower back, and he said, "Sure, Mom. That would be nice, thank you. I want to introduce Aubrey to Joyce, and then I think we'll head back to the inn so Aubrey can take care of the work she mentioned. Mind if I take the snowmobile?"

"It hasn't been used since you were here last winter," his father said. "Leon has kept it tuned up. You know where the keys are."

Knox nodded.

"Thank you for your hospitality," Aubrey said, trying not to sound upset about missing her family's party. "I look forward to seeing you at dinner." As she and Knox walked down the hall, she whispered, "Dinner with your *parents*? What are we, going steady now?"

He chuckled as he led her through an elegant sitting room with a beautiful view of the winter wonderland outside.

"Holy cow," she said. "Look at that snow. How long were we in the cellar?"

"Long enough for us to enjoy each other." He stood beside her and said, "I'm really sorry about missing your family's Super Bowl party. We can still try to drive in it, if you'd like."

She didn't like the idea of missing the party, but with snow falling outside and Knox's warm hands wrapping around hers, she could think of worse things than spending time at a gorgeous romantic inn with him. She was a little shaken by the idea of having dinner with his parents, but she'd seen love in Knox's eyes when he'd hugged them, even if the relationship between him and his father seemed somewhat strained. Knox was doing so much for her, she wanted to do this for him.

Or maybe I don't need a reason beyond wanting to do it for us.

She gazed into his eyes and thought, *For the us you want so badly, the one that challenges everything I believe I need to remain on top of my game.*

The us I think I might want, too.

"I'd rather not die on the roads, but I appreciate the thought. It's fine. I'll just text my mom and brothers and let them know." She reached into her back pocket and realized she'd left her phone in her suite.

"We can have our own Super Bowl party. Just you and me."

"You know what, Knox? That sounds great."

"Yeah?"

"Yes, it does." It truly did. "But don't say you haven't been warned. I can only be who I am, and as I mentioned, me watching a football game is not quiet *or* pretty. I know everything there is to know about the game, and I hold nothing back."

He pulled her closer. "Are you trying to turn me on? Because that makes you the perfect woman." He pressed his lips to hers and lingered, brushing them over hers. "Mm. No smart-ass retort? I think I'm breaking through that brick exterior of yours, Stewart. Let's go before you realize it and change your mind."

"Good plan," she teased. "What was up with the awkward hug between you and your father?"

"My father knows how to excel in business, but he's not quite as good in the parental department. He means well, but he's never been comfortable showing emotions. Although he's much better now than he ever has been. Paige's close call changed him. Come on. I want you to meet Joyce."

"Can we grab some food, too? Our wine-cellar tryst made me hungry. I'd love some finger food."

A greedy laugh escaped as he pulled her into another kiss.

"We are two of a kind."

"I meant like a sandwich and chips, *sex machine*, as opposed to fancy restaurant food *or* your body parts."

"Babe, you have a dirty mind. I meant that I was starved for real food, too."

"Mm-hm…"

He curled his fingers around her hip, stopping her just outside an enormous kitchen with two islands and loads of counter space. A thick-waisted woman stood with her back to them, humming as she cut vegetables. She wore a plum-colored dress with a pink apron tied around her middle. Her rounded hips swayed to nonexistent music. Her white hair was short and layered, like Aubrey's grandmother used to wear hers.

"That's Joyce, Leon's wife," Knox whispered. He stepped into the kitchen and began whistling the same tune Joyce was humming.

Joyce spun around, and a vibrant smile appeared, lighting up her dark eyes. "Knoxy," she said warmly. She set down the knife she was holding and wiped her hands on the apron as she walked into his open arms. "Sweetheart, I've missed you."

"I've missed you, too," he said, holding her a little longer than he had his own parents. "You look as beautiful as always."

"Pfft," she said, glancing at Aubrey. "Still the charmer, I see."

He took Aubrey's hand and said, "Joyce, this is my *special* friend, Aubrey Stewart. Aubrey, this is Joyce. If it weren't for her, I probably would have grown up to be a real cad."

Joyce beamed with his compliment but shook her head. "Nonsense. You don't have that in you." She opened her arms and hugged Aubrey. "It's a pleasure to meet you. Leon told me you two were heading this way. I was worried when you stayed in Belize for so long, Knox, but you look happy. Are you okay?"

Knox snagged a piece of cucumber and popped it into his mouth, raising his brows at Aubrey as he said, "Better than okay."

Witnessing the maternal kindness Joyce lavished on Knox made Aubrey happy, but she felt a lightening in her chest and knew something big had changed inside her. She'd been afraid to confess that she hadn't been with any other guys in so long, worried she'd feel too vulnerable and want to backpedal afterward. But she didn't feel that way at all. She was doing better than okay, too.

"WELL, THAT'S GOOD to hear," Joyce said. "Next time you disappear for months on end, you'd better come see me first."

Knox saluted. "Yes, ma'am."

Joyce was the only person other than Graham and Morgyn he'd told the truth about why he had stayed in Belize, but he'd done it over the phone. Landon had never been one to talk about relationships, and Paige would have wanted to fly out to be with him so he wasn't alone. She'd dealt with enough angst in her short lifetime. But for as long as Knox could remember, Joyce had taken the time to listen when he needed advice. She didn't judge or make him feel bad for wanting to stray from his family's legacy. She supported his desire for a less elitist lifestyle, and her advice was always sound. He'd never forget what she'd said when he'd called. *Some people look for love in all the wrong places. You're not one of them, Knox. You've never needed anyone else to make you feel whole. If you have such strong feelings for this gal that you need to run away to figure them out, then time in the jungle is not going to change them.*

She'd been right.

Knox snagged a piece of a carrot and offered it to Aubrey. "Want some, babe?"

"Sure, thanks."

When she took the carrot, her eyes lingered on his, and he saw something different in them. *Surrender* maybe.

"Where are my manners?" Joyce said. "Knox comes home and my brain turns to mush. Can I get you anything, Aubrey? A cup of warm tea? Hot chocolate?"

"Joyce makes killer hot chocolate," Knox said.

"Sounds perfect. Thank you."

"I just finished making Knox's favorite winter snack," Joyce said as she crossed the kitchen to another counter and retrieved a decorative tray full of tea sandwiches. "White bread and Smucker's Goober peanut butter and grape jelly, just the way you like it."

A warm feeling bloomed inside him. "You're the best. Thank you." He picked up a tea sandwich and held it out for Aubrey. "Finger food at its best."

"I might never leave this kitchen."

They chatted as they ate, and what was supposed to be a quick introduction turned into an enjoyable hour-plus visit with Joyce.

Later, as Joyce went back to preparing dinner, Knox kissed Aubrey's shoulder and handed her his phone. "Didn't you want to call your family?"

"Oh, yes. How did you remember when I forgot?"

"Guess you're more important to me than to yourself."

She snagged his phone and said, "Smart-ass. I'll be quick."

After she left the room to make her call, Joyce sidled up to him. "Tell me," she said quietly. "She's the one? The one you tried to forget?"

"She's the one."

"I like her. She seems sharp but cautious, and she makes you smile. That's all I have ever hoped for. That you, Paige, and Landon would find love like Leon and I share."

"Don't get too carried away."

"It's in your eyes, Knoxy." She put her hand on his and squeezed gently. "That means she's in your heart, too."

Chapter Seven

KNOX DROVE THE snowmobile to the side door, where Aubrey was waiting, huddled up against the cold. He climbed off and reached for her hand. "Climb on, tiger."

"Believe it or not, I've never been on one of these before, so don't flip me off or anything."

"I'll try to refrain from doing any movie-worthy stunts." He sat in front of her and guided her hands around his middle. She was trembling against his back. Whether it was from the cold or nerves, he wasn't sure. He pulled his coat down over her arms and then tucked her hands between his legs.

"Hey!" she complained, but she didn't move her hands.

"Warmth, beautiful. Hang on tight."

The engine roared to life, and snow sprayed around them as they cut through the powder, heading for the inn. He felt Aubrey shielding her face with his back. His tiger had more kitten in her than she cared to admit. When they cleared the woods, he slowed to a stop.

"Why are you stopping?" she hollered.

He climbed off and said, "It's your turn."

Her eyes widened. "Me? I have no idea how to drive this thing. I just told you that."

"Exactly." He patted the front seat. The snow was still coming down, and they were both covered, but he knew she'd warm up from sheer adrenaline once she got the hang of it. "Come on, babe. It's time to build your résumé."

As she scooted forward she said, "I'm sure this will come in handy in the media industry."

"Life is about enjoying all things, and I will take great pleasure in fondling you while you drive."

She rolled her eyes.

"Seriously, though. It's fun to drive, and a woman who can command an empire can surely drive a snowmobile."

He gave her a lesson in all things snowmobile related. "I want you to drive around this level area before trying the hill, okay? And as I said, kneel and lean forward as you take the hill. The deeper the snow, the more speed you'll need. Do you remember how to go faster?"

"Increase the throttle. I've got this. Climb on, big boy. It's your job to keep me warm."

"That's the confidence I adore. When you take the hill, don't stop until you get to the top. If you lose momentum, you may not be able to start climbing again."

She nodded and pulled her hat farther down on her forehead. "I can't tip it, can I?"

"Only if you try really hard." He wrapped his arms around her and teasingly put one hand on her breast, the other between her legs.

She glared at him over her shoulder, making him grin as he readjusted his hands around her waist. He planted a kiss on her cheek and said, "Take me home, Wattsy."

She drove slowly across the level ground, but as he'd anticipated, she quickly gained confidence, and twenty minutes later she was zipping up the hill. When they reached the top, she rode along the level ground and made a big U-turn, hollering, "Can I go down?"

He couldn't resist saying, "When you're with me, you can *go down* all night long…"

ALMOST TWO HOURS later, they parked the snowmobile at the inn.

"Do you have two snowmobiles? Are there trails we could go on? Sorry I got stuck a few times," Aubrey said giddily. She'd lost momentum on one ride up the hill and had gotten stuck in a drift at the bottom of another run, but overall she'd done spectacularly well. "Thank you for teaching me. I can't believe I've lived in Upstate New York all my life and have never done that!"

Excitement radiated around her as she went on about how it felt to control the snowmobile and her love of the power. He wrapped his arms around her and kissed her. Her nose and cheeks were icy cold. He deepened the kiss, and she curled her fingers into his coat, holding on tight. This was a different Aubrey from the one who had arrived at the inn last night. He wanted to do more for her, to keep seeing this carefree side of her, the side he had a feeling she always kept under wraps except in the bedroom.

When their lips parted, they were both a little breathless, and he said, "Ready to warm up?"

"That made me pretty warm," she confessed.

He lowered his lips to hers again, enjoying every second of

her surrender. He sent a few quick, preparatory texts as they headed inside.

"I should check my email," she said. "And get out of these wet clothes."

"How about if we put work on hold for just a little while longer? I have a little something for you first."

They crossed the lobby and headed through a back entrance to the day spa. He led her down the wide hallway, passing Anne, one of the massage therapists.

"Hi, Knox, Aubrey," Anne said, causing surprise to rise in Aubrey's eyes. "You're all set. Room six, and your delivery will be here shortly."

As they made their way to room six, Aubrey whispered, "Delivery?"

He pushed open the door, and just as requested, the fireplace was lit, the lights were dimmed, and soft music played. A bottle of wine and two glasses were on the counter, and the massage area was prepped.

"Knox! We're getting *massages?*"

"*You're* getting a massage." He closed the door behind them and poured her a glass of wine. "Take everything off and get comfortable under the sheet. The table should be warm by now. I'll be right back."

"Wait. Why aren't you getting a massage?"

"Because I'm needed elsewhere." He ducked out of the room, giving Aubrey time to digest his surprise. A few minutes later Paige came down the hall with the packages he'd asked her to pick up for him from the inn's boutique.

"Hey, big brother." She held up two gift bags. "You sure know how to dazzle a woman."

"Is it too much?" he asked, feeling nervous for the first time in as long as he could remember. "I know most women love to be pampered, but Aubrey's different. She loves her independence."

"So do I, but if I had a boyfriend who went to this trouble for me..." She smiled and said, "I wouldn't be able to resist him."

He exhaled. "I hope you're right."

"You're really into her, aren't you?"

He nodded.

"I've never seen you nervous a day in my life. Not even when you used to get in trouble. It looks good on you."

"It makes me ridiculous."

"It makes you *normal*, which is what you've always strived for when it comes to everything except business." She handed him the gift bags.

"You're awesome, sis. I owe you big-time."

"Hardly." She hugged him and said, "Now, get in there before she thinks you forgot about her."

AUBREY'S HEART RACED as she lay beneath the sheet on the heated massage table. She probably shouldn't be this nervous, but while she had no qualms about being touched by a man she invited to touch her, she had always felt a little funny about getting massages and shied away from them. But Knox had gone to all this trouble; she didn't want to seem ungrateful.

The door opened and she lifted her eyes, surprised to see Knox closing it behind him. He didn't need to see her this nervous! "You're back?"

He turned with two gift bags in his hand and set them on a couch by the fireplace. As he peeled off his coat and hat, looking a little nervous himself, he said, "Hello, Ms. Stewart. I'm Knox Bentley, and I'll be your masseuse today."

It took a second for her to realize what he'd said, and relief washed through her. But just as quickly, her nerves tingled again. "*You're* giving me a massage?"

"Yes, and don't get any ideas," he said far too primly. "Happy endings are *not* permitted at this establishment."

Feeling more at ease by his humor, she said, "Is that a challenge, Mr. Bentley?"

He rolled up his sleeves, grinning like a Cheshire cat. Any hints of nervousness she'd seen were obliterated by her *sexy* comment.

"Should I be worried about what's in the gift bags? Please tell me they're not adult toys. Not that I'm opposed to using them, but doing so in your family's inn would be way too weird."

"Damn. Guess I'll just save them until we're back at your place."

Her jaw dropped open, and he chuckled.

"Since you're unexpectedly stranded at the inn with a charming, handsome man, and meeting his parents for dinner, I had Paige get you some things to wear from the inn's boutique."

"As in real clothes? Not lingerie?"

"As in a plethora of things for you to choose from. Jeans, dress, skirt, blouse, sweater..."

"Knox, that's so sweet of you. And of Paige to take the time to shop."

"Well, apparently this is what *me* dating *you* is like, babe. The desire to send you the bouquet and gifts that I sent to your office sort of blew me away, like some other guy had whispered the idea into my ear and I couldn't shut him up. But it turns out that was all me, because it happened again. I like doing things for you. So I suggest we both get used to it."

He moved to the head of the table, poured oil into his hands, and rubbed them together. "Are you comfortable?" he asked with a British accent as his slick, warm hands met the backs of her shoulders.

"Yes." *And nervous again, thank you very much.* She wasn't used to being taken care of like this.

His hands moved down her back to the top of her ass. She held her breath, expecting him to get naughty, but in the next second his hands moved up beside her spine and then along her shoulders and down her arms. He massaged his way back up her arms and across the tops of her shoulders to her neck. It felt so good to be touched like this by him, she closed her eyes, enjoying it as he took care of her, patiently soothing her tension away.

"That's it," he coaxed, as if he could read her mind as well as her body. "You've had a busy week, a roller coaster of a day. Now it's time to chill." He moved beside the table, and using both hands, he massaged the far side of her body, pushing all the tension away from her spine.

"You're very good at this. You must have had a lot of practice."

"On the contrary. This is my first day on the job," he said in that seductive accent. "Maybe I'll earn a good tip."

She lay mesmerized, relaxed by the man who usually made her heart race. The sound of the music, the scents of the oils, and the hard press of his hands lulled her into a state of euphoria.

"Thank you, Knox," she said softly. "This feels amazing, and it was so thoughtful of you."

"I'm sure it's not as good as you're used to, but you got wrangled into staying at the inn and having dinner with my parents. It's the least I can do to make it up to you."

"You don't have to make anything up to me. I'm glad we're having dinner with your family. And I don't get many massages. I have a thing about strangers touching me."

His hands stilled for a second, and then they began moving again. "That's surprising. I assumed you love being pampered."

"I come from a football family. Pampering was never part of my life, and as an adult, it felt funny to let someone else do this for me. It was a big deal when Presley and Libby forced me to get mani-pedis with them after college. But massages are so intimate."

He moved to the other side of the table and kneaded the stress away from her spine. His hands were warm and strong, breaking through her armor one stroke at a time. She caught sight of him smiling and said, "What's so funny?"

"Are massages too intimate, or do you dislike them because they make you feel vulnerable?"

Her gut reaction was to deny feeling vulnerable, but wasn't that exactly how she felt, lying naked beneath a sheet, trusting someone to touch her body? Isn't that why she'd felt relieved as soon as she'd learned Knox was doing the massage? Because she knew she was safe in his hands?

She mustered the courage to be completely honest and said, "Maybe both."

"I'm the same way," he said as he pampered her. "You're exposed, laid bare for a stranger to touch as they see fit." He used both hands to massage her lower back. "Are you comfortable?"

"My goodness, yes. If you stop I might have to *kill* you…After my body turns from mush back to normal."

He laughed, and she lay quietly, enjoying his touch as he finished working her arms into limp noodles and focused on her legs. His palms covered the backs of her thighs, his thick fingers squeezing gently as they traveled from her ankles to the tops of her hamstrings.

"You know my childhood secrets," he said coyly. "I want to know some of yours. What was it like growing up with only brothers?"

"You mean growing up in a frat house? It was fun and loud, and there was always some sporting event going on in the backyard. My brothers played everything, so we had sweaty guys at our house *all* the time. They'd come over after practices and games to hang out and watch sports on television. It was like growing up with thirty-plus brothers instead of just two."

"I'm surprised with two brothers you've never ridden a snowmobile."

"Group sports are expensive, and we didn't have much money. There's a reason we went to the college where my father worked. Our tuition was free. When we were growing up my brothers had dirt bikes, and they'd take me on their friends' ATVs, but I grew up in a very different world from the one you're used to."

"I would have given anything to grow up in that world. Were you spoiled rotten by them?"

"Are you kidding? There was *no* spoiling in my family for anyone. We all worked hard at school, did chores, and whatever else our parents asked us to. It was expected as part of the family." She tried to figure out how to explain the strange, sometimes uncomfortable, wonderfulness of her childhood. "You know how you were groomed to follow in your father's footsteps? Well, I wasn't brought up to follow in *anyone's* footsteps. I was brought up to be part of the *Stewart sports family*. I don't mean that in a bad way. I was a tomboy, and I kept up well, playing tag football, baseball, basketball, and whatever else they were willing to play with me. But I had my own hobbies, too. I was a media nut, studying movies and learning all about the history and processes for television and film from the time I was in fifth grade. I was so passionate about it, my parents bought me a movie camera, and I drove everyone crazy making films, documenting our lives. It was silly and fun, but I wanted to do something bigger—to be the person who brought it all together."

"So much of who you are is starting to make sense to me now."

"You mean that I'm an eighties movie fanatic?"

He crouched by her face and looked directly into her eyes as he said, "That you're a self-made woman who followed her dreams and isn't willing to be sidetracked or ignored. It's impressive as hell."

"Well, I wasn't always so impressive. But by the time I went to college I had sort of had enough of being one of the Stewarts. I wanted something of my own, and even though I went to Boyer University *in* Port Hudson, there were enough people coming into the school from other areas that I saw it as a chance to break away. I told everyone I was part of the Stewart's soda family instead of my own football family. It's kind of pathetic."

"Ah, now I understand your Stewart's Orange 'n Cream soda fascination. But it's not pathetic at all. It's no different from me going to MIT and breaking the family's Harvard legacy, or refusing to be a productive part of my family's businesses."

"I've always loved Stewart's Orange 'n Cream soda. But it was freeing to have people think I was from a different family. I didn't have to wonder if people hung out with me to have an in with my brothers or my father. I acted like I came from a normal family who didn't keep a sports radio on at dinnertime or gawk at the television like it was an idol to worship."

"How'd that go for you?" He began kneading her hip.

"It was great for a while, until I went to a football game at school and hollered, 'Great play, Dad!' I sort of blew my cover."

Knox leaned down and pressed a kiss to her hip. "Can't hold back a football girl. You said you and your friends conceived the idea of LWW Enterprises while you were drunk? I'd love to know about that. I've never seen you drunk. I can't imagine it."

"We did. It was the night after my fake persona blew up in my face. I realized if I was ever going to stand out on my own, I needed to do it for real. Not playact. Presley and Libby and I got drunk and came up with the idea based on each of our strengths and our goals. The next morning we were even more excited and determined to bring it to fruition come hell or high water. We spent our college years networking, strategizing, coming up with and refining our business plans as we interned and learned about our respective fields. We worked our asses off when others were out partying, and it paid off. After graduation, Presley came into some money, which helped us secure loans to get started. I wasn't very comfortable with owing money to a bank or using Presley's inheritance. It didn't feel like I was standing on my own, but what options did I have? I couldn't qualify for a loan the size we needed on my own."

"It sounds like it was a good investment."

"It was, but there's a story there, too," she said, and he stopped massaging to listen. "My family has always supported my endeavors, and they were proud of me, but the bank loans scared them to no end. They were always asking about it, worrying. I swear I saw them age as the months passed. It was just out of their realm of understanding to think anyone would borrow so much money based on a hope and a prayer. I felt guilty for worrying them, and it started to take my focus away from building the business."

"I can see how that could happen."

"I was lucky. I had Charlotte, and she came to my rescue. She had inherited more money than she could spend in three lifetimes and never wanted to own a business or manage other people. It just isn't her thing. But she believed in me, and even more importantly, she had faith in the three of us—me, Presley, and Libby. I can't believe I'm telling you this. Even my parents don't know, but Charlotte paid off my loan to the bank and let me pay her back privately. I paid interest just like I had to the bank. The media division was doing well, and we were turning major profits, but my parents thought the company just took off like a bat out of hell and I was able to pay off my share of the loans quicker than the others. It obviously wasn't true, but taking the worry off of my parents' shoulders made it possible for me to focus on work. I knew I could pay the debt back. I just didn't want to cause my parents undue stress in the meantime."

"Damn, Aubrey. That's a hell of a secret."

"Does it make me a bad person? I worry that it might."

"No, babe. It makes you one hell of a daughter. Better than I am as a son. I threw everything I did in my parents' faces like they deserved it, when they were just doing what they knew. Repeating how they were brought up."

She reached down and touched his hand, bringing his eyes to hers. "And so were you. I think we're a lot alike. You might be more *in your face* about some things, but we'll both stop at nothing to do what feels right."

"Exactly. By the way, tonight's dinner? It's a *date*."

She rolled her eyes and smiled.

"Now flip over, hot stuff, and I'll do your front."

"I'm onto you, Bentley," she said as she turned onto her back. "Get me all relaxed and off guard and then drive me wild. Good plan."

He moved the sheet, covering her from her breasts to the tops of her thighs, and using that feigned luxurious accent he said, "I told you, no happy endings on my table. You've had your way with me once today. Dating is about respect for all parts of each other. Right now I'm respecting your need for relaxation. Later I plan to respect your need for titillation."

Laughter burst out before she could stop it. "I'm sorry! *Titillation?* Really?"

"It sounded more romantic than saying that later I was going to get you so hot and bothered, you'll beg me to take your clothes off. And when I do, I'm going to take you in every sinful way I can imagine. Then we're going to come up with several more ideas *together*, each one dirtier than the last, and I promise you, sweetheart, I won't stop until you're completely, utterly satisfied."

"Trust me," she said softly. "You don't need fancy words or an accent. That was better. *Much* better."

"Yeah? It didn't seem very romantic." He put his hands on her thigh, caressing just inches from where she now desperately wanted him, and said, "So, I could have just told you that if happy endings were what I were after, I'd lift that sheet and tease your breasts with my tongue until you were wet and needy? Or that I'd like to bury my face between your legs until you come so many times your legs go numb?" His fingers brushed painfully close to her sex, causing her body to clench with anticipation. "That I'd like to take off my clothes and hold your hot, oiled body against me as I slip inside you—"

She sat up, holding the sheet against her chest, and panted out, "Aren't we going to be late for dinner?"

"We have plenty of time. Want some wine?"

"Yes!" She thrust her hand out and said, "Give me the bottle."

Chapter Eight

DINNER AT THE Bentley house was very different from dinner with Aubrey's family, and it wasn't just the four-course feast of the richest, most magnificent food she'd ever eaten. The room was painfully quiet, though conversation was pleasant enough, cycling between rather formal topics such as their parents' upcoming travel plans, events Paige was handling for the resort, their father's recent business deals, and investments Landon managed. Interestingly, Knox didn't say much, one hand resting casually on Aubrey's leg as he listened to his family. Every once in a while he'd whisper in Aubrey's ear to explain what was being discussed. When his father and Landon's conversation got a little heated, Knox's fingers pressed into her leg, his eyes shifting between the two men. Aubrey realized this was how he kept a pulse on his family's dynamics, and she wondered how often he stepped in—and whom he protected. Initially she thought he would always support Landon, but the looks Landon sent him told her it could go either way.

"Aubrey," his mother said, "why don't you fill us in on the project you've come to discuss."

Aubrey told them about the new channel she was launching, Charlotte's movie, and her interest in filming at the inn.

"Oh, how lovely," Elizabeth said. "And at such an opportune time, with the ski resort attracting so many of our potential guests."

"I'm sure Aubrey doesn't want to talk about work tonight," Landon interjected, effectively shutting down the conversation.

The rest of dinner passed with long stretches of silence broken only by occasional comments about the weather, food, and other impersonal topics, magnifying the clinking of utensils.

It was during one of those stretches of silence after dessert was served that Aubrey took her first bite of the decadent raspberry and white chocolate mousse Joyce had made. It was *divine*. She closed her eyes, savoring the mouthwatering dessert as it melted in her mouth. "Hm-mm. Hm-mm." Never in her life had she tasted anything so delicious.

She licked her lips, and when she opened her eyes, everyone was looking at her. Elizabeth wore an amused smile and Paige stifled a giggle, while Landon and their father looked a bit uncomfortable. Aubrey glanced quickly at Knox, who was squeezing her leg. He looked ready to tear her clothes off.

Oh shit.

Griffin cleared his throat, and suddenly everyone was focusing on dessert, stuffing forkfuls into their mouths. Aubrey wanted to shrivel up and disappear.

"That was quite a *moan*," Knox said softly, the heat in his eyes morphing to amusement. He leaned closer and whispered, "If we were in a restaurant, I'd have gotten the check and hauled your ass out to do all those things I promised earlier." He slid a forkful of dessert into his mouth as if he hadn't just made the matter worse. Now she was flustered and embarrassed.

"Aubrey's right. Joyce has outdone herself this time," Elizabeth said. "This is one of her specialties."

"It's delicious," Paige agreed.

"The peak of a scrumptious meal," Landon said, earning a glare from Knox. "The perfect climax to the evening."

"Agreed," Griffin said so seriously, Paige stifled a laugh.

Aubrey felt her cheeks flame and decided to just get it over with and own up to her loud faux pas. "It was a *hum*, not a moan," she said loudly, bringing Griffin's serious eyes to hers. She was aware of the shock on Landon's and Paige's faces and of Knox's hand tightening around her thigh, but she was done being embarrassed. "I'm an expressive eater. I can't help it. I'm sorry. I've always done it. When I like something, everyone around me knows it. My brothers used to call me Hummer."

Paige, Knox, and Landon burst into hysterics, while their parents looked completely confused.

"I'm sorry," Knox said between laughs, pulling her close. "I'm sorry, babe, but...*Hummer*?"

"What is so funny? I think it's an adorable nickname," his mother said as her children tried to pull themselves together. "What a sweet term of endearment. *Hummer*. Why, I can see Landon saying something like that to Paige."

Aubrey lost it, along with the rest of them. She turned her face away, trying to stop laughing, but his mother was on a roll.

"Why, it's so *cute*, I can see your father saying it to me. Right, sweetheart? You'd call me Hummer, wouldn't you? In fact, I can hear you saying it. *How about lunch, Hummer? A dip in the pool, Hummer?*"

"Yes," he agreed with a serious expression as the rest of them fought hysterics. "Remember when we were dating and I called you my hummingbird?"

"Yes. In fact I think you did call me Hummer sometimes," Elizabeth said.

Aubrey clutched her stomach, laughing so hard no sound came out. Knox buried his face in her neck, his body rocking with hysterics.

"Stop, stop, *stop*!" Paige said through her chortles. "Mom!" She leaned over, covered her mouth, and whispered something that made her mother's eyes go wide as saucers.

"Oh dear," Elizabeth mumbled. "Surely her brothers didn't mean that."

"No!" Aubrey chimed in, knowing just what Paige must have said.

"What am I missing?" Griffin demanded.

Knox looked at Landon, and the two exchanged a look that clearly translated to, *I'm not telling him!*

"Oh, for goodness' sake." Elizabeth got up from her seat, marched to her husband's side, and whispered in her husband's ear.

His expression remained irritated.

Elizabeth straightened her spine and walked gracefully back to her seat as the rest of them finally got their laughter under control, but not their unquenchable smiles.

Griffin lifted his spoon, eyes locked on his dessert. The room fell silent, and Aubrey thought whatever chance she had of being invited back had just been shattered. As she opened her mouth to apologize, Griffin scooped up some mousse and said, "Things were much easier when you kids were younger and you'd blurt things out without thinking."

Knox and his siblings exchanged worried glances as Griffin put the spoonful in his mouth. A few stressful seconds later, the edges of his lips curved up and he said, "Like when Landon came home from school the summer after fifth grade and announced he got erections."

The room erupted into another round of hysterics.

"Or when I said I needed a bra because I wanted boys to snap it?" Paige belted out, which made Landon and Knox glower.

Griffin pointed his spoon at Knox and said, "And don't think you were too cool for any of that. I seem to remember a summer when you were about the same age Landon had been when he discovered…*that*…and you said you needed rubber boots. When I asked why, you said you didn't want to get any girls pregnant."

"Oh my gosh!" Aubrey doubled over in laughter again. "What a stud you were!"

"Parenting is an interesting job," Griffin said sternly, quieting their giggles. "It's *trying* and *amusing*, and all you want for your children is for them to grow up happier and more successful than you did."

Knox's jaw was tight as his father looked directly at him and said, "And then one day you realize they've done it, and maybe their paths weren't what you had planned." Griffin shifted his gaze to Landon. "Or that their choices were unexpected." He looked at Paige and said, "Or that they're stronger than you could *ever* be." He reached for his wife's hand, and as he looked into her eyes he said, "And you realize that you did the best you could."

"And then you realize that your best wasn't always enough." Elizabeth glanced lovingly around the table at each of her children and said, "But by the grace of God you realize you have been blessed with more time, more chances to do the right thing, and so you press on and never give up."

Aubrey's eyes teared up as Knox hugged her, pressing a kiss to the side of her head, and whispered, "Thank you."

Chapter Nine

KNOX LAY ON his back beside Aubrey Sunday morning, his body still shuddering from their lovemaking. Aubrey's eyes were closed, her body glistening from their efforts. Her breasts rose with each breath. He brushed a lock of damp hair from her cheek and said, "Hey, beautiful. Come back down to earth yet?"

She smiled and turned toward him, snuggling closer, her eyes fluttering closed again. "Shh. I'm still in the clouds."

He put his arm around her and ran his fingertips along her back. "After last night and this morning, I don't think we need to hit the gym for a week."

"I'm not sure I can move. Is it still snowing?"

There had been a foot of snow on the ground yesterday evening and it had been still coming down when they'd left his parents' house last night. The staff had plowed a path from the house to the inn, and Aubrey had surprised him by wanting to walk back despite the cold. For the first time in all his years, he'd felt *romance* in his life. They'd walked home hand in hand, talking about the difference in their families and their shared hope that Landon would approve the use of the inn for the movie. By the time they reached the inn, thoughts of work and family had been lost to tender kisses, which turned to laugher when the branch they were standing under dumped a heap of snow on them. Aubrey had surprised him by starting a snowball fight, and soon they were rolling in the deep white powder making out like teenagers.

The truth was, she was surprising him at every turn, like with her explanation of her nickname at dinner. Only Aubrey could bring out a side of his father Knox had never seen.

"Snow...?" she whispered.

He glanced at the window. "Still snowing. Sorry, babe."

She groaned and flopped onto her back, eyes open. "Okay," she said. "Then we have lots of Super Bowl prep to take care of. We can't get to the store, so I hope they have what we need. Do you think your family will mind if I use a little space in the inn's kitchen?"

"The kitchen?" He perched on his elbow. "Clyde, the hotel chef, can whip up a great spread for the Super Bowl if that's what you're thinking."

Her brow wrinkled. "A *chef?* No way. Super Bowl food isn't made by chefs. Okay, I lied before. Or rather, I *fibbed* when I said I wasn't groomed to follow my parents' leads, but I didn't mean to fib. I was brought up to follow in my mom's Super-Bowl-prep footsteps. Pregame, the kitchen is *our* domain."

"Wait a second. You can cook?" He nipped at her jaw and said, "What other secrets are you hiding from me?"

"I cook like a rock star, but don't get any ideas. I told you I'm not a baby-making, housekeeping type of girlfriend. I wonder if Paige would want to cook with me. It's more fun cooking with someone else. Maybe your mom would want to join us, too."

"Don't count on it. I've never seen my mother do anything in a kitchen besides give orders."

"Really? Well, that's just sad, but Joyce is so amazing, it's not surprising."

After dinner last night, Knox and Aubrey had made their way into the kitchen to say good night to Joyce and had caught Joyce and Leon kissing. It was the sweetest thing he'd ever seen, and it had stoked memories of seeing them embracing and touching hands as they'd passed each other in the house, sharing secret smiles. While his parents had been teaching him how to be a businessman, Joyce and Leon had been teaching him how to love.

"Did I tell you what your mom said to me last night before we walked home?"

No, his girl didn't talk *at all* after sex... "That she was sorry you'd miss your family's party today?"

"Well, that," Aubrey said. "But while you were helping Paige climb onto the back of Landon's snowmobile, she told me she wasn't sure if you and I were seeing each other when she first met us at the top of the cellar stairs. She said she thought she'd seen a new, *special* glimmer in your eyes. *Mother's intuition*, she called it. She said you had always been a handful, but that she's never seen you look happier. And then she thanked me for bringing laughter to your dinner table."

"She said all that?" He wasn't surprised his mother had seen a look in his eyes. He'd be surprised if everyone didn't see it, because his feelings for Aubrey were so strong, he couldn't suppress them. But the fact that she'd thanked Aubrey for bringing laughter into the house was surprising.

"Yes! I really like your parents, by the way. Your dad might be a little uptight and conservative, and it sounds like he was a tough father to grow up with. But I've been thinking about what he said at dinner, and it seems like he and your mom are really trying to be better parents. To be more aware. Maybe not so stuffy?"

"They are. We all are. I'm trying to be more tactful about expressing my feelings, and Paige is sharing more, holding in less."

"And Landon?"

"I don't know," he said honestly. "He's distracted lately. I want to go see him this morning, make sure he's okay and discuss the project again."

"Did you notice he got a million texts last night? Or at least that's what it looked like. He kept looking at his phone, and every time he'd get a pinched expression."

"That's one reason I want to talk to him. Working with my father can be stressful. I'll see if I can help him out."

"If my project is causing him stress, I can keep looking for another place."

"Not yet. I don't think it's your project that's causing the issues." *It's his broken heart.* "I'm pretty sure he'll come through for us."

"Okay, but the last thing I want to do is cause trouble in your family when you guys are working so hard to make things better."

He shifted over her, and she smiled up at him. "For a girl who fought the idea of dating, you're pretty good at this boyfriend-girlfriend give-and-take stuff."

"It's just common sense. Don't get any crazy ideas."

"You're good with my family, a tigress in the bedroom, and a master in the kitchen. I'm getting ideas, babe. *Lots* of ideas." He kissed her tenderly, then dragged his tongue along her lower lip. "Does this mean you're *all in*?"

She opened her mouth to respond, and then she closed it,

her brows knitting again, like she was making the most important decision of her life. Did she know she was making the most important decision of his?

"Admit it," he said. "You like being snowed in with me and my crazy life."

She tried to stop a grin, and it made her look even more beautiful. "It's better than a toothache."

He tickled her ribs, and she squealed, curling onto her side.

"A toothache?" He trapped her hands against the mattress and began kissing his way down her neck, causing her to giggle and squirm. "Admit it, Wattsy. You want to date me."

A tease rose in her eyes as she said, "I like making out with you."

"Say it. Say you like dating me." His tongue circled her nipple and her hips rose, brushing against his arousal.

"Convince me," she said playfully. He nipped at the taut peak, and she bowed beneath him with a hiss. "Do that again," she pleaded.

He did, and she moaned, trying to shift her body to align with his.

"All in?" he whispered, brushing the head of his cock against her slickness.

Her eyes narrowed. "Is there any other way to do it?"

"You kill me, baby..."

He entered her slowly, enjoying the heat spreading from her cheeks to her eyes. Her fingers curled into his and she angled to take him deeper. When he was halfway in, he stilled.

"Don't stop. Please don't stop, Knox."

The emotions in her voice drew his forehead to hers, and he said, "Why do you torture me? Is it because you've had to fight so hard for your independence? To be seen for who you are and not as part of your impressive family?"

After a long silence, "Yes" came out like the secret he was sure it was.

"I see *you*, Aubrey. I've always seen you. If I met you on a train and had no idea who you were, the moment we started talking I'd still see you as fierce, creative, and sensitive, even though you think otherwise as far as the sensitive part goes. I'd never want to change who you are, babe, or stand in the way of what you want to become."

Her fingers relaxed, and he released them. She wound her arms around his neck and said, "I know you wouldn't. I'm all in, Knox. I think I've been all in for a very long time, but after having an edge in all aspects of my life for so long, I'm not sure I know how not to have that edge with you without also losing it everywhere else."

His heart swelled with her confession, and for the first time in months he felt like he could finally breathe. "Sure you do. You've done it a million times with me in private without losing your edge elsewhere. Besides, I like your sharp edges as much as I like your sweet, soft curves. You keep me on my toes, Wattsy, and I keep you on yours. We're a perfect match."

As he lowered his lips to hers and their bodies became one, he felt the world shifting around them. He'd wanted this for so long, and now that he had her heart, he was never going to let her go.

LATER THAT MORNING they ordered room service and enjoyed a feast of crepes, bacon, fruit, and loads of coffee and kisses. By the time Knox returned to his suite so they could both catch up on work, Aubrey didn't feel like working. She was too distracted by her newfound happiness, which confused and elated her at once. But she knew if she didn't go through her emails, she'd never get out from under them tomorrow. Plus, when she'd gone through emails yesterday, she'd gotten the documents from their legal department to present an offer on film rights for a screenplay written by actor-turned-screenplay-writer Zane Walker, and she'd forwarded them to his agent. She sifted through her emails as quickly as she could, which wasn't quick at all, hoping to find a response from his agent, though she knew that was wishful thinking. Part of the negotiation game was waiting until the last minute to present a counteroffer. Two hours later her chest was still fluttery.

She needed to get these feelings out before she burst. She snagged her phone and called Charlotte.

"Hey there, snow bunny," Charlotte said when she answered.

"I did it!" Aubrey blurted out.

Charlotte gasped. "You got the inn?"

"No! Maybe! I hope so. We're still working on that, but Knox is pretty confident it'll go through. But that's not what I meant. I'm officially dating Knox!"

"Wow! His big wand really does work magic. You know I never bought the whole *we just hook up when we run into each other* thing, right?"

"What do you mean? That *is* what we were doing."

"I know that, but I also know *you*. He's the only guy you've talked about for as long as I can remember, and before him you rarely saw a guy more than once or twice."

Aubrey sighed. "I know. It's true."

"Besides, Becca told me that she and Taylor have been purposefully booking you guys at the same functions."

"What?" she snapped. "For how long?"

"Mm-hm. I guess they saw a huge difference in your personalities after you two first hooked up, and they got to talking and decided to put their very capable little minds to matchmaking. You know the second time you two hooked up? Five or six weeks later? Apparently that was Taylor's idea, contrived after Becca said you were bitchy and needed to get laid."

"I'm going to kill Becca for *real* this time!"

"Oh please! Because she knows you as well as I do?" Charlotte said. "You and Knox started hooking up all on your own, and Becca and Taylor didn't *make* you two continue sleeping together. They just facilitated the exposure, and I'm glad they did. I've never heard you so happy. I mean before you heard about their matchmaking."

"I feel like I'm on *The Bachelorette* or something."

"Hot guy, gorgeous inn. Now, there's an idea! Hey! Why don't you start a reality television show about matchmaking hookups?"

"No way!"

"It's fun to push your buttons," Charlotte said. "Guess who else tried to seed the whole Knox-Aubrey idea?"

"Oh Lord. There's more?" Aubrey pressed her hand to her temples and said, "Do I even want to know?"

"Okay, I won't tell you."

"Charlotte!"

"Fine!" She laughed. "Libby said she tried to set you and Knox up on a blind date before you guys ever hooked up because you had similar business experiences and personalities."

"Our personalities aren't *that* similar."

"Outside of the office they are. Anyway, you told Lib you don't do blind dates. I remember when it happened because I was in town meeting with Presley about my publishing contract, and we were all at Quarters having drinks. So, really, if you think about it, Libby should be given credit for conceiving of the whole *Knoxley* phenomenon in the first place."

"Do *not* call us that. And what made you think it was a good idea to keep all of this a secret from me?"

"I didn't know any of this until after Knox decided to stay in Belize just before Halloween. In my defense, I wanted to talk to you about it, but you weren't exactly in the best mood while he was gone. We were all a little worried about you, and every time we brought up Knox's name you got pissy."

Aubrey sat on the bed and flopped onto her back. "It's happened, hasn't it? I've gone all girlie, and it's affecting everything I do. My family won't even recognize me anymore."

"Do you even hear the ridiculousness coming out of your mouth? You've always been girlie. You're just a tough girl who likes football and confrontations, whereas I'm a frilly girl who prefers to live my life like a fairy tale."

"That's true." Aubrey smiled, remembering how Charlotte used to flit about in dresses, dreaming of her Prince Charming.

"This is a good thing, Aubs. It means Libby has good taste in matchmaking, except for herself, of course. We need to find her a man. And like it or not, it means Becca and Taylor saw something real and likable in you and Knox. It might have started out as a way to satisfy you sexually so you wouldn't kill someone at the office, but think about it. For the first time in forever, you're happy about something other than closing a business deal."

"I am happy, but I'm going to have a talk with Becca. She

needs to keep her nose out of my personal life."

"Whatever. I know you. You'll bitch at her and then she'll promise, and she'll do what she wants anyway. It's not like you'd ever fire her. If you're the backbone of the media division, she's the ligaments that keep you functioning."

"She is, but paybacks are hell—and this one will be *so* gratifying."

They talked for a few more minutes, and when they ended the call, Aubrey found herself smiling again. She sent a text to Becca. *Hey, Matchmaker. Watch your back. Love and kisses, Knoxley.*

Her phone vibrated, and she read Becca's response. *There's officially a Knoxley!? I'm texting Tay! Yay! Sooo NOT sorry!*

A knock sounded on the door adjoining her suite to Knox's, and as Aubrey rose to her feet, Knox stepped in looking fit and handsome in a black T-shirt and jeans. He hadn't shaved, and his hair was a little messy, which for some strange reason made him even more appealing.

"Almost done working?"

"I'm done." She slipped her phone into her pocket. "Did you know that Taylor and Becca have been making sure we ended up at the same events so we could hook up?"

"No, but I'm glad they did."

"It doesn't bother you?"

He put his arms around her and pressed his lips to hers. "Why would that bother me? I went to most of those events hoping to see you. Do you think I like dressing in a monkey suit? I mean, I know I look like James Bond and all…"

She laughed.

"I can donate without showing up, which is what I did pretty often before my friend dragged me to an event and a certain beautiful blonde entered the picture. Does what our loyal assistants did bother you?"

The truth came easily. "I wanted it to more than it did."

"That's because you're a control freak."

"Admittedly."

"Face it, Stewart. We belong together." He kissed her again. "Let's get out of here so I can introduce you to the kitchen staff and then find Landon before the game."

On the way out the door Aubrey said, "Let's find Paige first. If she's not too busy, I'd like to ask her to help me in the kitchen. Oh, wait. Does she have food issues I should be aware of? Is it a bad idea to ask her to help?"

"No. It's a great idea. But I love that you care enough to ask."

They found Paige in her office working on the computer.

"Hey, guys. I'm glad you're here. Have you read anything by Emma Chase?" She motioned for them to come around the desk.

Knox looked at the monitor and made an annoyed sound. "Why would I read something called *Getting Schooled* or *Royally Screwed*?"

"Not *you*," Paige said. "Sorry. I meant Aubrey. My online book club is delving into new-to-us authors. This month it's my turn to choose, and I want something really romantic."

"I haven't read her books," Aubrey said, "but my partner Presley loves them."

"Great! Thanks." Paige pulled up her email.

Knox crossed his arms and said, "I'm not sure how I feel about you reading books with those titles. Can't you pick a book called something like, *I'll Never Get Schooled or Royally Screwed*?"

"Haha." Paige shook her head.

"Your sister is a beautiful woman," Aubrey said. "She's going to meet lots of guys and drive you batty, so get used to it."

Knox slid his hand into his pocket and said, "Why do I feel outnumbered?"

"Because you are. Paige, I'm going to whip up a few things in the kitchen for the Super Bowl while Knox is busy with Landon. Want to help?"

Paige wrinkled her nose. "Hasn't Knox told you? I can make cereal and burn toast, but the one time I tried baking I nearly burned down the kitchen."

"No problem. I'll teach you," Aubrey offered. "It'll be fun."

"She says she's a rock star in the kitchen," Knox said.

"Okay. Sure. I have to make a few phone calls for the Gratitude Ball, but I'll come find you after I'm done. Now, please take him out of here before he finds my copies of the Wicked Boys After Dark series."

"No time to waste. Super Bowl prep takes time." Knox scowled as Aubrey ushered him toward the door. In the hall she asked, "What's a Gratitude Ball?"

"A dog and pony show my parents throw every year to honor their colleagues and clients."

"That's nice of them."

He grunted something inaudible as they headed for the restaurant.

They passed through the restaurant and entered the double doors at the back that led them into a large commercial kitchen. The staff bustled around stainless-steel counters and massive stoves, unfazed by the steam rising from large pots and pans. The din of their banter quieted as Knox and Aubrey approached.

"Who let the riffraff in?" The jovial voice rang out from a burly, pink-cheeked man closing in on them from across the room.

"Paige left the back door to the inn open and we snuck through it," Knox teased as he embraced him. "It's good to see you. It smells delicious in here, as always." He placed his hand on Aubrey's back and said, "Chef Clyde, this is my girlfriend, Aubrey Stewart."

Alarm at the term *girlfriend* rang in Aubrey's head, and just as quickly, happiness pushed it away.

"My boy has a *girlfriend?*" Clyde clasped Aubrey's hand between his meaty palms, smiling warmly. "You are far too beautiful to be hanging out with a man who prefers Goober sandwiches to my delectable meals."

"Hey, now," Knox said. "Don't dis my snacks. Aubrey is partial to Cheetos, orange-cream soda, and finger foods."

"A woman after your own heart." Clyde raised his brows and said, "Where did you two meet? Junk Food Junkies Anonymous?" He laughed heartily and smacked Knox hard on the back.

The other staff chuckled while continuing to man their stations.

"Aubrey's used to cooking with her family for the Super Bowl, but since we're staying at the inn for the game, I thought she could take over a corner of your kitchen," Knox explained.

"Corner? Nobody should cook in a corner." He turned toward the others and said, "Chester, Adrian, please prepare a workspace for our guest."

"Thank you," Aubrey said. "I don't need much space."

"Then you're not cooking right." Clyde winked. "Shall we

ditch the *Goober eater* and begin?"

Knox smiled and kissed Aubrey's cheek as Clyde stepped discreetly away. "You going to be okay?"

She looked at the giant refrigerators, freezers, and all the accoutrements she could ever need and nearly burst with excitement. "Yes. I just need to know one thing. Besides Goober sandwiches, what's your favorite food?"

His eyes smoldered. "Don't you know by now? It's you, Wattsy."

"Sustenance-wise," she said, trying to ignore the way her pulse kicked up.

"If it's made with your hands, I'll love it. Surprise me."

Chapter Ten

KNOX SAT ACROSS from Landon in Landon's office as his brother wrapped up a phone call. Landon had always seemed untouchable to Knox, impressively couth, confident, and unflappable. But he'd watched his brother closely last night, and the slightly twitchy, highly irritated man they'd had dinner with wasn't the brother he was used to. The first few times Landon's phone had vibrated, his face had become pinched, as Aubrey had noticed. He'd seen Landon silence his phone, but then Knox noticed he'd continued checking his messages throughout the evening, as if he had a love-hate relationship with whoever had been leaving them. Now, as Landon assured whoever was on the phone that he would have documents in his possession by the middle of next week, he appeared to be back to the confident businessman Knox knew him to be.

Landon set his phone on the cradle and said, "Sorry. We're negotiating the purchase of an overseas property."

"No worries." Knox crossed his ankle over his knee as Landon shuffled papers on his desk. "Aubrey's cooking for the Super Bowl, so I thought I'd come hang with you for a little while. Unless you're too busy?"

"Not too busy to spend time with you. Aubrey was pretty

funny at dinner last night. She reminds me of you. A bit rebellious."

"I think the word you're looking for is *forthright*, not rebellious. She'd rather shake the tree so everyone knows her apples are good than feel like a bruised apple when she's not one. Have you ever seen Dad so playful? Is that even the right word? *Emotional?*" He relaxed into the chair and said, "What was that?"

"You've got me, but I think it was a much-needed breakthrough. He's been struggling with being more approachable."

"Yeah, I know. I'm glad to see it. But he seemed a little hard on you about that Bruckner deal."

Landon shrugged. "Not any harder than usual. You know him. When it comes to business, he wants to be sure all t's are crossed and i's are dotted."

Knox set his foot on the floor and leaned forward. "Can I ask you something?"

"Go for it."

"Why are you here overseeing the resort instead of working in one of the Bentley offices in the city? The inn is so remote. There can't be much of a chance to meet single guys out here."

Landon pushed to his feet and came around the desk. Knox was struck anew by how similar Landon's gait and appearance were to their father's. He moved with purpose and dignity. His brother was a classy dude.

Landon sat on the edge of the desk and said, "You always wanted to get away and strike out on your own, but I never felt that. I have friends here and I like being around the staff that we've known for so many years. Besides, someone has to be around in case Mom or Dad need us."

Knox wasn't sure he was buying his brother's explanation or

not, and that uncertainty bugged him to no end because it magnified the distance between them. Hopefully he could make strides in closing that distance by finding some common ground. "Don't you get lonely for companionship?"

Landon's lips quirked up. "I have male friends who live nearby, Knox. It's not like I can't get laid if I want to."

"Sorry. My bad." He eyed his brother's upside-down cell phone on the desk. "I noticed your phone blowing up throughout dinner last night. Everything okay?"

Landon shifted his eyes away. "Fine."

Nope. Not fine.

"Something happen with work yesterday?" Knox asked.

"No."

"Argument with a dude? A hookup?"

Landon glowered. "No."

That left only one thing. Knox knew he was going to push his brother's buttons with his next question, but he didn't like seeing Landon so cagey and not being able to help. "Carlos?"

"Why do you care, Knox? It's over with him. Done. Let it go."

"I care because you're my brother, and I don't think you're being honest with yourself. You're not over him. I've never seen you as edgy as you were every time your phone vibrated last night." He put his hands up in surrender and said, "You can be pissed, but I love you. I want you to be happy, and knowing some dude hurt you makes me want to fix it or pound the fuck out of him."

"Some things can't be fixed, and he's not worth going to jail over." Landon took a few steps away.

"But you are." Knox rose from the chair. "If that's him blowing up your phone, just talk to him. Hash it out. If you don't want him back, then end it for good. Stop the calls. And if you do want him back, then get off your ass, track the fucker down, and lay it on the line for him. All or nothing, that's the way you roll."

"No, Knox. That's the way *you* roll." Landon scoffed. "You almost had me there. I almost believed you were watching out for me. But then I remembered your girlfriend wants to use the inn. You know where I stand on that, and pushing me to get over Carlos isn't going to change that."

"Damn it, Landon. Why is it so hard to believe I care about you? Yes, Aubrey wants to use the inn, but that's not my reason for being in your office right now. You can't tell me you're okay and expect me to believe it. I'm not Dad. I see *you*, not what you can do for a business. I know you're hurt and I get that. It would suck to have your existence denied the way Carlos did to you. But if he's still texting you after all this time, he's not over you, either. You need to shit or get off the pot."

"Not everyone is like you, Knox. We don't all bully our way into other people's lives."

"I'm a risk taker, not a bully."

"You're a *bulldozer*. You nearly got kicked out of high school for fighting."

Yeah, to keep the assholes from giving you shit about being gay. Knox gritted his teeth. His brother didn't need to know what he'd done to protect him when they were younger, and he sure as hell didn't need to hear it now. Just like he didn't need to know that after Landon came out to their parents, it was Knox who'd spent long nights helping their father understand the complexities of innate sexuality that a percentage of his generation had a hard time grasping.

"No response," Landon said sharply. "No surprise there.

That's just like you, willing to risk everything for your passions—in work and in your personal life—without regard for the ramifications to anyone else."

"You're right. In certain cases I am willing to do that, because if I know *one* thing about myself, it's that I have to be true to what I feel. I want to live an authentic life, and yeah, sometimes that means pissing people off. That's why I'm willing to go head-to-head with you about Aubrey using the inn and why it is driving me batshit crazy that you won't go to the same efforts for yourself with Carlos. Trust me on this. Figure out what you want and go for it. I spent months in Belize trying to get over what I felt for Aubrey, trying to convince myself it wasn't real, or that I—the great Knox Bentley—didn't *need* her." He lowered his voice and said, "Dude, I couldn't do it. All it made me realize is that there is no *great Knox Bentley*. That guy who blew through life like a rebel? He suddenly realized he was missing a piece of himself. Don't get me wrong. I'll always be a badass, but I'm not too proud to admit that I have *never* wanted to be with anyone the way I want to be with Aubrey. I think of her and my heart goes wild. I see her, and I'm all live wires inside, which really messes with my head, but, man, she's it for me. For her, I'm all in, no matter what it takes. And regardless of what you're telling yourself right now, this guy might be your *Aubrey*. He might be it for you."

"Don't act like you know me."

"Oh, I'll act like it, because I *do* know you. We may not have been super close growing up, but I know you in ways nobody else can. I was there for you when you realized you were into dudes, remember? It was me you talked to and cried with until three in the morning when we were kids because you thought you'd let Dad down by being yourself."

"I was *fourteen*."

"No shit. And now you're a man with bigger issues, and you need a swift kick in the ass or you're going to hurt forever."

"The guy who spends more time away from his family than with them is suddenly an expert in relationships?"

"No," Knox said honestly. "But I know how it feels to have a rift between me and the people I love, and I know how hard it is to come back from it. I learned from my mistakes, and Paige made sure that we *all* learned from Mom and Dad's mistakes. I don't want to see you suffer when all it might take is putting your ego aside long enough to figure out if Carlos was ever worthy of you or not. Had I been less worried about my fucking ego and more worried about getting through to our parents in a more tactful way, maybe things would have been different. Maybe I'd have been around more and I could have seen what Paige was going through earlier on—or better, maybe her life would have been different and she never would have gone into modeling and down the rabbit hole. Maybe I could have been around when the shit went down with Carlos and helped you somehow. I don't know. But this isn't about me. It's about opening your eyes to why you're so unhappy and trying to get to the heart of it so you're not so damn miserable."

Landon's jaw clenched. His hands fisted and unfurled. His eyes became hooded, and he said, "Don't you think I'd like to be as aggressive as you? To not care if I got turned away again? To barrel through life with your confidence and arrogance?"

"Not really. You don't like the way I do things."

"That doesn't mean I'm not impressed by it, or a little pissed at myself because you can do things I can't."

"Then *do* them!" Knox challenged.

"I can't, because I *do* care about being turned down again. I care a whole hell of a lot more than you can imagine." He paced, averting his eyes from Knox as he said, "I was devastated when all that shit went down. It took everything I had to stand up for what I needed in my life. And now I ask myself a hundred times a day if I was stupid to end our relationship. If I'm still being an idiot and should take his calls." He met Knox's gaze with a deeply troubled expression. "But I can't because I don't know if I can survive that again."

"But you're not alone this time." Knox stepped closer. "I will be here whenever you need me. I'm not saying we'll be best buddies tomorrow, but I'm trying, Landon. It kills me to see you so unhappy. And this conversation, me being here for whatever you need, that has nothing to do with Aubrey wanting to use the inn."

There was a knock on Landon's office door, and then their mother peered into the room. "Hi, boys. I'm sorry to interrupt. I was looking for Aubrey."

"She's with Paige in the kitchen," Knox said.

"Oh, okay." As she pulled the door closed Knox heard her say, "The kitchen…?"

Landon's office phone rang, and the two men stared at each other, at an impasse. When it rang again, Landon said, "I should get that."

Knox nodded curtly, knowing a dismissal when he heard it. "Come by the media room to watch the Super Bowl with us later?"

"You know football's not my thing." He reached for the phone, hesitating long enough to say, "But I'll stop by."

134

AUBREY WAS IN heaven. Clyde had everything she needed for a perfect Super Bowl spread, and he even let her stream music from her phone as she worked. She began by making her mother's famous guacamole, her father's favorite salsa, and tiny pizza pockets. Paige had arrived while she was making lasagna, and they'd been working side by side ever since.

Aubrey pulled a tray of miniature cinnamon buns from the oven.

Paige looked up from the dough for the pigs in blankets she was turning out and inhaled the sweet aroma. "I want to be you when I grow up."

"No you don't. I'm a big pain, but I can cook, that's for sure." She set the tray on the counter. "And now, so can you. Look how beautiful our cinnamon buns are. While these cool, we'll finish the pigs in blankets."

"Okay. Don't forget to show me how to turn the guac into a football field."

"That's so easy. Right before it's served we'll use sour cream in a frosting sleeve to put lines across the guacamole, like yard markers on a football field. Then we'll put a few pigs in blankets upright on either side of the fifty-yard line, like teams. We'll cut black and green olives in half and put the black on the tops of the pigs in blankets on one side and green on the others, like helmets. Then we'll put a piece of sausage in the middle as a football. It'll be really cute."

"You're a Super Bowl food savant. I want to be able to do all of this, too, not just for Super Bowl parties, but for other events we can host here at the inn. Will you email me your recipes and instructions? Or even better, maybe we can continue to get together sometimes and do stuff like this? Just for fun?"

"I'd love that."

"Yay!" Paige looked over the dishes littering the counter and the enormous rectangle of dough before them and said, "I swear we have enough food for thirty people."

"I know. It's a downfall of mine. I can cook for big groups, but I'm not as good when it comes to paring the dishes down. Maybe your parents and some of your friends can join us for the game? The more the merrier."

"I would say don't count on my parents, but after Dad's slip into normalcy last night, who knows what he'll do. I'm kind of excited to find out."

"I think Knox is, too." She wondered how things were going with Landon, and she realized that while this trip had started because of the inn, it had turned into a life-altering weekend of learning about Knox *and* herself. Finding an unexpected friendship with his sister was icing on the cake.

Paige handed Aubrey a pizza cutter. "You should cut the dough. I know you said to just cut it into ninths diagonally since it's so big, and then slice each section into ninths vertically, but I'll mess it up. I think I'll just eat a cinnamon bun while you show me how." She reached for a bun with a mischievous smile.

Despite Knox's reassurance, Aubrey had wondered if Paige would act different around all this food, but she was just as effervescent as ever. Aubrey was glad she hadn't hesitated to taste nearly everything.

"It's going to be so fun to watch the game with you guys. I've never watched a Super Bowl before," Paige said as Aubrey cut the dough.

"Really? I'm sure Knox told you that my brothers play pro football and my dad's a football coach. My whole life has been sports."

"No, he didn't. How fun was that growing up? Are your brothers older? Younger?"

"They're older, and Troy, the oldest, has a little girl, Danielle. She's almost three, and we call her Dani. She is a little firecracker. I was a total tomboy and she's a girlie girl, but she copies *everything* I do. It's the cutest thing, and my brother is an amazing father, which is good, because her mom isn't in the picture. Dani loves the loud get-togethers, and all our family's friends adore her. Our house has always been *the* gathering place. When we were kids we had friends over all the time. I swear every team member my brothers ever had called my mom Mama Stewart. I've been helping her prepare feasts like this for as long as I can remember."

"You're lucky. Your family sounds amazing. I've never done anything like this with my mom, and our house was pretty much like dinner was the other night. We attended parties as a family and sometimes my mom and I would shop for fancy dresses, but she was so busy keeping up with my father's social schedule, we didn't have much mother-daughter time. Although she did little things for me when I was younger. When I was home from school on break she'd come into my room just before bed and brush my hair and tell me stories about my grandparents. I wanted to know everything about them."

"You never knew them?"

"They were older when they had my mom. I knew them as a toddler, but I don't remember them." She popped a piece of cinnamon bun into her mouth and said, "I would have loved growing up in a loud, busy house. When we were young, Knox used to drag me places that we shouldn't go. Sometimes we'd wear baseball hats and hang out at the inn's pool. He'd tell everyone we were the Joneses or some other made-up name. He said I needed to experience being a *regular* kid."

Aubrey's heart warmed. "He loves you and Landon."

"I know. He saved my life, although he'll never tell you that."

"He told me about your eating disorder. I'm so sorry you went through such a hard time."

"Thanks, but we all have hard times. Mine just manifested in the only thing I felt I had complete control over." She paused, and then she said, "The funny thing was, it had control over me."

"Knox said you're in a better place now?"

"Much," she said earnestly. "Thanks to him. He's always been there for me, but when I went through treatment, he also saw a counselor and got Landon and my parents to as well, so they would know how to help me. He worried that he was the cause of my issues, because he was so rebellious. But it wasn't him. It was a mix of my own insecurities and trying to fill a hole by becoming what I thought was perfect. But I know better now."

"I'm glad to hear that. Is it hard for you to be around all this food?"

"No. It would have been at first, but I have a healthier relationship with myself now and with how I treat my body. More importantly, my relationship with my parents is getting better. And Project ME helps a lot."

"Project ME?"

"Project Mindful Eating. Knox didn't mention it?"

Aubrey shook her head. "No."

Paige smiled. "I'm not surprised. I swear his heart is bigger than anyone's, but he doesn't like to let people know that. Project ME is a nonprofit that Knox founded when he realized what I was dealing with. It provides support for people with eating disorders and their families—treatments, education, the whole nine yards. I spend tons of time there helping others, and doing so has helped me, too. I think that's the real reason he started it, to give me something of my own to focus on. Not that I own a piece of it—it's a nonprofit—but you know what I mean."

"I do. And you're right. He has a very generous heart, but he covers it up with cockiness sometimes."

"He's always been good at acting like a bad boy."

As Paige went on about Knox, Aubrey thought about their time together. She was enjoying her time with him and his family. Even dinner had ended on a happy note. But that was only part of what was drawing her to the big-hearted, cocky man. Knox was so loving toward her, she felt herself not only responding, but also intensely aware of her feelings blossoming into something much bigger than anything she'd ever known. He'd touched parts of her that she'd kept walled off for a very long time, and she wondered if he'd been that loving toward her all the time and she'd just been too protective of her heart to see it, or if it was new. While the changes were a little frightening, she liked the way it felt to finally accept, and return, his affection. She liked giving their relationship the depth and strength she'd come to realize it deserved, and she would be sad to leave their time together behind and go back to real life when the snow let up. But she was still a realist, and she wondered if they would last when they returned to their lives. Knox lived in New York City, and she lived in Port Hudson. They were only a little more than an hour apart, but what would their relation-ship become? Would they be weekend lovers? Would that be enough after this? Would it be too much and have a negative effect on her business life?

"Aubrey? Hello?" Paige waved her hand in front of Aubrey's face, snapping her out of her thoughts. "Daydreaming about Knox?"

"Something like that," she confessed, and returned her attention to the pigs in blankets. "Let's roll up the sausages and get these in the oven."

The kitchen doors flew open and Elizabeth breezed in, walking swiftly toward them in her designer dress and high heels. Her hair was perfectly coiffed, and her slanted brows made Aubrey's nerves prickle. The kitchen staff shifted into a line, their hands behind their backs, shoulders square, chins up in greeting.

"Good afternoon, Mrs. Bentley," Clyde said with a smile that Aubrey could tell was more strained than the ones he'd been sharing with her and Paige.

"Hello, Clyde. It smells wonderful in here," she said as she strode toward Paige and Aubrey.

Clyde turned to the staff and nodded, and they went back to work.

"Paige," Elizabeth said with a question in her voice, eyeing Paige's apron.

"Hi, Mom. We're cooking for the Super Bowl," Paige explained. "You should try one of these." She offered her a cinnamon bun.

Elizabeth waved it away. "No, thank you. I don't want to get all sticky."

Paige's shoulders sank, and Aubrey felt so bad for her, she couldn't keep quiet. She handed a napkin to Elizabeth and said, "They really are delicious. Paige did such an amazing job on the cinnamon spread and the dough, it'll melt in your mouth. I'm

sure Clyde won't mind if you wash up in his sink afterward."
She was being pushy, but she cared about Paige. She didn't
know what might send her over the edge with her eating
disorder, but Aubrey would be heartbroken if her mother
negated her efforts like that.

"I guess you're right," Elizabeth said kindly.

Paige's eyes brightened as her mother took the cinnamon
bun with the tips of her fingers and thumb and lifted it to her
mouth, pinkie extended. She bit daintily into it, and her entire
body seemed to exhale as she chewed. Her eyes fluttered closed,
and she moaned. *Moaned!*

"You like it!" Paige exclaimed, full of pride.

Elizabeth's eyes flew open, and she dabbed at the corners of
her mouth. "It's delightful. Sweet and light and simply perfect.
You made this, Paige?"

Paige nodded. "Aubrey is showing me how to make everything. You should join us. We're doing pigs in blankets now.
It's fun, Mom. Please?"

"Oh, I don't know…"

"Yes, please join us." Aubrey took off her apron and said,
"You can wear my apron so you don't get dirty. I'm sure you
have some old family recipes you can share, and I'd love to
know about Knox's favorite dishes."

Elizabeth looked at the apron like it was something so foreign she didn't know what to make of it.

"Please, Mom?" Paige pleaded. "Aubrey has great memories
of cooking with her mother, and I feel like I missed out."

"I'm sorry," Aubrey quickly interjected. "I didn't mean to
make you feel bad about that."

Elizabeth set the cinnamon bun and napkin on the counter
and touched Aubrey's arm. "Don't ever apologize for the things

you enjoyed with your family, sweetheart. I'm sure you didn't mean to point out the areas in which I was lacking as a mother."

"Oh, no. I didn't mean—"

"It's okay." Elizabeth looked at Paige with an apologetic gaze and said, "Our priorities weren't always in the right place for making memories. But it's never too late to start." She slipped the apron over her head and reached behind her back to tie it.

Paige's eyes teared up, and she embraced her mother. "Thank you."

Clyde came to Aubrey's side and handed her another apron with an approving nod before going back to work.

"I was actually looking for you, Aubrey," Elizabeth said. "The storm has shifted. Leon said the transportation crews have been plowing all night. He took the Rover to see if he could make it into town. You might just make it to your party after all."

"Really?" The excitement she felt at joining her family was dampened by the idea of leaving Knox's family. She looked at Paige and saw the same mix of emotions.

"I hope you can," Elizabeth said. "We should know if the roads are clear shortly."

"Oh, Paige, we'll miss watching the game together if I leave."

"I know," Paige said solemnly. Then she smiled and said, "Can we watch the next game together if I come down to Port Hudson?"

"This marks the end of football season, but how about if we watch a baseball game together?"

"Perfect!" Paige exclaimed. "I know nothing about baseball either, though, so you'll have to teach me."

"Stick with me, girl. I'll teach you all the sports lingo you could ever want to know."

"Sounds like you two have become fast friends." Elizabeth looked at the dough and said, "I don't know anything about sports, but I do know a little something about rolling sausages." She laughed softly and said just above a whisper, "That sounded dirty."

Paige and Aubrey laughed.

"And as for my son's favorite dishes, have you ever heard of Goober sandwiches?"

Paige and Aubrey exchanged surprised glances.

Elizabeth held her finger in front of her mouth and whispered, "Shh. Boys like to think they hold secrets, but really it's the moms who hold them the closest."

"Did you know all of my secrets, too?" Paige asked.

"I thought I did," Elizabeth said. "But it turned out I didn't know the most important one of all." She exhaled loudly, as if to push past that sad memory, and said, "Aubrey, did Knox ever tell you about the talk Leon had with him about girls when he was fifteen?"

"You knew about that?" *Holy cow.*

"Who do you think sent Leon down to the cellar?" She winked and said, "Let's get cooking, so you can get home to your mama and she can pretend she doesn't know your secrets, too."

Chapter Eleven

AFTER THE LONGEST goodbye Knox had ever experienced, he and Aubrey headed back to Port Hudson. Leon and Joyce had fawned over them, and Joyce sent them home with Goober sandwiches and a six-pack of Perrier, which Aubrey was thrilled about since she'd devoured all of her Cheetos and drank all the orange soda Knox had given her. Paige and Aubrey must have hugged a dozen times with promises to text and call and God only knew what else. Knox heard mumblings about a baseball game and a girls' night out. He was glad they had hit it off so well. He still didn't know how Aubrey had convinced his mother to wear an apron, much less cook with them, but when she'd said goodbye, she'd embraced Aubrey for what seemed like forever. And then, as if he couldn't tell how fond of his girlfriend his mother was, when she'd hugged him goodbye she'd whispered, "She's beautiful, inside and out, just like you." His father and Landon were the only two who said their normal goodbyes, hugging them briefly with no added fanfare beyond how nice it was to see them.

Aubrey was quiet for the first few miles, giving Knox space to think about how their time together had felt more like a month than a weekend. He wondered if Aubrey felt that way, too. But she'd been thrust into so much Bentley drama, he didn't ask. He was sure she needed time to decompress.

"Hey," she said a little while later. "Can you believe your family is going to watch the Super Bowl?"

"No," he said honestly. "I'm hoping they do, for Paige, but I'm not counting on it."

Paige had suggested they open the media room to the guests and host their first annual Bentley Super Bowl Party with all the food they'd made. Elizabeth, who Aubrey had said seemed *drunk on fun* by the time they were done cooking, had heartily agreed. Clyde offered to make even more food for the event, and his mother had said she wanted more of the same foods Aubrey and Paige had made. Knox had never seen Paige so happy.

"Oh, they'll do it," Aubrey said. "At least your mom and Paige will. Your mom wanted to see what all my family's excitement was about."

"Sounds like you made quite an impression."

She smiled, relaxing against the headrest, and said, "It goes both ways. Hey, since we're dating now, does that mean you'll go to a party with me?"

He reached for her hand. "Whatever you want, you know that."

"Good, because I told your mom we'd go to the Gratitude Ball."

"Why would you do that? I'm not going to that dog and pony show."

"Well, I'm going, and you're my boyfriend, so if you don't want to attend with me, then I should probably rethink this whole dating thing we have going on."

He gave her a deadpan look.

"What?" Her brows shot up with her grin. "You guys are trying so hard to change old habits. Don't you think it would be a nice gesture to show them you're willing to make changes, too, and support their endeavors? Besides, Paige said they're doing a *Great Gatsby* theme, which I *love*. But if you want to deprive me of seeing you as Gatsby and you have no interest in seeing me in a sexy little flapper dress, I'm sure I can find another date."

"Playing dirty?"

She leaned across the seat and ran her finger along his thigh. Her eyes flamed, and his cock twitched behind his zipper as she said, "I can play as dirty as you'd like."

"Jesus, Aubrey. You keep looking at me like that and I'll pull over in the snowbank and take you up on that offer."

She giggled. "And I'd be all over that if I hadn't already texted my brothers to let them know we were on our way. They'll worry if we're late. Go with me to the party, Knox. Let your parents show you off. You're an impressive guy, and even if things weren't what you'd hoped when you were growing up, they had a little something to do with the way you turned out."

"Yeah, they fueled my fire. I'll go for *you*," he relented. "I really hate these things, but I was planning on circling back to Landon then anyway about your using the inn for the movie. This will allow me to do it face to face. But you'll see that party is just an excuse for my father to flaunt his wealth and show off his family."

"I don't care if that's all it is. I'm glad we're going. Your mom was happy when I said we'd be there."

"I guess she knows me better than I thought."

"Why?"

"Because she must know I'd do anything for you." He laced

his fingers with hers and said, "So, what do I need to know about your family before meeting them?"

"Nothing," she said lightly, but her secretive smirk told him to be ready for anything.

When they entered the quaint college town of Port Hudson, fifty miles north of Manhattan on the Hudson River, Aubrey gave him directions to her parents' house.

"I just realized something," Knox said as they drove along the main drag, passing a host of cute shops.

"That you have wrangled an awesome chick to be your *girlfriend* when you said you just wanted me to *date* you? You sure pulled a fast one on me, Bentley. You got me all swept up in your family dynamics and wowed me with the snowmobile, then romanced me in the moonlight."

"There was no moon, babe. It was snowing. I romanced you in the Knox light."

"Cheesy. I like it. What did you realize?"

"That this is our second real date."

"Have you always been this *high school*?"

"Not a day in my life," he said as he turned off the main drag toward her parents' house. "But I like it. I'm going to have to give you my letterman jacket."

Her head fell back with a laugh. "And I'll doodle your name on my notebooks."

"Don't pretend you haven't been doing that for months," he said as they turned onto her parents' street, which was lined with bumper-to-bumper cars. "Guess your parents' neighbors like football, too. Where should I park?"

"Joey said he saved us a spot in the driveway."

She pointed to the end of the street, and sure enough, in the driveway of a modest two-story Colonial with a partial front porch there was an empty parking spot. He parked and came around to open Aubrey's door.

"Nervous?" she asked as they walked up to the door.

"About watching a football game?" He scoffed. "Hardly."

"You're nervous about meeting my family." She lifted their joined hands. "You're about to break my hand."

He released her hand. "Shit, babe. Sorry. I didn't realize..."

"It's kind of cute." She pushed open the door and hollered, "I made it!"

As they stepped inside Knox was shocked at how many people were packed into the surrounding rooms. There was standing room only.

"Hummer!" Deep voices boomed through the house, followed by thunderous footfalls.

Everyone turned toward them as Aubrey's brother Troy, a wide receiver for the New York Giants, burst through the crowd to their right and lifted her into his arms, spinning her as the crowd began chanting, "Hummer! Hummer!"

Aubrey's laughter was as loud as the chants as her other brother, Joe, the starting quarterback for the New York Jets, barreled in and hauled her out of Troy's arms, hugging her tight.

"Okay, okay! Put me down before I give you a noogie," she threatened, and greetings rang out from the crowd. "Hey, Aubrey!" "Glad you made it!" "About time!"

Joe set her on her feet and said, "Missed you, Hums."

"Stop calling me that," she said sharply. "Can't you see I brought a date?" She waved to Knox. "Knox Bentley, meet my brothers."

Standing shoulder to shoulder, her brothers stepped closer to Knox, their arms crossed and their sharp eyes narrowing more by the second. They were *massive*. Though the three men were all close in height—a couple inches over six feet—her brothers had an easy forty or fifty pounds of sheer muscle on Knox.

"Be nice," Aubrey warned, pointing at her brothers. "Or I'll personally kick each of y'all's asses."

"How's it going?" Knox offered a hand.

Joe shook his hand with a grip so strong, it sent a very clear message. *Don't fuck with my sister.*

"*Joey*," he said. "Nice to meet you. How did you and Aubs meet?"

"At a charity function a couple of years ago. We've been close ever since."

"Then why haven't we met you before this?" Troy asked.

"Didn't you get enough of this *scare the bejeezus out of my male friends* stuff when we were young?" Aubrey smacked Troy's arm.

A lopsided grin appeared, and Troy clapped a hand on Knox's shoulder. "Just giving you shit, dude. Come on in. Grab a beer."

Knox glanced at Aubrey, who lifted her palms toward the ceiling, amusement dancing in her eyes as she said, "You wanted to date me!"

She laughed as Troy draped an arm around Knox, guiding him through the crowd with Joey flanking his other side. Troy raised his voice and said, "Hey, everyone, this is Knox. He's with Aubrey!"

Greetings rang out around them. Knox looked over his shoulder and saw Aubrey with a group of women huddled around her. The cutest little girl with golden ringlets barreled into her legs, yelling, "Wee!" Aubrey's entire face brightened as she picked up the little girl and smothered her with kisses.

"But seriously," Troy said, forcing Knox's attention back to her brothers, "you hurt our sister and you'll wish you never walked into this house."

"If I hurt your sister, she'll castrate me before either of you have a chance to blink."

"He's right," Joey said. "Aubs is vicious."

"*Tough*, not vicious," Knox clarified.

Troy pulled open the fridge and tossed Knox a beer.

"We got us a wordsmith here, Troy," Joey teased. "Yeah, she's *tough*."

"You ever play any ball?" Troy asked.

"Sure. I played a little ball in school, but hockey was my best sport."

The brothers exchanged a humorous look. "Hockey," they said in unison. "Cool."

Troy and Joey kept close to Knox, introducing him to their friends and family and grilling him in a non-confrontational way. Knox didn't mind. After all, he had a sister, too. He understood their protective nature.

Much later, Knox sat on one of four couches in the lower level of Aubrey's parents' house between Aubrey and her father, Hammond Stewart, whom everyone called Coach. He was a dead ringer for Craig T. Nelson, and as nice as a man could be. Her mother, Debra, sat beside Hammond on the edge of her seat, eyes glued to the projection tv, like her sons. Debra had caught him coming in from outside earlier, where he'd taken a phone call, and they'd talked for a while. She was warm, funny, and confident. With parents like Hammond and Debra, it was easy to see where Aubrey's confident, outgoing personality came from. And with brothers like Troy and Joey, Knox knew Aubrey had to be tough as nails to keep up.

He glanced at her burly brothers, sitting on another couch surrounded by friends Knox had met, though he had trouble keeping track of their names. There were at least thirty or forty people watching the game, and everyone seemed to have two or three nicknames. Aubrey had already been called Hummer, Hums, Shortcake, Bruiser, and Cheeto Girl. Knox had learned that the little girl he'd seen with Aubrey earlier was Troy's Danielle, but everyone called her Dani or Dani Girl, and she called Aubrey *Ree*, which came out as *Wee*. Troy was a loving, attentive father. Dani's mother wasn't in the picture, but Aubrey's family made up for it by showering her with love.

"*Another* fumble! How did he miss that?" a guy hollered from across the room, and was joined by other exclamations from the crowd—*You suck! Get him off the field! What the heck was that?*

"Are you kidding me?" Aubrey threw her arms up in the air. "What'd you do? Bathe in butter, for Pete's sake? Come on, McDonnel! My grandmother could have caught that ball!"

Dani threw her arms up and yelled, "Why you do that, Donel?" Her eyes were trained on Aubrey, as they'd been most of the game, as she parroted almost every move Aubrey made.

Everyone laughed, and Troy kissed Dani's head. "That's my girl."

Aubrey had been hollering at the game all night, a far cry from the woman who handled herself gracefully at professional functions, careful to say and do the right things, and *man*, he loved this side of her.

"*Comeoncomeoncomeon!*" Aubrey yelled at the television, mimicked by Dani. "*Catchitcatchit!* Yes!"

Aubrey leaped to her feet, giving high fives all around as

cheers—and disgruntled gripes from those cheering for the opposing team—rang out for the touchdown. Dani wiggled off Troy's lap and high-fived those close to her, too. Aubrey collapsed next to Knox and took a swig of his beer, which she'd been doing all evening. It was halftime, and the room vibrated with conversation as everyone moved about.

"Did you *see* that?" Aubrey asked, wide-eyed.

"Hell, yes, I saw it, and it was *hot*." He hauled her in for a kiss. He liked sports, but he found Aubrey far more fascinating.

Dani climbed onto Knox's lap and put her adorable face *this* close to his as she said, "See dat?"

Knox laughed. Damn she was cute. "Yes. It was pretty exciting."

Dani nodded vehemently. "Touchdown!" Her hands shot up, and Knox tickled her belly, earning the sweetest giggles.

"Sorry to break this up, but it's potty time for my Dani Girl." Troy's big hands wrapped around his little girl, and he hoisted her onto his shoulders, making her giggle as he carried her away.

"That was about the sexiest thing I've ever seen," Aubrey said softly.

"Oh yeah?" He nuzzled against her neck and said, "I'll have to hold her more often." The warmth in Aubrey's eyes made his stomach get all funky.

"No, don't," Aubrey said. "I'd rather picture you doing dirty things with me, and that adorable image gets in the way."

He pulled her close and whispered, "Babe, nothing will get in the way of me doing dirty things to you. I'll take you upstairs right now and we can sneak into your childhood bedroom, or a closet, or bathroom, like high school kids."

Her eyes darkened and she said, "You're not turned off by

all this at all, are you?"

"Are you kidding? This is what life is supposed to be like. No pretenses and lots of warm family fun."

"Crazy and competitive is more like it," she said. "I have three hundred dollars riding on this game."

"Why doesn't that surprise me?"

She gave him a quick kiss, then popped up to her feet and said, "I have to use the bathroom. Be right back."

Aubrey disappeared up the stairs, and as Knox pushed to his feet, her father greeted him with a heavy clap on the back. "She's a pistol, isn't she?"

"Rapid-fire," Knox said.

"Troy says you've known her a couple of years." Hammond raised his bushy gray brows. "That true?"

"Yes, sir. But we kept things quiet on the dating front until now."

Her father chuckled. "Her choice is my guess."

"Sounds like you know your daughter pretty well. I don't blame her. She's created an incredible business, and she doesn't want to be sidetracked from future success."

Hammond leaned closer. He was a thick-chested man, easily six four, with a receding hairline that began around the middle of his head. His deep-set hazel eyes were more golden and green than brown. "My daughter has got more gumption than both of my boys put together, but sometimes it backfires. I like you, Knox. My wife likes you, and my boys and their buddies do, too. None of that really makes a heap of difference to my daughter."

"With all due respect, sir, I think it does."

Hammond inhaled deeply and blew it out slowly. "Well, that's good to hear. But where I was going with it was that *she* likes you, and bringing you here is a testament to just how much."

"I sure hope so, because I'm crazy about her. She's incredible."

"Don't I know it." Hammond laughed and walked away mumbling, "Don't I know it."

Knox made his way toward the stairs to see if he could intercept his girl for a few stolen kisses before halftime ended. The lower level of her parents' house was decorated with sports paraphernalia and pictures of Aubrey and her siblings through the years playing in the yard, fishing, laughing with friends, and all dressed up in fancy clothes beaming at the camera. They'd captured her brothers in action on the football field and Joey's proud moment when his team won the Super Bowl. A copy of the picture he'd seen in Aubrey's office with her, Presley, and Libby standing in front of the LWW building was featured prominently, along with several others of Aubrey and the girls. There was also a plethora of pictures of Aubrey and Charlotte as kids riding horses, swimming, and sitting in the grass holding plastic cups and with red juice stains around their lips. Knox fell a little harder for Aubrey with each and every one, but his favorite picture was of Aubrey wearing a football uniform, complete with cleats and a helmet, standing between her brothers. She couldn't have been older than seven or eight. She clutched a football to her chest with both hands, her fiery spirit beaming out from beneath the helmet in her proud amber eyes. Troy was leaning on her helmet, flashing that crooked smile, and Joey stood on her other side, scowling, as if he'd been on the losing team while his siblings had been on the winning team.

"She was a spitfire," her mother said as she sidled up to him.

"Still is."

Aubrey shared her mother's height, curvaceous build, amber eyes, and blond hair, though Debra wore hers cut just above her shoulders.

"That picture was taken on the field at the university, after one of Hammond's practices. Aubrey and her brothers swindled Ham into letting them hold a game with all their friends on the university field. Joey was supposed to catch the ball and run the play, but Aubrey snuck right in front of him and snagged that ball. She ran like a bat outta hell all the way to the end zone, and of course Troy took her brother and just about everyone else on the field down to make sure she made it."

He chuckled, imagining Aubrey's delight at making that touchdown. "It's nice to see nothing has changed. She's still beating men to the end zone."

"That she is. Aubrey said you have a brother and a sister? It sounds like she and your sister really hit it off."

"Yes, they sure did."

"I heard they made plans to go to a baseball game together. That's good. She works so hard. It's nice to finally see her reaching beyond the doors of LWW."

"Her devotion to the company is impressive."

"From what I hear, you're pretty darn impressive, too," she said sweetly.

"Thank you."

"I don't mean just in business. I know what men are like, how big egos can get in the way. I raised two of them. But I also know what it was like to raise a daughter who was dead set on conquering the world. It takes a strong, intelligent man to put up with a strong, intelligent woman, and two years, even if kept quiet for most of that time, tells me all I need to know."

Knox was shocked Aubrey had told her mother they'd been together for two years. Nothing could have made him happier. "She's a tough nut, but I'm no pushover."

"That's good, because if I know my girl, she wouldn't have brought you home if you weren't important to her. This was probably the most important test of all, seeing if you can handle the razzing from her big brothers. No matter what she tells you, their opinions, along with her father's, matter a lot to her. I know mine does, too, but they've been her sounding boards and protectors for a very long time. She's their princess, even if she doesn't think she is."

He couldn't even imagine Aubrey's reaction if she heard her name tied to the word *princess*.

"The next time Troy and Joey give you a hard time," Debra said quietly, "call them Chipmunk and Pinkie."

"Are you trying to get me killed?"

"No." She glanced across the room at her sons, who were talking with a group of people. "When Aubrey was little, she saw a chipmunk run across the patio and it ran so fast, she started calling Troy Chipmunk. And *Pinkie*...well...at three years old she accidentally walked into the bathroom when Joey was getting undressed for a bath. She was so bothered by the idea that boys had *pinkies* and she didn't, I wondered if she'd ever get over it."

As Aubrey descended the stairs, Knox's heart beat a little faster.

Her mother winked and said, "I'm glad to see she has."

AFTER THE POSTGAME celebrations, Aubrey and Knox headed back to her place. As Knox carried her bags from the car to her front door, she was still high from not only the evening's festivities, but seeing how easily Knox had fit in with her family. He rolled with the punches, unfazed by her brothers and their buddies' teasing barbs. By the end of the night he was giving it right back and hollering at the television with the rest of them.

She unlocked the door, swamped with emotions. Butterflies took flight in her stomach as they stepped inside. She'd never been needy or clingy, but when he set down her suitcase and gathered her in his arms, smiling down at her with a sexy look in his eyes, she didn't want him to leave. She liked sleeping with his arms around her, waking up to his husky morning voice and scratchy whiskers. She enjoyed having coffee together as wakefulness rolled in. She'd had relationships in college, but this was different. This was *I want you to stay*, not *you're fun to hang with, but everything else comes first.*

"What's going through your pretty little head right now?" he asked, searching her face for answers.

"I was just thinking it's a long ride back to the city and it's late. Maybe you should stay."

His lips quirked up. "Why can't you just tell me you want me to stay with you? Why do you need to take baby steps?"

"They're big-girl steps, thank you very much. It's all new for me, Knox. I don't know how to do this without being afraid of losing myself."

"Then let me help with that." He lifted her into his arms and guided her legs around his waist as he strode toward the staircase.

"Knox!" She held on tight.

"This is when you say, 'Knox, I loved spending the weekend

with you and don't want to spend a single night without you,'" he said as he carried her up the stairs.

"Knox, I loved spending the weekend with you," she repeated as he carried her toward the bedroom, earning the cockiest expression yet. "But *every single night* might be excessive."

He set her on her feet beside the bed and cradled her face between his hands. His big body pressed temptingly against her as he said, "I like excessive."

His lips came coaxingly down over hers, changing those butterflies in her stomach to embers, heating her up from the inside out. She put her arms around him, expecting him to kiss her harder, to stake his claim urgently the way they usually couldn't keep themselves from doing. Instead, his tongue swept through her mouth like a smooth and all-consuming wave, tantalizingly persuasive. One hand circled her waist, and the other dove into her hair, angling her mouth as he pressed his hardness against her, kissing her so thoroughly she went up on her toes, eager to give him more. She was light-headed with desire, pawing at his shoulders, his ass, anywhere she could find purchase. When his lips slipped away, trailing kisses along her jaw and down her neck, she longed for their return. He pushed her coat off her shoulders, and it landed by her feet in a heap.

"No more baby steps," he whispered.

He sealed his mouth over the base of her neck. The sharp graze of his teeth clashed with the softness of his tongue, causing zings of electricity inside her. Lost in the world of Knox's enticing mouth, in his hands slipping under her sweater and cupping her breasts, she heard herself moan. He pinched her nipples between his fingers and thumbs, causing her to cry out. He captured her cries in a scorching kiss. Her body shook and shivered as he took the kiss deeper and her urgency took over.

She reached for the button on his jeans, but he grabbed her wrist and tore his mouth away. His eyes were dark as night, his chest heaving with his lustful breaths. Never before had she seen so much desire staring back at her, and Lord help her, she wanted every ounce of it.

"By the time I'm done with you," he said in a sexy, gravelly voice, "you're going to crave *excessive*."

He lifted her sweater over her head and tossed it to the floor. His gaze dropped hungrily to her breasts, and he dipped his head, kissing the skin along the edge of her bra. He licked her through the lace until her nipples burned and tingled. Her eyes fluttered closed as he taunted and teased, lavishing each breast with a sinful amount of attention. She pushed her hands into his hair, arching against his mouth, but he grabbed her wrists without stopping his tantalizing seduction and he held them by her sides. She had no idea how long he focused on her breasts, but it was long enough to drench her panties and for her legs to turn to jelly.

"I will never, ever get enough of you."

His warm breath spread over her skin as he blazed a trail using his teeth and tongue down the center of her body, still holding her wrists. Her body thrummed like a winter storm building, pressure mounting, *pounding* inside her vying for release. Her nails dug into his skin as his tongue dove into and around her belly button in slow, mind-blowing strokes. He used his teeth to tear open the button on her jeans. Then he licked the patch of skin he'd exposed, sending shivers of heat to her core.

"Knox, *please* take them off."

He answered with a low moan and nipped at her hip. Then he released her wrists, his big hands claiming her waist as he circled her and stood behind her. His hands moved up her body and she closed her eyes. He kissed her shoulder. Once. Twice. Three times. Each feathery touch of his lips sent rivers of heat coursing through her. One hand covered her breast, the other held her belly, keeping her tight against his cock as he sucked her earlobe into his mouth.

God...

She had no idea how her legs were keeping her up. Her muscles tingled and twitched, her sex pulsed and clenched, and when he whispered, "I've waited a lifetime to find you. Being excessive with you sounds perfect to me," her heart opened even more.

When his hand left her breast she mourned the loss, but he worked her zipper lower and pushed his hands down the front of her jeans, using one to tease between her legs, while the other wreaked havoc with the magical spot that he homed in on with laser precision. She melted back against him, and he pushed his fingers deep inside her, stroking her in all the best places. His teeth sank into her ear, and she went up on her toes. She pushed at her jeans, trying to get them off, but they stuck at her knees. His tongue delved into her ear, and she moaned out his name. At least she thought she did. She was so lost in the overwhelming sensations consuming her, she couldn't be sure. Then his mouth was on her neck again, and she thought she might die as raw passion tore through her, her orgasm consuming her. She bucked wildly, every nerve ablaze. She wasn't even sure she was breathing as scintillating charges went off like fireworks inside her. She clutched at his arms to remain upright, panting and moaning, utterly lost in him.

He circled her again, going down on one knee, and removed her boots, socks, jeans, and panties from her trembling body.

He rose to his feet and unhooked her bra, pushed the cups to the side, and took her breast in his mouth, sucking and loving her so exquisitely, she felt another mounting storm.

He tore his shirt off, pinning her in place with a dark stare. Then he guided her to the bed and lowered her to the edge. He knelt before her, his hands on her thighs. His eyes never left hers as he parted her knees, spreading them wide. He leaned in as if to kiss her mouth, but stopped short. His breath tickled her face as he licked her lips in quick, taunting motions and then slid his tongue slowly over them until she was panting even harder. She leaned forward trying to take a kiss, but he leaned back, remaining in total control of her pleasure. He pressed a kiss to the crest of one breast, to the taut peak of the other, and then he flicked his tongue over it.

"Please, Knox." She reached for him.

He caught her hand and brought it to his lips, kissing the center of it. Then he opened his mouth and pressed it to her palm, sucking and licking with fervor. She never knew her palm could be so erogenous, but she felt his tongue as if he were licking between her legs. He kissed all the way from wrist to shoulder, down her body, and then he brought that magnificent mouth of his where she needed it most. In one slow slide, he coaxed her orgasm to the surface, perched and ready to explode. His mouth covered her needy sex, one hand clutched her hip, keeping her rocking body right where he wanted it. His shoulder held one leg, and his hand gripped her other thigh, spreading her legs wide open—and holding her there. He slid one hand up her belly, pushing her down to the mattress. She went willingly, his wanton lover. His hand moved from her thigh to her sex, dipping inside before traveling lower, to her bottom. He teased over her tightest hole as he ate at her sex, fucking her with his tongue. She'd never let a man touch her ass like that before, but she wanted all that he had to give. In that moment she knew she'd become *his*.

She lifted her hips, giving him the green light for the naughtiness he offered. His thick digit pushed into her at the same moment his tongue plunged forward. Lights exploded behind her closed lids. She arched and thrust as her climax tore through her, churning and pulsing for what felt like forever.

When the whirlwind finally abated, he stripped off the rest of his clothes and moved them both to the center of the bed. He came down over her, her body still reeling with pleasure. As he slid inside her, she didn't even try to hold back. "Keep loving me like this, and I just might let you stay forever."

He nuzzled against her neck and whispered, "'As you wish,' *princess*."

"Did you just quote *Princess Bride*? And call me *princess*?"

"My girl's a movie buff. I'm counting on it being among your favorites."

She laughed softly, feeling whole and happy as she said, "You're becoming one of my favorites, too. Now shut up and remind me why."

Chapter Twelve

THURSDAY EVENING, AUBREY wiped the sweat from her face as she left the treadmill and fell in step with Presley and Libby on their way to the mats for crunches. They were just as red faced and worn out as she was, while their evil trainer, Trinity—who also worked as a columnist at LWW—headed to the juice bar with an all-too-pleased-with-herself grin.

"Why do we let her do this to us all the time?" Presley complained.

"Because we care about our health," Libby said.

"And because Knox wasn't around last night, so I had lots of extra energy to burn off," Aubrey said as they lowered themselves to the mats. "I swear the more I'm with him, the more I want him."

As they began doing crunches Libby said, "Like an addiction?"

"Worse," Aubrey responded. "You know how you feel when you want a guy, all hot and bothered? Then after you're satisfied it's like, *Okay, that was fun. Move on…*And you go on with your life."

"Um, no," Libby said.

"Okay, not *you*, specifically, my pure friend," Aubrey said.

"Let's talk about me. I haven't thought about a man after doing the deed in ages."

"You're always focused on work," Presley said as she did crunches. "You'd better do crunches as you talk or Trin will crack her whip."

"Exactly, and you're right." Aubrey began doing crunches. "When Knox isn't around, I can't stop thinking about him. He's slept at my house *three* nights this week. You'd think I'd want a break. You know how much I like my movie and sweats nights."

"Well, at least you're still getting the *sweat* part in," Presley teased.

"That's just it. It's so easy being with him, I still lounge around in sweats. They just don't stay on very long." She smiled, remembering how he'd chased her around the pool table the other night. "We watch movies together and I can actually talk with him about more than just if they're good or funny. I didn't realize he was that interested in media, but he is."

"He's interested in you, Aubs, and he's probably become interested in media because of you. I think you've met your match," Libby panted out. "He's the one my friend told me about that I wanted to set you up with for that blind date. I knew you'd hit it off."

"Why didn't you tell me when you first met him? Or for that matter, when I started hooking up with him?"

Libby lay on her back and shrugged. "If we tell you we like a guy, you tend to run the other way."

"I do not."

Presley stopped midcrunch and said, "Jack Keener."

"Caleb Martin," Libby said. "Oh, and Tim Larren."

"Whatever. They weren't right for me. It was just coincidental that you liked them so much. And if that were true, Libs, you wouldn't have tried to set me up for a blind date with Knox."

"It's different," Libby said, doing more crunches. "I didn't know him. I knew *of* him. Can we get back to your sexual addiction? I'm seriously lacking in that department and living vicariously through you."

"It's not a sexual addiction. It's an everything-with-him addiction."

"So, let me get this straight," Presley said. "You went from not sure you want to commit to dating to having a live-in lover? Oh man, this is one for the books. Nobody gets you to do a one-eighty like that. He must be a master in the bedroom."

"In the bedroom, the spa, the snow, the kitchen," Aubrey said with a laugh. "And look who's talking. You and Nolan have been shacking up for months." She lay on her back to catch her breath. "He's not living with me. And it's not all about sex, even though the sex is amazing. I always thought if I had a guy in my life, I needed to keep him separate from all the other parts of my life."

"No drama," her friends said in unison.

"Yes! It is weird though, isn't it? Suddenly we're in each other's lives in a big way. I'm sleeping in his T-shirts, and my sheets smell like him. And God, you guys, since when do I even *notice* things like that?"

"Since you finally stopped allowing yourself to *only* be Aubrey Stewart, self-made billionaire, and realized you deserved a fuller life." Libby touched her hand and said, "This is a good thing."

"It feels good. *Weird*, like I said, but really good. We're having dinner with Graham and Morgyn tomorrow in the city,"

Aubrey said.

Morgyn's sister, Amber, had attended Boyer University with them. Amber was part of their LWW sisterhood and had lived in the LWW house. They'd met her five sisters and her brother several times. Aubrey had hired Amber's oldest sister, Grace, a screenplay writer/producer who had recently married and moved from New York City back to their hometown of Oak Falls, Virginia, to write the screenplay for Charlotte's book. She'd done a fabulous job.

"That should be fun. And I just have to say that you've come a long way, baby. Double dates are serious dating," Presley said.

"She *has* been with Knox for two years," Libby reminded her. "I think this was bound to happen. That's a foundation that can't be overlooked."

Presley lay flat on her back, breathing hard, and said, "Always the voice of reason."

"Thank God, because you and I aren't always the most rational. Libs pulls us back down to earth. But she's right. Maybe that's why we fit so well together, you know? My family can be a lot to handle, and he waltzed right in like he'd known them forever. He doesn't care if I'm Aubrey Stewart the billionaire or Aubrey Stewart from a football family. He likes me for *me*, and he's not intimidated by me."

"I'm intimidated by you," Libby said. She reached over and squeezed Aubrey's hand. "Not really. But once upon a time..."

"I was intimidated by you too, Libs. You were the sweetheart I could never be."

"Good thing we wore off on each other," Libby said.

"And you both wore off on me," Presley said. "I'm a killer bitch with a sweet-as-sugar touch."

They all laughed.

"So, did Mr. Everything score the Monroe House for you?" Presley asked. Presley and Libby had been traveling the first half of the week, and this was the first time they'd had a chance to catch up.

"We'll know within a few weeks. His brother, Landon, is mulling it over. He's gun-shy because of the media craziness that followed the engagement of actor Carlos Ruiz, but Knox is *finessing* the situation. He thinks we'll get it. It's gorgeous, and perfect for the movie."

Presley smirked. "That man knows how to *finesse*, that's for sure."

You have no idea. I'm pretty sure he could finesse an orgasm from a nun. Aubrey kept that thought to herself and told them about his family, Joyce, and Leon, and about her humming debacle at dinner and how it had somehow brought out a more emotional side of his father. "Knox thanked me for it, and I hadn't even meant to do it. But I have to confess, when Knox whispered *thank you* to me? I can't remember ever feeling like I had done something so important, so meaningful. All that just from two whispered words. It's crazy."

Libby and Presley exchanged a knowing look.

"I think this is bigger than *dating*, Aubs," Presley said. "I know when things changed for me and Nolan, I finally realized I was holding myself back. I needed to give myself permission to love him."

Aubrey did more crunches and said, "Let's not get carried away. It was a big *moment* for sure, but don't force me down the aisle just yet."

They exchanged another look, and Aubrey said, "Stop. I have to be able to tell you guys these things without pressure to say it's more, okay?"

"You're right." Presley coughed as she said, "Jack Keener." *Cough, cough.* "*You'rearunner.*"

"Shut up," Aubrey said. "Do you see me running? We're going to a Gratitude Ball his parents are hosting for their colleagues and clients. That's not dodging commitment. Do either of you have a flapper dress I can borrow?"

"No, but Becca will." Libby sat up and exhaled loudly. "That girl must have a closet in her apartment for every era."

"Oh, right!" Aubrey said. "Why didn't I think of that?" And then she realized why. She'd tried to give Becca a harsh talking to about nosing into her love life, but it was hard to be mad when things had ended up so good. Becca had been gracious enough to apologize and to promise never to do anything like it again, but as she'd left Aubrey's office she'd poked her head back in and said, "We LWW sisters have to stick together. I just wanted you to be happy..." To which Aubrey had given her a *yeah right* look. Becca had laughed and said, "Okay, fine. I wanted you to get laid so you wouldn't be so edgy all the time, but you can't really complain when your man is smokin' hot. Send him my way if you get bored. I wouldn't mind being his rebound girl!" She'd been smart enough to duck out of the office before Aubrey had a chance to throw something at her.

"Did I tell you I got the film rights to *Beneath It All* by Zane Walker?" Aubrey said. "I cannot wait to bring it to the big screen."

"That's fantastic," Libby said.

"I'm thinking about trying to get Brad Parlor for the lead. He was named Sexiest Man Alive a few years ago by *People* magazine. He's the right age, and I'm tight with his PR rep, Shea Steele. She said it's the perfect role for him."

"Sounds promising," Presley said. "Back to *Knoxley*…"

"Don't even…" Aubrey glared at her, still doing crunches, while Presley and Libby were both sitting up, reaching for their water bottles. She spotted Trinity heading their way and said, "He called me *princess*."

Libby's and Presley's eyes widened.

"Uh-oh," Libby said.

"Did you deck him?" Presley asked.

"No. It was weird. I kind of liked it…"

"Let's go, slackers," Trinity said as she approached. "Give me twenty-five push-ups." She clapped her hands, and the girls flipped onto their stomachs, obeying her command.

"I hate you," Aubrey said.

"So you've told me," Trinity said flatly. "If you keep bitching I won't share my newest exercise with you. The one that promises better orgasms."

"I'm out!" Aubrey rolled onto her back and said, "If they get any better I might die."

Chapter Thirteen

AUBREY WANDERED THROUGH Knox's loft Friday evening admiring the gorgeous paintings hanging on the walls. They were meeting Graham and Morgyn for dinner, and Knox was wrapping up a business call. The longer she studied the two abstract paintings before her, the more pangs of sadness they brought. If she looked hard enough at the first sea of muted earth tones, she could make out a little girl wearing a dress walking away while looking over her shoulder with a lost expression. Dim shades of clay, yellow, gray, and browns blended together and yet somehow also stood out, as if each color were swallowing a piece of her. Another painting boasted bolder colors. Shades of peach, purple, magenta, and green came together to form a woman wearing a long dress. She was walking forward, toward the viewer. Her features were blurry and indistinguishable. Her neck was bent as if she were looking at the ground, her hair curtaining half of her face. Within her body was another shadowy blur. Her edges were frayed and felt almost transparent, though she looked real enough to walk off the canvas and right past Aubrey.

Aubrey startled when Knox's hands circled her waist. Knox had asked her to stay for the weekend, and after missing him so much last night—regardless of how needy that sounded in her head—she'd wanted nothing more than to do just that.

"Paige painted those," he said softly. "They were some of her first paintings when she started therapy as an inpatient at the treatment center. I had no idea what to think of art therapy, but it was a great outlet for her in many ways. None of us, including Paige, knew she was so talented."

"They're so emotional. I can feel that lonely little girl pleading for something."

"To be seen," he said as he came to her side. "She titled it *Unseen.*"

"It's her?"

He nodded. "She said it's how she felt as a child. And this one"—he pointed to the woman walking—"she calls *Alone.*"

"That's the saddest thing I've ever heard."

"For me, too, especially since we've always been close. But it's not about us as her family. She said it's a depiction of her and her illness. If you look hard enough you can see it inside her, the darkness."

Aubrey put her arms around him, hoping to ease the sadness in his voice. "She must have been terrified. How does someone get past so much pain?"

"Therapy helped, but I think love helped more. Kids need to feel like they matter as individuals. Like their parents see them not as part of a group, but really see them each for who they are—faults and all. She needed to be embraced as *Paige*, the little girl playing dress-up, the teenager wanting to laugh or fight with her parents. Unlike me, she was afraid to push the limits, afraid of disappointing them, I think. So she got all tangled up inside, and then she found something of her own in modeling, but that toxic environment wasn't what she needed, either."

Sadness simmered in his eyes, taking Aubrey's emotions even deeper. "You feel responsible, don't you?"

"Somewhat, even though I understand it's misplaced guilt. I think some battles can only be shifted when you face down the right opponents."

"Your parents," she said more to herself than to him. Knox had made no secret of how their oppressive lifestyle had fueled his rebellion, and now that she knew more about Paige, her mind also traveled to Landon. Landon was different from either of his siblings, more reserved, yes, but she'd also felt another vibe coming from him. She'd sensed Landon embracing a level of responsibility that was different from Knox's. She'd written it off to his being the oldest, but now she wondered if it was driven by something much bigger.

"I'm glad things are changing for all of you," she said. "And I'm glad I had a chance to meet your family and be part of that change."

"I was surprised, and happy, that you stuck around and had dinner with them. You definitely struck a unique chord with my father."

She smiled and said, "I was intrigued by the dynamics between all of you. I wanted to see what played out."

"So we were like a puzzle you wanted to piece together?"

"Your life was, and each of them had a hand in how you turned out. And you, Mr. Bentley, had a hand in how they turned out, too. So, yes. I wanted to understand the Bentley puzzle. But your family isn't just made up of straight edges and rounded tabs. Yours is ever changing, and I think it would take a lifetime to fully understand it."

"Careful, babe, a guy could read a lot into that statement."

He took her hand, leading her across the room, and stopped before another painting.

The second the words *it would take a lifetime* had left her mouth, she'd skipped to that very same conclusion. And she wasn't sure she minded the idea.

"Is this one of Paige's paintings, too?" she asked while trying to refocus her thoughts.

This one was completely different from the first two, with an invitingly soft background of eggshell and buttercream. A tornadolike twist of vibrant colors swirled up from the corner of the canvas, guided by a strikingly sharp backbone of black brushstrokes. As the colors widened toward the top, they formed twists of chunky letters and words with tiny fissures throughout each one. *HAP* swirled into *PY*, followed by what looked like shards of glass, and then thicker swirls formed into wide green leaves, the type that grew on peace lilies.

"She painted dozens of pictures between the others and this one. I think they tell her story." He led her to another painting in the hallway. Thick dark lines that reminded Aubrey of prison bars formed a background of vertical streaks, the colors of the rainbow. In front of the bars were five figures with lanky limbs, narrow, stretched bodies, and ovals for heads. They seemed to be dancing, their colors brighter than the background. Two of them faced outward, one leg stretched back toward the center of the painting, bisecting each other. The bodies of all five were arched, one arm of each angled and reaching toward the top of the painting, the other arms coming together in the center. Their bodies and arms formed a heart. There were no faces to indicate moods, just a visual feast of happiness.

"Can you see it?" Knox asked.

"The heart?"

"No. What's missing."

Aubrey studied the picture. "Joyce and Leon?"

Knox smiled. "That was my guess, too, but no. There's no darkness in any of those bodies." He pointed to the right side of the canvas, where she now recognized a shadowy figure disappearing off the edge. "The darkness she'd painted so viscerally in many of her paintings, she'd painted *leaving* in this one. This painting wasn't hanging here when I left for Belize. She'd hung it up while I was away. She still has a key to my place in case she ever needs me. I guess you should know this about me. My place is always open to Paige, and she'll always be a priority in my life."

Aubrey's throat thickened with emotions. "I can see that, and I'm glad. Family is so important." She glanced at the pictures again. "Her paintings are all beautiful. Why didn't your parents have any in their house?"

"Paige never gave them any. At first they wanted her to show them in galleries, but Paige didn't paint them to show them off. My parents pushed a little, thinking it would help her to have that sort of attention, but they relented on the advice of Paige's therapist and doctors."

"Thank goodness. But why did she give them to you?"

"She said she didn't want them in her place, but she wanted them to be with someone she trusted. Landon has some, too."

"So she still doesn't trust your parents?" Aubrey's heart hurt for his family.

"I think she does, at least more now than ever before, but she feels like they'd always wish she'd put them in a gallery even if they no longer talked about it. She wants her paintings to be seen for what they represent, not to be ogled by strangers. They're her personal journey, one that will always shadow her, and along with them come good and bad feelings."

"I can understand that. She feels safe with you, Knox. That's so special."

"Yeah. I know. But I think she also gave them to me as a reminder of what holding things in can do to a person."

"Mr. Pushy? You blurt out everything that pops into your head."

He gathered her in his arms with a cocky smirk and said, "Like how you're lucky we're meeting Graham and Morgyn in half an hour, because I'd really like to devour *dessert* before dinner?"

She pressed her smiling lips to his, amazed at how quickly he'd switched gears. "Yes, just like that. Speaking of dinner, we'd better go. You can tell me what you hold in on the way. I want to hear about the secret thoughts of Knox Bentley."

His eyes smoldered as his gaze dropped to her diamond-studded leather choker, and lower, lingering where the draped neckline of her royal-blue sweater exposed a deep valley of cleavage. He licked his lips, his lustful leer igniting fire in her veins as his eyes traveled down her second-skin leather pants all the way to her heeled suede boots. He made a guttural noise in the back of his throat. She'd chosen the outfit hoping to turn him on. As he helped her on with her bomber jacket, his jaw clenched tight, and she knew she'd chosen perfectly. She loved when he had to try to restrain himself, as he would over dinner, because when he finally let loose, they were combustible.

"Don't worry, Wattsy," he said roughly. "I plan on sharing all my darkest secrets with you, starting with what I'm going to do once I finally peel those leather pants off you."

GRAHAM AND MORGYN arrived at the restaurant moments after Knox and Aubrey. The girls squealed and ran into each other's arms like they hadn't seen each other in years, which was funny, considering Aubrey had just finished telling Knox that she'd seen Morgyn last summer in Oak Falls.

"I was so bummed to have missed you when I saw Grace and Amber before Christmas. I can't believe my little Morgyn is *married*!" Aubrey gushed.

"I know, right?" Morgyn waved her wedding ring. "And I can't believe you got to see Brindle's proposals and I didn't. Life changes so fast." Morgyn was a bohemian girl through and through, from her colorful serape and wide-brimmed hat to her embellished boots, torn jeans, and long sweater. She and Graham had met at a music festival last summer and had been inseparable ever since. "I couldn't believe *you* were the woman who had Knox all tied up in knots when we were in Belize!"

Aubrey glanced at Knox with a warm expression as she said, "Neither could I."

"Good to see you finally made your move," Graham said as he embraced Knox.

Graham and Knox had hit it off at MIT. Graham was half adrenaline junkie, half careful, methodical engineer. But he had a knack for investing, and he and Knox shared a passion for helping the environment. Together they'd formed B&B Enterprises, an investment company that specialized in eco-friendly businesses. They helped companies get off the ground, and they also owned several eco-friendly businesses themselves. Graham knew the good, bad, and the frustrating about Knox and his family. Knox had also confided in him after he'd first gotten together with Aubrey, confessing that even after spending only one incredible night together, he couldn't stop thinking about her.

Graham winked and said, "Looks like you didn't need Taylor as your wingman after all." Before leaving for Belize, Graham had teased Knox about needing Taylor as his wingman. At the time, they'd both believed Taylor to be a man.

"Dude," Knox said as his friend embraced Aubrey. "You're not going to believe this, but Taylor is a *woman*."

"What? No way." Graham looked like Knox was trying to pull one over on him.

"She is," Aubrey said. "A *beautiful* woman. She uses a male persona for work to keep creeps away. She's my assistant Becca's sister. I had no idea Knox thought she was a guy until the New Year's party! You should have seen his face when he found out. It was epic."

"Epically ridiculous," Knox said. "Taylor and I email each other all the time, and sometimes we joke around. I kept trying to remember if I'd ever made any jokes that could even remotely be considered offensive."

"Apparently you never said anything bad," Aubrey said. "It turns out Taylor and Becca were matchmaking and sending us to all the same events."

Morgyn took off her hat and ran her fingers through her long blond hair. "You never spoke with her on the phone?"

"No. We've always done everything online. She was experienced, came highly recommended, and her resume spoke for itself. I mean, let's be real. She said she uses a male persona for a reason, and she's *very* good at keeping her real identity under wraps." Knox explained. "But you can be damn sure that from now on I'm talking directly to *anyone* I do business with."

"Damn, that's crazy." Graham reached for Morgyn as they headed into the restaurant.

The trendy restaurant was one of New York's hot spots, known for the atmosphere more than the food. Various street artists had decorated the space with urban-abstract murals and other artwork that depicted the history of the city. Graffiti, faces, skulls, birds, and other enormous, vibrant images adorned the brick walls. Textures came alive with a mix of brick, iron, glass, and wood. Strings of lights hung from the ceiling, and ivy and other verdant plants were plentiful, bringing nature indoors.

They were seated immediately in leather chairs surrounding a small round table near the windows. As they settled into their seats a waitress took their orders. Morgyn caught Aubrey up on her and Graham's latest adventures. She'd recently closed her secondhand shop, where she'd sold gently used items that she'd repurposed. She had begun selling them on consignment through other businesses, several of which were high-end venues in the city. "We spent the fall and Christmas holiday in Oak Falls so I could build up more inventory, and as you know, since I heard you were in Oak Falls right before New Year's, we spent that holiday with Graham's family in Pleasant Hill, Maryland. It was wonderful. And today we spent the day with Graham's cousin Josh Braden and his wife, Riley."

"Josh and Riley *Braden*? The fashion designers, as in JRB Designs?" Aubrey's eyes widened. Josh and Riley were world-renowned designers.

"Yes!" Morgyn exclaimed. "They're so down to earth, and they're opening a boutique on Cape Cod, where Josh's oldest brother, Treat, owned a resort. What was the name of it?" She glanced up at the ceiling and said, "Ocean Edge, that's it. Anyway, they want to work with me to bring an eclectic vibe with a mix of our designs. It's so exciting!"

"Holy cow, Morgyn," Aubrey said. "You've gone from small-town consignment-shop owner to big-time *designer*."

"No," Morgyn said, lowering her gaze to her lap.

"Yes, she has," Graham said. "I'm so proud of her."

"Oh, please." Morgyn waved her hand. "Anyway, Josh and Riley have the cutest little girl. Abigail. She's two and all chubby cheeks and big brown eyes."

Graham looked at Knox and said, "That reminds me. Pierce sent me new pictures of their little boy, Theo." Pierce was several years older than Graham. He'd taken Graham under his wing and showed him the ropes of investing when Graham was in college. Knox had met Pierce several times, and their companies now held a few joint assets.

"Look at that face," Graham said as he handed the phone to Knox.

"I want to see!" Aubrey leaned closer, *ooh*ing and *ahh*ing over the adorable little brown-haired boy.

"Scroll through," Graham said. "I have pictures of Jake and Fiona's little boy, Cannon, and Emily and Dae's daughter, Seraphina." Jake and Emily were two of Pierce's younger siblings.

Knox scrolled to the next picture, and his heart melted at the two little ones sitting in the grass with three puppies crawling over their legs.

"My ovaries are going to explode," Aubrey declared.

"The puppies are my cousin Ross's. Ready for Ross and Elisabeth's adorable twins?" Graham pointed to the phone and said, "Go to the next picture."

Knox did, and Aubrey put her hand over her heart. "Oh, Graham. I can't...I just can't..."

Knox laughed at her reaction to the little boy and girl sitting on a blanket with Ross and Elisabeth. The little girl had blond hair and bright green eyes. The boy had darker hair and dark eyes, Braden traits.

"Declan and Delaney," Graham said. "And don't ask about ages, because I can never keep any of them straight."

Aubrey pushed the phone away. "God, Morgyn. I hope you didn't drink the water when you visited."

"Right?" Morgyn said. "Geez, between all his cousins' children and Brindle and Trace's baby being due next month, it's baby *overload*. And Graham's cousin Luke and his wife, Daisy, adopted a little girl from Guyana. Her name is Kendal. She's a little over a year old and *so* stinking cute."

Aubrey gulped down her drink and moved away from Knox.

"What's wrong, babe...?"

"I just got used to the whole dating thing. This makes me nervous." Aubrey crossed her legs.

Morgyn giggled.

"Thanks, buddy," Knox said to Graham. "Any other scary news you'd like to share?"

Graham slipped his phone into his pocket and said, "Hey, I was just catching you up on family pictures. I didn't know Aubrey was afraid of babies."

"I'm not. I want children one day in the *very* distant future. I have a niece I adore. I get to love her up and send her home. For now I'd like to keep my baby relations that way."

Knox chuckled as Aubrey reached for his drink. At least they were on the same page. Knox was in no hurry to start a family, but he wanted one eventually.

"Let's see what else we can find out about Aubrey. How do you feel about threesomes?" Graham asked.

Aubrey choked on Knox's drink.

Knox laughed as he patted her on the back. "Don't worry. Graham isn't into threesomes. He was just trying to lighten the conversation."

The rest of the evening they steered clear of baby talk. Over dinner they discussed various projects they were working on, like a sustainable community they were developing in Seattle, which had been Morgyn's brilliant idea. They were starting the project in early spring, and they talked about taking a trip out together, the four of them, for the ground-breaking ceremony.

"That sounds fun." Aubrey looked at Knox and said, "It will be exciting to see one of your projects from the start, and I've never been to Seattle."

He loved that she was thinking in terms of a future for them and wondered if she realized how much had changed or if she was just caught up in the moment.

Graham asked about the movie for Charlotte's book, and Aubrey told them about the Monroe House. She was so enthusiastic, describing all of the elements in the inn that made it perfect for the film, right down to the trees for the dream-scape scene. Knox silently vowed again to do whatever it took to change Landon's mind. He'd come up with a plan earlier that week to try to get Landon thinking more clearly, and the gears were already in motion. His brother had been avoiding his calls, but Knox knew Landon would eventually see that the benefits to the inn outweighed his discomfort. And damn it, it wasn't like Knox *ever* asked for favors. A little voice in the back of his head reminded him that Landon didn't ask for favors either.

The difference was, Landon never had to ask. Knox had always done what he could to help his siblings—even when they didn't realize they needed him.

"The inn is perfect, but Landon has a thing about the media. I know Knox is finessing the situation, but just in case it doesn't work out, I'm still researching backup locations. I found one that looks promising in Maryland. The only thing that's missing from either of them is Snow White's cottage," Aubrey said.

Snow White's cottage?

"That was my favorite scene!" Morgyn exclaimed. She turned to Graham and said, "Remember, I read it to you? It's the one where she shows him the house her great-grandfather built? The replica of Snow White's cottage?"

"Oh yeah, I remember. I've actually seen the house her great-grandfather built. It's pretty damn remarkable," Graham said.

"Wait," Knox said. "Why is this the first I'm hearing about this cottage?"

Aubrey shrugged. "I don't know. I was so focused on securing the inn, and this is something really specific. Char's great-grandfather built one on her property, but she likes her privacy and doesn't want to use that cottage for the movie. We figured we'd just use interior shots and build a set for those scenes."

Knox took out his phone and said, "Maybe you won't need to. When we were scouting properties in Seattle there was a house like that for sale. They even called it Snow White's house." He navigated to the house on his browser and said, "I remember wondering who would build, much less *buy*, a house like that with droopy roof lines and short doors."

She snagged the phone from his hand, studying the images.

"Oh my God. How can there be another fairy-tale aficionado as *out there* as Char's great-grandparents?" She poked around on his phone and said, "Maybe we can convince the owners to let us use it. I hope you don't mind. I'm texting the link to myself and also to Becca so she can jump on it. I'm sorry. This is rude to do in a restaurant, but I'm too excited to wait."

"I like your determination," Graham said. "You and Knox are two peas in a pod. The man waits for nothing and no one."

If you only knew how long I bided my time with Aubrey. He glanced at her and could see the gears in her mind churning as she typed on his phone. *You were worth the wait.*

The conversation eventually circled back to Charlotte and Beau's wedding.

"Will we see you guys there?" Graham asked.

"You're looking at the maid of honor right here. Char has been my best friend since we were kids. I wouldn't miss her wedding for the world." Aubrey glanced at Knox with a playful expression as she said, "I probably need a date for the wedding, huh?" She shifted her attention to Graham and added, "Which of your brothers are still single?"

Knox hauled her against him, chair and all, and said, "Don't even..."

Graham and Morgyn laughed along with them.

"Oh, did *you* want to be my date?" Aubrey teased, grinning like the jokester she was.

"Damn right, for that and every other commitment we make."

"Gosh, you guys are so cute together," Morgyn said. "I can hardly believe this is the same Aubrey who just last summer told me she preferred being a *free agent* to being tied down in a monogamous relationship."

"Don't let her fool you." Knox set a serious stare on Aubrey and said, "She wasn't a free agent last summer. We were both just too stubborn, scared, or simply too damn stupid to admit that what we had was bigger than either of us."

"Yeah, well…" Morgyn gazed at Graham with so much love, it radiated across the table. "The heart is a powerful thing. I met my soul mate and realized the only thing to be scared of was a life without him."

"Aw, sunshine." Graham brushed his lips over hers and said, "It's been the best adventure of my life, and I look forward to every day with you even more than I did yesterday."

Knox glanced at Aubrey, catching her staring at him with a soulful look in her eyes. She didn't move a muscle, didn't mouth silent love for him, or do a single thing other than look so deeply into his eyes, he felt, rather than saw, her emotions. She slid her hand into his, weaving their fingers together the same way he felt their hearts becoming one. Was this what Landon felt with Carlos? Like he couldn't imagine a day without him and his heart was going to beat right out of his chest. He was vaguely aware of Graham's voice, but he couldn't take his eyes off Aubrey's. Everything around them faded away, until there was only him and Aubrey and the unbreakable bond forming between them.

When they finally left the restaurant, Knox was still a little light-headed from his discovery, and he could tell by the look in Aubrey's eyes that she felt it too. He had the urge to tell her how he felt, but he wasn't sure if it would make the scared bunny in her scamper away.

"Don't forget to let me know when you get your stuff in the boutique on the Cape," Aubrey said as she hugged Morgyn. "I'll talk to Presley about getting your designs on the cover of

LWW's fashion magazine."

"That would be awesome," Morgyn said. "Thank you."

Graham opened his arms, embracing Aubrey warmly. "It's nice to finally meet the woman who has had my buddy flustered for all these months. I look forward to doing some traveling with you guys as a couple, starting with Seattle."

Aubrey stole a glance at Knox. Her cheeks flushed as she reached for his hand. "I hope so. Maybe we can get together again. Are you staying in the city for the weekend?"

It didn't matter that Knox knew Graham and Morgyn had other plans. Aubrey's efforts to plan another double date filled him with happiness.

"We're actually heading to the airport to meet my cousin Ty and his wife, Aiyla. We're going cross-country skiing. I was going to invite you two, but Knox said with the movie project, you probably can't get away."

"He's right," she said with a hint of disappointment. "Maybe another time."

Knox and Graham made plans to connect the following week about an investment Graham was looking into, and then they climbed into separate cabs. After giving the cabbie his address, Knox put his arm around Aubrey and said, "If I'm not mistaken, my non-dater just tried to arrange another double date and agreed to travel to Seattle in a few weeks for a weekend double date. Sounds like a long-term commitment to me."

"Yeah." She leaned her head on his shoulder and said, "Dating isn't so scary after all. I really like you, Knoxy boy, and I like our worlds coming together."

Knoxy boy. Her endearment tweaked something deep in his chest, and his emotions tumbled out. "Aubrey, I'm fall—"

She silenced him with a sweet touch of her lips, and then she whispered, "Some things are bigger without words."

Chapter Fourteen

SHORTLY AFTER NOON on Saturday, Aubrey stood in a Manhattan theater waiting as Knox purchased tickets for *Jaws*. The theater was hosting a throwback films month and was showing movies from the seventies. Knox was talking to the guy in line in front of him. Though Knox wasn't wearing anything special to make him stand out in the crowd, she couldn't take her eyes off him. He knew how to fill out a pair of jeans. His boots and leather coat gave him a rugged appearance, softened slightly by the red and black scarf hanging around his neck. He hadn't shaved, and his hair was messy from the gray hat that now peeked out of his coat pocket, but damn, the man looked *hot*.

Knox glanced over and winked before returning his attention to the conversation. Her pulse quickened, and her mind reeled back to earlier that morning. She'd been awake long before Knox, and she'd lain in his big, beautiful bed surrounded by the scents and sights of the man who had captured her heart so many months ago. She'd waited for panic to set in as she thought about how much had changed between them. Her clothes were hanging beside his in the closet, her toiletries were no longer in a bag, ready to be zipped up and carried away until the next event when she'd see him again. As if what they had hadn't been real when they weren't together. That thought made her laugh now. How could she have even tried to deny what she felt?

They'd spent a lazy morning tangled up in each other in bed and hit a café for breakfast before roaming through shops, grabbing hot dogs and pretzels from a street vendor for lunch, and finally deciding to see a movie. For the first time in forever, she wasn't thinking about work.

She was thinking about them.

Ever since she and the girls had opened LWW, she'd spent almost every day working, even if working from home, researching or strategizing. It had been a very long time since she'd enjoyed this type of down time and even longer since she'd had a man in her life the way Knox was. Her first year of college she'd had a boyfriend for a few months, but he never felt irreplaceable the way Knox did.

A group of women did a double take as they passed Knox. Jealousy streaked through Aubrey. It was a different, and annoying, feeling. How could she be jealous now, when she'd spent two years not having any idea where he was or what he was doing in between their sexy hotel trysts?

Gawk your fill, ladies, because he's definitely taken.

She smiled to herself. Wouldn't Knox love to know what she was thinking right now?

She imagined the smug look he'd flash, the snarky comments he'd make, and her smile grew bigger. He looked so easy and unguarded right then, but didn't he usually appear that way? It was one of the things she loved about him. Her smile faded as she remembered the way he'd tensed up around his father.

Knox had mentioned over breakfast that morning that he had to go to Los Angeles Monday to take care of some *family business*. He didn't offer any details, and she didn't ask, but she wondered if he was helping Landon and if he was glad to be working on something for his family again. He didn't know how long he'd be gone, *a few days maybe*. And here she was, wondering why she was already starting to miss him.

She slipped her phone from her pocket and snapped a quick picture of him as he paid for their tickets. At least she could look at the picture while he was gone and remember the incredible weekend they'd had. She glanced down at the picture, studying his beautiful face. *You came out of nowhere…*

"Work catch up with you?" Knox asked as he came to her side, tickets in hand.

"Oh, it's nothing." She pocketed her phone. "Can we get popcorn?"

"Heck yes." He took her hand and they waited in the refreshment line. When it was their turn he said, "A large popcorn and a bottle of water, please."

"And two bags of Cheetos and one box of Reese's Pieces," she chimed in.

"Guess that hot dog and pretzel didn't fill you up?" Knox asked as he paid for their treats.

"I'm never too full for movie-theater food." She snagged the bucket of popcorn, Cheetos, and Reese's and said, "Come on."

At the condiment counter she dumped out some of the popcorn, poured the Cheetos and Reese's into the bucket with the popcorn. Then she put her hands in the bucket and mixed it all up. Knox watched with amusement.

"Let me just wash my hands." She ducked into the ladies' room. When she returned they headed into the theater, and

Knox dragged her down the back row. "Don't you want to sit closer?"

"Are you kidding? I've got you in a dark theater. I'm not missing out on making out with the hottest girl in New York in the back of a theater."

"Another teenage fantasy?"

"Oh yeah. And don't think I'm above tearing a hole in the bottom of the bucket and giving you a whole lot more than popcorn and candy."

She gasped, and as the lights dimmed, he tugged her into a salacious kiss.

Two hours later they left the theater in a lusty haze, having seen only parts of the movie. They hadn't dumped the treats—*that would have been sacrilegious*—but since they were the only people in the back row, they'd gotten sinfully handsy.

The brisk air stung Aubrey's cheeks, clearing the fog from her brain.

Knox ushered her into a cab and said, "Rockefeller Center, please," to the driver.

"Do you have this whole day planned?" she asked.

"Babe, I spent months in the blazing heat of Belize trying to get over you, and when that didn't work, I thought of all the things I would do with you if you were my girl. At the top of the list was getting you out of a hotel room and into my bed." He pressed his lips to hers. "Second on that list was getting an invitation into yours."

"Wow, you really skipped courting me, didn't you?"

"I'd only been thinking about having you naked in *my* bed since our first night together. What do you expect?"

"What other locations made your *Nail Aubrey* list?"

"That's a whole different list, and to answer your question,

I'm not sure there's a place on the planet where I haven't thought about taking you to pound town." He snickered, and she couldn't stop grinning. "But this list, my Things I Would Do with Aubrey If She Were Mine list, is made up of all the places and things I've gone and done since meeting you, when I'd *wished* you were with me."

"Does that mean you were making out in the back of a theater with another woman and thinking about me?"

He frowned. "That would make me a prick. I went to see *Under the Pie-Filled Sky*—*alone*—and wished you were there."

"You saw that movie?" It was an LWW Production, an endearing tale about a young girl whose mother baked pies for the homeless. It spanned two decades, following the lives of the little girl and two of the homeless people she'd come in contact with. It was a real tearjerker and had been touted as *a movie for the biggest of hearts.*

As they climbed from the cab at Rockefeller Center he said, "I've seen all of your movies. That probably makes me a sap."

"Yup," she teased. "I'm not gonna lie. It pretty much does."

He grabbed her around the waist and crushed his mouth to hers, taking her in a rough, possessive kiss. "Do I need to prove to you how manly I am?"

"Yes," she said a little dizzily. "Over and over again."

KNOX SHOULD HAVE known better than to assume he could skate circles around Aubrey to impress her. She skated like she was born with blades on her feet and a rink in her basement. They skated for a long time, racing around laughing and kissing as people flew past, and even though he couldn't *wow* her with his skating, her giddy laughter proved she'd had a blast.

Knox had stolen a look at his phone while she was in the ladies' room, and he learned there was a chocolate festival a few blocks away. They left Rockefeller Center hand in hand and headed for the festival.

"I don't think I've ever done so much in one day," she said, her cheeks pink from the cold. She was adorable, wearing a pretty white hat that matched her sweater and her blond hair spilling over the shoulders of her coat.

"Would you rather take a cab?"

"No. This is nice. It feels good to be outside, seeing all this life around us. It's been a long time since I've done anything besides work or hit the gym. Then you barged into my life with Cheetos, lingerie, and lipstick, offering to help me secure the best possible location for my project. And now I'm hanging out in the city acting like I could be just any old girl on a Saturday without a business to run."

"You could never be just anyone, Wattsy. Besides the fact that you're too smart, sexy, and funny, you're with *me*," he said arrogantly, with the sole purpose of making her laugh. "You know I could never be with just anyone."

She laughed softly as they followed a crowd across the street. "It's strange for me to take all this time off, and I'm not even freaking out about it or checking my phone every five minutes."

He draped an arm over her shoulder as they came to the park, which was bustling with festivalgoers who were eating, dancing, and shopping. Kiosks and tents offered everything from clothing and gifts to food and crafts. A DJ played music from atop a platform, and colored lights hung from all the trees.

As they headed into the crowd he said, "And LWW hasn't gone to hell in a handbasket because of it. Come on, let's get some hot chocolate."

"Why aren't *you* working more?"

Knox spotted a vendor selling hot chocolate and held Aubrey close as they weaved through the crowd. "I work my ass off when I have to, but I love life too much to give it up for money. I used to work twenty-four-seven, but I quickly realized that wasn't how I wanted to live my life. I love taking road trips on my motorcycle, hitting the slopes, or going backpacking. Hell, give me a week at a beach with you and I'll be a happy dude."

They joined the end of the line at the hot-chocolate vendor, and Aubrey said, "No trips to Paris or Italy on your agenda?"

He shrugged. "Sure, if I'm going with you or friends, but I went there enough when I was a kid." He gathered her closer, moving up as the line progressed, and said, "Think of me as a regular guy with a few bucks."

"Says the *regular* guy with a Ducati bike."

"Okay, a regular guy with good taste and expensive toys. So what, Aubrey? Does that make me a bad guy? Your house had to cost a few mil."

"I didn't mean it that way. I just meant that at our level, we're not just regular people." Her eyes became hooded and she said, "Do you ever worry that if you let up, it'll all fall apart?"

"Sure I do. I think anyone in our position would. But does that mean I'll give up weekends like this just to make sure that doesn't happen?" He lifted her face with a finger under her chin and said, "I did that for years, Aubrey, and I wouldn't trade this for anything." He pressed his lips to hers, and she made an appreciative sound, so he did it again.

"As much as I didn't want to be like my father, I worked

day and night when I first began investing. I was in college then, so I was also going to classes and studying." He paid for their hot chocolates, and they stepped away from the booth. "Our second year of school, Graham asked me to go with him on a ski trip over winter break, and I said I had too much work to do. I was always researching prospective investments, tweaking my strategies. He came back refreshed and invigorated, and though my portfolio was thicker, I wasn't living the life I'd imagined for myself. But success was like a drug. The more I achieved, the more I wanted."

"I feel that all the time," she said. "Don't you wonder if that's part of what made your father the way he is?"

"I'm sure it is. I also thought I had to prove something to him, but I realized the only person I needed to prove a damn thing to was myself. But changing those habits wasn't easy, and believe me, that made me appreciate how hard my father is trying now."

"How did you break free from it? How did you change your ways?"

"I did what I do best. I gave myself a deadline. A goal. Something else to achieve."

"Brilliant, Bentley." She bumped him with her shoulder.

"You're just learning this about me? Sheesh, Wattsy. Think about it. You say *don't come yet*, I meet the challenge every time."

"You're impossible," she said with a grin. "Deliciously impossible."

He chuckled. "I'm great with goals and deadlines. My deadline was graduation. I worked my ass off until then, and once I graduated, I made a fresh start. I was already only making deals that spoke to me on a personal level—eco-friendly investments—but from then on I made sure that while I worked hard, I also played hard."

They window-shopped as they walked along the kiosks, and he said, "Every time I got that knot in my gut about taking time off, I thought of that winter break. And if that didn't work, I thought, 'What would my father do?' And *that* was enough to make me see the light."

"Did you have a deadline with me?" She sipped her hot chocolate, watching him over the rim of the cup.

"Sort of," he admitted. She looked a little hurt, which made his gut ache, but he wasn't going to lie to her. "You knew we were supposed to be in Belize for only eight to ten weeks. That was my timeline. But when that time passed, I was still so hung up on you, I figured I just needed more time to get you out of my head. But months later, after spending every minute with those amazing, happy people who had nothing to speak of except one another, I knew what I had to do. And yeah, I gave myself a new deadline. New Year's Day. I knew if you were at the New Year's Eve party, we'd wake up together the next day, which we did. And when you blew off my offer to take our relationship outside the bedroom, I gave myself a new deadline."

She tilted her head and said, "So, your New Year's *deadline* didn't really mean anything? Seems like a character flaw to me."

"It meant *everything*," he said firmly, stepping closer. "You tried to be strong and brush off my request for a real date, but then we reconnected after the next event. You remember that one, don't you, Wattsy? It was only two weeks ago. You couldn't *really* blow me off. You made love to me the next morning in the bathroom *despite* knowing it would throw off your entire schedule. At that point my deadline became when *you* were ready. If you hadn't agreed to go to the inn with me, I would have tried again the next day, and the next, until finally you gave in to what's between us."

She breathed a little harder, gazing up at him with wide, wanting eyes. "And what's that?"

He brushed his lips over her cheek and said, "Worth waiting for."

THE AFTERNOON BLURRED into a blustery evening, full of music, dancing, and all types of savory foods and rich chocolate dishes. It was after midnight when they finally stumbled into his loft.

"I had no idea you were such a good dancer," she said as they shed their coats and shoes by the door.

"I had no idea you were a dirty dancer." He kissed her on the neck as she yawned. "Aw, I wore you out today."

"Hardly. Let's watch a movie. I just want to put on something warm and comfy."

He patted her ass and said, "Go. I'll light a fire."

Aubrey headed into the bedroom and returned a few minutes later carrying the comforter from his bed and wearing sweatpants and his favorite sweatshirt. Paige had given him the sweatshirt with JUST DO IT emblazoned across the front when he'd decided to buck the family's Harvard legacy and attend MIT.

Aubrey climbed onto the couch and covered herself with the blanket, stifling another yawn.

"We can light the fireplace in the bedroom," he suggested.

"No. This is great. Let's see what's on."

He grabbed the remote and sat beside her. She cuddled against him as he surfed through channels. "Where'd you find that sweatshirt?"

"It was on a shelf in your closet. Do you mind?"

"Not at all. I had no idea you were a snooper."

"I noticed it when I hung my clothes up earlier." She smiled up at him and said, "Finders keepers."

Could she be any cuter?

"That!" She pointed at the television. "*Armageddon* is *so* good."

"Let me guess. You have a thing for Ben Affleck."

She made a face like he'd suggested she liked to eat dirt. "Not a chance. I have a thing for Bruce Willis. He's my hall pass, by the way. Who's yours?"

"I'm not telling. I know how this works. You pretend not to care, but suddenly we can't go see movies she's in anymore." He pressed a kiss to her head and said, "By the way, I'm burning my *Die Hard* and *Fifth Element* DVDs."

"You suck."

"You weren't complaining when I had my lips all over you this morning."

They settled in to watch the movie, and a few minutes later she said, "Outside of work stuff, I think today might have been the best day of my life."

He reveled in her confession, and after a while he said, "Today was the best day of my life, too. From waking up with you in my arms and making out in the movie theater, right down to dancing and seeing you in my favorite sweatshirt. I like what we've become, Aubrey, and I know you didn't want to hear it last night, but I want to say it. I'm falling in love with you." He pressed another kiss to her head and said, "Actually, I'm past that, and I don't want to hold back anymore. I've never felt this way about anyone. You're it for me, Wattsy. I love you more than I ever thought possible."

She made a noise, and he leaned forward so he could see her face. Her jaw was slack, her eyes closed, and she was snoring softly. He chuckled softly and shook his head. "And just like that, I fall deeper in love with you…"

Chapter Fifteen

SUNDAY MORNING AUBREY hummed along to "Out of the Woods" as she cooked French toast. She'd woken up at some point in the night to Knox carrying her into the bedroom. He'd helped her change into one of his T-shirts, and she remembered his body cocooning hers. She must have fallen back to sleep, because this morning she'd woken with the sun and felt so full of energy and well rested, she was afraid she'd wake him. The sleepyhead had been out like a light when she'd snuck out of the bedroom. She'd made coffee, turned the stereo on low, and raided his kitchen.

Using the spatula like a microphone, she sang along with the stereo about a car accident and stitches.

"I had no idea I was dating Taylor Swift."

She spun around without missing a beat and continued singing to him as she tiptoed over. He reached for her and she turned again, her back to him as she sang the chorus, shoulders and hips swaying as she circled him. He chuckled and grabbed her around the waist, showering her face and neck with kisses and making her squeal with delight. His body was still warm from sleep, and as she melted against him, she felt every hard inch of him through his dark boxer briefs.

"Morning, beautiful."

"Good morning, handsome. I'm a much better girlfriend than Taylor Swift. She goes through boyfriends like I tear through miles during my workouts."

He followed her to the stove and placed his hands on her waist, peering over her shoulder. "Smells almost as good as you do."

"I hope you like French toast. Unfortunately, you live like a guy who has been staying with his girlfriend half the time." She transferred the French toast onto two plates and said, "I found eggs, milk, butter, and beer in the fridge, and your pantry was almost as bare."

"You're my sustenance." His hands slid down her hips and beneath the T-shirt. "Jesus, babe. You're naked under here."

"*Oopsie*," she said innocently. Then she turned with a plate in each hand and said, "Breakfast is served."

His eyes turned hungry as a wolf's as he grabbed her around the waist and lifted her onto the counter. "I'm ravenous."

"Me too…"

He tore off a piece of French toast and fed it to her. "There you go, sweetheart. Enjoy your breakfast." He knelt before her with a greedy look in his eyes and said, "I know I'm going to enjoy mine."

He lowered his mouth between her legs, obliterating all thoughts of food. He licked, stroked, and devoured her into a writhing, trembling mess. She fisted her fingers in his hair, a stream of pleasure-filled noises escaping her lungs as he took her right up to the edge.

"Knox," she pleaded.

Her vision blurred, her insides seared and sparked like live wires, and he finally, *blissfully*, sent her soaring.

When she came down from the peak she panted out, "Bedroom. *Now*, please."

He lifted her off the counter, capturing her mouth as he turned to carry her out of the kitchen.

"Wait!" She snagged the syrup, earning the biggest grin she'd ever seen.

Like a man on a mission, he made a beeline into the bedroom.

Several sticky orgasms—and one shower that didn't stay *clean* for long—later, they nuked the French toast, then spent the rest of the day lazing around the loft, watching movies, stealing kisses, and catching up on emails. They ordered pizza for lunch, Chinese food for dinner, and Aubrey was completely relaxed and euphorically happy. The last thing she wanted to do was leave, but Knox was catching an early flight to L.A., and Aubrey had an eight o'clock breakfast meeting with Zane Walker and his wife, Willow, about his upcoming movie. She couldn't chance being late by staying in the city. She told herself it would probably be only a few days before she saw Knox again, and she certainly could make it on her own. But she didn't know how to handle the emptiness forming like lead inside her at the prospect of spending that time without him. It felt needy and weak, and she didn't like that *at all*.

She was folding her clothes, trying to pull herself together, when Knox carried her suitcase into the bedroom and set it on the bed.

"Why don't you leave some stuff here for next time?" He picked up her black lace bra and said, "Surely you won't need this in Port Hudson while I'm gone."

She snagged it from him. "I need it for the Gratitude Ball next weekend, and God only knows what shape it would be in when I got it back." She threw it into the suitcase and flopped down on the edge of the bed. Her chest constricted, and it just kept getting worse, like she was already missing him so much her heart was swelling, taking up every ounce of space inside her.

What is going on with me?

He sat beside her and said, "We can FaceTime while I'm in L.A. I'm sure we can come up with the best use of that black lace bra without tearing it to shreds."

She laughed and rested her head on his shoulder. "FaceTime sex? That'd be a first for me."

He kissed her cheek and said, "Me too, Wattsy. The truth is, I like seeing your stuff here, mixed with mine. It'll make me feel closer to you when I'm back in town, on the nights when I'm stuck here in the city and you're in Port Hudson." He reached for his favorite sweatshirt, which was among her things, and set it in her lap. "You can take this if you'd like."

"I was going to wear it home."

He chuckled.

"Finders keepers, remember?" she said quietly. "So, you'll be gone for a few days?"

"Probably. But you know we'll talk every day. I'm going to need my Aubrey fixes. As soon as I know when I'll be heading home, I'll let you know."

"Okay, well…" She pushed to her feet, feeling flustered and edgy, and went back to folding her clothes, trying to play it cool. "Did I tell you Becca has the perfect dress for the ball? She's even got a headpiece. I texted a picture of it to Paige, and she loved it, too. I hope you don't get held up in L.A. and have to miss the ball Saturday night. Paige and your mom are thrilled that we're coming."

He pushed to his feet and took a pair of jeans from her hands. "You've folded and refolded the same pair of jeans twice, and you're talking faster than I can listen. What's wrong?"

"Nothing. I'm just excited about the ball." She tried to take the jeans from him, but he held on tight. She lifted her gaze, meeting his worried eyes.

"Talk to me, Aubrey." He set the jeans on the bed.

Her chest constricted again, and she turned away, speaking through gritted teeth. "*God. I hate* this so much."

"Then leave it all here. I told you I'd rather you did that anyway."

She spun around with her heart in her throat and said, "It's not the stupid clothes. I'm going to miss you. Okay? A *lot*. And it makes me feel all…" Her shoulders rose, and she squirmed.

"Out of balance?" he asked, pulling her into his arms. "Like you have no control for the first time in your life and you can't figure out what to do with that bizarre feeling?" His eyes narrowed. "You kind of want to outrun it, but at the same time you know that would only make it worse?"

She buried her face in his chest and nodded.

"I hate to tell you this, Aubrey, but there's no outrunning what you're feeling. Trust me. I went halfway around the world trying to do just that."

She looked up at him and said, "I hate you for doing this to me."

"I have a feeling *hate* is not the word you're looking for."

Her heart raced. "Maybe it's not the right word, but if this is"—*love*—"what being together makes me feel like, then I need to rethink *everything*." She began pacing. "How can I work when my heart feels like a cannonball? It's not like you're moving away! You're leaving town for work. No big deal, right?

Right! This is nuts. It's utterly and completely idiotic that I could get this way just thinking about missing you." She began throwing her belongings into the suitcase. She didn't want to take her stuff. She just wanted to feel normal again, *in control.* She groaned, dumping the suitcase on the bed. "I'm leaving it all here. All of it. Do you care?"

His fingers circled her wrist, and he sat on the bed, bringing her down on his lap. He smiled up at her and tucked a lock of hair behind her ear. She must look like a madwoman, because she sure felt like one.

"Breathe, Wattsy. Just take a deep breath with me, okay?" He inhaled slowly, and she rolled her eyes. "Please? For me?"

He inhaled again, and to humor him, she did, too.

"Good. I just wanted to be sure you were still in there somewhere, still able to process what I'm going to say next."

"Please don't! Don't say something so big that I lose my mind."

"I think I know you well enough to know when to hold back and when not to. Aubrey Stewart of the football dynasty, not the Stewart soda company, you are a brilliant woman. You can negotiate the hell out of business contracts and bring men to their knees with a single sideways glance. I have faith in your ability to pull up your big-girl panties and accept that thing we're not talking about. And you have to know that's horribly difficult for me to say, because now I'm thinking about pulling *down* those big-girl panties and not talking at all."

She touched her forehead to his and sighed. "Are you for real? Or are you a figment of my imagination, because I didn't think men like you really existed."

"They don't." He pressed his warm hands to her face and looked directly into her eyes as he said, "I'm the only one, and lucky for you, I'm all yours."

Chapter Sixteen

"JUST TO RECAP," Becca said to Aubrey as they left the conference room Friday afternoon. "I'm going to schedule a meeting with Salvatore for early next week and find out the availability of your top three casting agents for Zane's film. And what about the Monroe House? Any word on that yet?" Salvatore was a sought-after director.

"Ugh. I forgot to tell you."

"You've been pretty distracted this week."

"No kidding. Knox is meeting with Landon tomorrow before the ball, but just in case Landon's still on the fence, Knox offered to see my second choice while he was in L.A."

"The Brookstone? And...?" Becca asked. She looked like she'd walked off the set of *I Love Lucy*. Her hair was in a sleek half updo with her signature victory rolls above her forehead, and she wore a vintage midcalf-length black dress with three-quarter sleeves and a peekaboo triangle of black-and-white polka dots from hem to waist. Cherry-red lipstick completed the look.

"It's not the Monroe House, but it'll do. I appreciate Knox trying to work things out with Landon, but we really can't wait any longer. If there's no decision tomorrow, we'll make do with the Brookstone."

"Got it," Becca said. "I'm glad you're closing in on a decision because Char's fans are going crazy about the movie. I can't wait to announce the leads. Her social media pages have been blowing up for *months*." Becca handled all of Charlotte's social media pages so Charlotte could focus on writing.

"Once the location is nailed down and dates have been confirmed, you can announce the leads."

The elevator doors opened as they walked past, and Presley barreled out, colliding with Aubrey. She had a mouthful of food and held a monstrous cookie in one hand.

"Geez, Pres!"

"Sorry," she said, covering her mouth with her free hand. "Don't judge me. I've got an author who's going to miss her deadline."

"Yeah, well, I've got a grouchy boss who hasn't been with her man for nearly a week." Becca held out her hand, palm up.

Presley broke off a piece of the cookie and handed it to Becca, who popped it into her mouth and said, "Thank you. I'm going to get things ready. How late are we working tonight?"

"I'm not working late," Aubrey said anxiously. "Knox's flight arrives at six, and then he's coming over. I want to surprise him with dinner for Valentine's Day, and I've got to run to the grocery store first. I'll probably take off around four."

Becca's jaw dropped open. "You're leaving *early*? Wow. If I'd known all it would take is a hot guy for you to leave work early, I'd have paid Knox to *live* here."

"Good for you, Aubs. I guess that means no drinks with me and Libby, either. That makes three weeks in a row," Presley pointed out.

"I know, but that's why we had drinks Wednesday night,

remember?" Those drinks had helped loosen her up for her and Knox's steamy FaceTime session. She'd been forcing herself to focus on work and had been greatly productive, but every night when they hung up the phone, she missed him even more. When he suggested a little video-chat playtime, she'd been more than ready. That night she'd slept like a baby all wrapped up in his cozy sweatshirt.

"Besides, your man owns the bar where we have drinks," Aubrey pointed out. "It's not like you're giving up a night with him, like I would have to with Knox. I have to run, though. I've got to make a few calls before leaving. Good luck with the author. I'll tell Trinity to work you double time this weekend to rid you of that stress."

"You wouldn't dare. If I don't see you before you take off, have fun at the ball," Presley said. "I want pictures of you in that dress."

"She looks hot in it," Becca said.

"Thanks. I cannot wait to see Knox in his tux. Correction, I can't wait to see him *out* of it!"

Presley laughed. "She is really gone over him, isn't she, Bec?"

"You should have seen her staring off into space daydreaming about him earlier." Becca lowered her voice and said, "It was kind of unnerving seeing Miss Large and In Charge all moony over a guy."

Aubrey headed for her office and said, "*Aaaand* you're fired again!"

"You can't fire me," Becca called after her. "You *love* me!"

KNOX PARKED BEHIND the Ladies Who Write offices while speaking through his Bluetooth, leaving a message for Landon. "Hey, it's me again. I know we're scheduled to talk before the shindig tomorrow night, but if you're around, I'd like to touch base before we get to town. Call me." He ended the call, grabbed the gifts he'd bought for Aubrey, and headed into the building to surprise her. He hadn't told her his meeting had been canceled at the last minute and he'd caught an earlier flight.

His pulse raced as he rode the elevator up to her office. When he stepped off, the receptionist smiled and he held a finger in front of his lips as he approached the desk, silencing her just in case Aubrey was nearby.

He leaned on the desk and said, "I want to surprise Aubrey. Is she around?"

"Yes, Mr. Bentley. Should I tell Becca you're heading back?"

"No, thank you. I can handle Becca."

He headed for Aubrey's office, hoping she didn't have any meetings planned for the rest of the afternoon. He wanted nothing more than to steal her away for an evening alone before spending the weekend bombarded with family and two hundred of his parents' associates.

Becca wasn't at her desk. As Knox neared Aubrey's office he heard her and Becca talking. His drew in a deep breath, telling himself to calm the hell down, and stepped into the doorway. "Knock, knock, beautiful."

"Knox!" Aubrey shot to her feet, looking sexy in a tight black skirt and low-cut blouse.

"Hey, handsome," Becca said as she sauntered toward the door. "I'm pretty sure it's not good boyfriend etiquette to call me *beautiful* in front of your lady, but..." She nudged him farther into the office and said, "I'll just close this for you on my way out."

As she pulled the door closed, Aubrey raced across the room in her sky-high heels and leaped into his arms. "You're early!" *Kiss, kiss.* "You ruined your surprise." *Kiss, kiss.*

"Want me to leave?" he asked, his words getting lost in another kiss.

"No! Lock the door!"

He reached behind him and locked the door, and Aubrey took his hand, dragging him toward a door behind her desk.

"Where are we going? I brought you a present."

"You're my present," she said as she led him into another room with a couch and a coffee table and closed the door behind them. "This is my dressing room. There's a bathroom through there." She pointed to another door on the far wall.

"God, I missed you."

He dropped the gift bag and reached for her, pouring all his pent-up passion into their hungry kisses. They tore at each other's clothes, sending their shirts flying through the air. His pants puddled at his feet, and he ground out, "Can't wait!"

He hoisted her skirt up, grabbed her panties between his fists, and tore them in half. They sailed to the floor as he lifted her into his arms and lowered her onto his throbbing cock.

"Oh God, *yes*—"

Her words were muffled by the urgent crush of his lips as he pounded into her. He held her ass, helping her move in sync to his efforts. Her nails dug into his shoulders, her slick sex tightened around him, drawing his release closer to the surface.

"Don't stop," she pleaded.

"Never."

He sank his teeth into her neck and teased her bottom,

knowing just how to make her lose her mind. She cried out, and their mouths slammed together as they surrendered to their passion, and he followed her over the edge, loving her through his own spectacular release. He leaned back against the door, holding her as their bodies jerked with aftershocks. She rested her cheek on his shoulder, and he kissed her softly, both of them breathing heavily.

"I didn't expect that," he confessed.

"Everything about us is unexpected." She nuzzled against his neck and whispered, "I missed you."

"Yeah, this was tougher than when I was in Belize. *Crazy.*" He felt her smile against his neck and said, "The best kind of crazy there is."

Sometime later, after their hearts stopped hammering and their legs were no longer numb, they got cleaned up, righted their clothes, and he gathered her in his arms, kissing her slowly and sensually, savoring every second.

"Let's try this again," he said softly. "Hi, beautiful. I brought you a present, but what was that you said about ruining a surprise? Because trust me, you surprised the hell out of me."

Her lips curved up in the sweetest smile, sending his heart into palpitations again. Damn, he loved her.

"I was going to leave early and make you dinner."

"Look at you, going all domestic." He kissed her again and said, "I'd say I'm sorry for showing up early, but I'm not. I look forward to eating a home-cooked meal from my favorite girl. Now it's my turn." He reached into the bag and handed her the gift box. "Happy Valentine's Day, sweetheart."

"You didn't need to buy me a gift."

"I had it made just for you."

She slid the pink ribbons off and lifted the lid, smiling at the football jersey with BENTLEY printed across the back. Her eyes darted up to his. She went up on her toes and kissed him. "My favorite team. Thank you."

"I can't have you wearing some other dude's jersey on game days."

"You are so possessive." She ran her fingers over the jersey and said, "I like that about you, but only because I'm the same way. Only your jersey would say *Taken by Aubrey Stewart*, because I want those ogling bitches to know how lucky I am."

"God, I adore you." He pulled her closer, kissing her deeply.

She took the jersey out of the box and her real gift tumbled out. "Oh!" She bent to retrieve the small gift box, eyeing him as she rose to her feet. "What have you done?" She opened the gift, and the breath rushed from her lungs. "Oh, Knox...This is gorgeous."

He lifted the diamond bracelet with a gold heart-shaped lock charm from the box and hooked it around her wrist. "You deserve the world, Wattsy, and I'm going to make sure you get it. But first..." He reached into his pocket and handed her another small box.

"Knox. You've given me so much already."

"That's for you to give me, because I'm a selfish dude like that."

She laughed and said, "Oh, okay. Knoxy boy, this is for you. I hope you love it."

"Oh, I will." He opened the box and held up a silver necklace with a key hanging from it. "You just gave me the key to your heart. Now you're stuck with me."

As he lowered his lips to hers she whispered, "You never needed a key. You've had my heart all along."

Chapter Seventeen

BY LATE SATURDAY afternoon the inn was bustling with preparations for the evening's party. Guests arrived throughout the day in limousines and expensive sedans, vying for face time with the two *discreet* society-page photographers, the only media allowed to attend. Aubrey was used to black-tie affairs, but now she understood the difference between the events she'd attended and Knox's parents' ball. The air of entitlement and importance filling the inn was more oppressive than the norm and vastly different from the serenity of Aubrey's first visit to the Monroe House.

She hadn't expected to see his parents before the event, assuming they would be busy with preparations and visitors, but they'd surprised her and Knox by greeting them at the doors with warm embraces and genuine, heartfelt appreciation. Aubrey and Paige had been texting all morning, excited to see each other again and attend the fabulous event. Aubrey assumed it was Paige who had tipped her parents off to her and Knox's time of arrival—and she loved Paige even more for it. Seeing Knox and his parents making strides toward being a true family made Aubrey all kinds of happy.

Lately, *happy* had taken on a new meaning for Aubrey. She

glanced at Knox in the bathroom mirror in their luxurious suite as they got ready for the party and thought, *That's all because of you*. Before Knox had inserted himself into her daily life, she thought being one of the world's most successful female business owners and all that entailed had given her happiness. Now she realized there were many types of happiness. There was the sense of accomplishment and pride she took from her LWW success and then there was the happiness she enjoyed from being with her family and friends. But she hadn't allowed herself to explore this other thing she'd tried so hard to ignore, when she'd unknowingly tried to fill her undiscovered emptiness with work. When she'd forced herself to believe the feelings she'd been tamping down and the man who earned them could only lead to unnecessary drama.

She watched Knox's big fingers fumbling with the tiny buttons on his tuxedo shirt, his bow tie loose around the collar.

He looked into the mirror, catching her staring, and said, "What?"

Everything, was on the tip of her tongue. So were the three words she'd been holding back. She stepped closer in her heels and glittery silver flapper dress and gently moved his hands so she could do the buttons for him. She'd always known she was into Knox in a *big* way, but what she felt for him now obliterated every definition of the word *big*. She glanced at her beautiful bracelet shimmering in the bright lights and then at the silver key hanging around his neck. Knox wasn't the type of man to which a woman could just blurt out *I love you*. It was too important of a confession, and simply saying what she felt wasn't enough. She wanted to *show* him in a way that would let him know he was as special to her as he made her feel to him. She wanted to do something that he would know she'd *never* do for anyone else.

"Did I mention how hot you look tonight?" he asked in a low voice, his hand resting on the curve of her hip.

"Only five times, but who's counting?"

"Well, it's true. Thank God you're my date, because if you weren't I'd have to steal you away from whoever you were here with, and that would just be embarrassing for that dude."

"That *fictional* dude," she reminded him. "Were you always this cocky?"

"You say cocky; I say charming." He pressed his hand over hers and said, "Thank you for making me come to this party. It was the right thing to do."

She smiled, glad he felt that way, too. "I'm glad we're here."

"Do you still want to talk to Landon before the party?"

She'd gotten so lost in her thoughts, she'd almost forgotten she'd mentioned wanting to speak with his brother. She did want to speak with him to give him her best sales pitch, to ease his worries about the media, and have a chance to overcome any other objections he might have. That conversation should be the most important thing on her plate today. But it no longer was.

"Actually," she said as an idea came to her, "I want to talk to Landon, but I just remembered something else I need to take care of first. I need to find Paige."

She finished buttoning his shirt and grabbed her headpiece. She rushed out of the bathroom hurriedly placing the ornate silver headband with leaf and pearl accents atop the professionally styled finger waves she'd had done earlier with Paige at the inn's salon.

He followed her through the bedroom. "I'll come with you. We have about an hour, and I was hoping to talk with you about something before the party."

"No!" she said, reaching for the door. "I need to do this alone. It's a girl thing. I'll meet you downstairs before the party and we can talk then." Her heart raced as she pulled open the door, took one last look at the man who had conquered her heart, and knew in that moment that nothing she'd ever done in her life was as important as what she was about to do. More determined than ever, she stepped into the hall and took off running for the stairs.

A couple came out of a neighboring suite, and Aubrey slowed to a fast walk as she passed. She descended the stairs and navigated through the crowded lobby and busy restaurant, trying to act like her heart wasn't slamming inside her chest. She pushed through the kitchen doors, hit with the shock of seeing three times as many people as the last time she'd been there working at various stations. Every surface was covered with food and utensils, as the white-coated staff prepared for the party. Steam rose from the stoves; dishes were set into ovens and pushed across counters. And there she stood, frozen like a mannequin, wondering what the heck she'd been thinking.

"Coming through," a man carrying a large tray of dishes said as he came through the doors and pushed past her.

Her heart took a nosedive, her romantic plans squashed.

Maybe she could borrow a car and see if Joyce could help her. That would take even more time, and she barely had enough as it was. Knox had done so much for her. Everything he said and did showed her his true feelings. Now it was *his* turn, and she'd be damned if a busy night would stop her from showing him exactly what he meant to her.

She squared her shoulders, scanning the room for Clyde. Her eyes locked on the big man, barking orders to the people around him like a military commander coordinating a mission, precise and confident. She closed the distance between them and waited for him to finish.

"Excuse me, Clyde?"

He smiled as if he weren't doing a million things at once and said, "Aubrey, you look lovely. How are you?"

"Fine, thank you. I'm sorry to bother you, but I need a big favor." She followed him as he headed across the kitchen to two women who were chopping vegetables and waited while he gave more orders.

On the move again, he said, "A favor?"

"Yes. I need a place to bake something. Just a corner of a counter, or a chair, or a cardboard box where I can set the bowls down as I mix the ingredients. Heck, I'll do it on the floor if I need to, *please*."

He chuckled. "There will be no *floor* cooking in my kitchen. Come." He walked around three men who were cutting meat to the counter behind them and began shifting dishes. "Stephen, clear this area, please. Thank you."

The tall, slender man he'd spoken to said, "Yes, sir," and helped him clear the area.

"Thank you. Thank you so much. I…um…" *God, this is so embarrassing.* "May I please borrow a phone for just a few minutes, a piece of paper, and pen or a pencil?"

Clyde's thick brows rose in amusement. "Of course." He nodded toward the far wall, on which hung a phone, and beside it, a clipboard with a pen dangling from a tether.

She threw her arms around his neck and said, "Thank you!"

As Clyde went back to preparing for a scrumptious night, Aubrey retrieved the clipboard and made her call. "Mom? I need Grandma's love cookie recipe, fast, please."

"EXCUSE ME," KNOX said as he moved between two couples, making his way out of the hallway that led to the executive offices and toward the ballroom in search of Landon. He wanted to talk with him before Aubrey got to him. He'd tried to text him, but his text had gone unanswered. He should have known his oh so perfect brother wouldn't think of carrying a phone to an event such as this.

"There you are!" Paige said as she emerged from the crowd. She touched Knox's arm and said, "You sure do clean up well, big brother."

His gaze swept down her floor-length beaded lavender-gray gown with capped sleeves and a neckline that plunged nearly to her belly button. "Not quite as well as you do. You look stunning, but why don't you go put something on under the top of that dress."

"Not a chance. This is pure Gatsby style." She looked around and said, "Where's Aubrey?"

"I thought she was with you."

Paige shook her head. "I haven't seen her since we got our hair done."

"She said she needed to find you to do *girl things*."

"I was down at the house for a while. Maybe she looked for me then? Want me to help you look for her?"

"It's okay. I'll find her. Have you seen Landon?"

"Mm-hm. He and Dad were in the hall by the side entrance to the ballroom a few minutes ago."

Her gaze slipped over Knox's shoulder, lighting up like she'd seen Zac Efron or Duncan Raz. He turned just in time to see a bearded, bespectacled photographer's lips curve up in an interested smile aimed directly at his sister. Knox ground his teeth together, wishing Paige would cover herself up. Would he ever get used to his baby sister being an adult woman?

The photographer stepped beside Paige and put a hand on her lower back. His light brown hair was cut close on the sides, longer on top, and slicked back in a trendy style. He wore a crisp white shirt, a gray-pinstriped vest, slacks, and a dark purple bow tie. Were those tattoos peeking out from beneath his collar?

"Hello, beautiful," the photographer said.

"Oh, Hawk." Paige blushed. "Have you met my brother Knox? Knox, this is Hawk Pennington."

"Nice to meet you." Knox offered a hand and was met with a firm handshake.

"May I take a photograph of the two of you?" Hawk asked.

"Yes, please." Paige moved beside Knox, smiling as Hawk took several pictures.

"Thank you," he said to Paige, holding her gaze a little too long. "Enjoy the party," he said to Knox. Then his gaze shifted to Paige again, and he said, "Maybe I'll see you later?" earning another blush that made Knox's blood simmer.

Paige sighed as the guy walked away.

"A little *informal*, isn't he?" Knox said quietly.

"Shut it, Knox," she said sternly. "He's an incredible photographer. We were lucky to get him."

"Let's just hope he keeps his eyes behind that lens and his hands on the camera."

She rolled her eyes. "Don't you have a girlfriend to track down?"

He motioned with two fingers from his eyes to hers, silently letting her know he was watching her, and then he went in search of Aubrey and Landon, who he hoped were not together. He found Landon and their father talking in hushed voices exactly where Paige had said she'd seen them. The hair on the back of Knox's neck prickled. They were both standing pin straight, a habit they shared when trying to gain the upper hand. He hoped to hell they weren't having an argument.

"Landon, Dad," he said as he approached.

Both men said "Knox" at the same time.

Landon looked from Knox to his father, a slow grin spreading across his face. "Well, it looks like now we know which one of us is more like our father."

Knox glanced at their father. It took a moment for him to realize Landon was referencing their clothing. Landon wore a white tuxedo jacket, black slacks, and a black bow tie, while Knox and his father had gone for classic black jacket with satin lapels, black slacks, and matching bow ties.

"We just don't have as much style as you do," Knox said. "Bold move, the white jacket."

"This is classic Gatsby." Landon swiped a hand down the front of his jacket.

"Funny," their father said with a small smile. "I always thought Knox was the louder of you two, but perhaps I've had you boys wrong all this time. If you'll excuse me, the party is starting shortly. I need to find your mother."

Music filtered out of the side doors to the ballroom, and Knox noticed more people gathering around the tables and dance floor. He brought his attention back to his brother, who was watching their father walk away, and said, "You look sharp, Landon."

"Thanks. You too," Landon said, looking past Knox at the

empty hall.

Knox stepped into his line of sight. "Want to tell me why you've been avoiding my calls?"

"I don't need another one of your armchair-therapist diatribes, okay?" Landon started down the hall.

Knox grabbed his arm, stopping him. "How about an easy conversation, brother to brother?"

"We don't seem capable of those," Landon said solemnly.

"We're more than capable. You've been dodging more than *my* calls lately, haven't you?"

Landon's jaw clenched. "Leave it alone, Knox."

"No. I won't this time. I love you too damn much to watch you go down this road. You're making shitty business decisions because you're still in love with Carlos."

Landon stepped closer, nostrils flaring. "You have no idea what decisions I'm making."

"Bullshit. You want to turn Aubrey's movie away because you're too stubborn and your ego is too fucking big to face the man you love and hear him out. It's easier to shut yourself off from the world. To pretend the inn doesn't need the exposure, when you know damn well it does." Landon's hands curled into fists, and he knew he'd struck the right nerve this time. "What else are you going to screw up, Landon? How much do you have to lose to see what's right in front of you?"

"You don't give a fuck about me, brother." Landon's tone was ice-cold steel. "You think you can change my mind about using the inn? Well, guess what. I made no bones about my decision. You've known I wouldn't allow it since you showed up with Aubrey two weeks ago, and just because you're sleeping with her will not change my mind."

A sharp gasp and a loud crash caused them both to spin

around. Knox's gut sank at the sight of Aubrey, frozen in the middle of the hallway, shards of china and food at her feet. She turned and rushed away.

"Goddamn it, Landon."

"I'm sorry," his brother pleaded. "I never meant for—"

Knox got right in his face, speaking through gritted teeth. "None of this was about the inn, you idiot."

"Landon?"

Knox swallowed hard, recognizing Carlos Ruiz's accent.

"Carlos...?" Landon said to the handsome dark-haired man standing at the side entrance to the ballroom wearing his heart on the sleeve of his royal-blue tuxedo.

"I've been trying to open your eyes to the huge-ass personal mistake you're making," Knox said as quickly and evenly as he could, when he really wanted to haul ass down that hall after Aubrey. "But you've been so damn wrapped up in protecting your delicate ego, so intent on *sharing* your misery, you went right for the throat, hurting the only woman I've ever cared about. You want to keep fucking yourself up, go right ahead. I already planned on telling Aubrey the inn wasn't an option."

Chapter Eighteen

AUBREY FLEW INTO her suite in a fit of rage, eyes stinging, heart racing, as Landon's words blazed in her mind. *You've known I wouldn't allow it since you showed up with Aubrey two weeks ago, and just because you're sleeping with her will not change my mind.* Knox had known the entire time that she couldn't use the inn. If that hadn't crushed her, then Landon's accusation would have.

The door to the suite opened and Knox barreled in. "Aubrey—"

"Don't even come near me," she seethed.

He stepped closer. "Let me explain. Please, baby."

She held up her hands, shaking her head. "You knew this whole time he wouldn't let me use the inn. You lied to me! You cost me two weeks when I could have been looking at other inns!"

"I never lied," he said anxiously. "I told you it would take finesse and that was true. There's a lot more to all of this than you know."

She crossed her arms, so angry and hurt she could barely breathe. "I know that never in my entire professional career have I used my body to gain a single thing, and in two weeks' time you managed to make it look as if I were trying to do just that. To use sleeping with you to get the inn."

"Goddamn it, Aubrey." His voice escalated. "You know I'd never do anything like that on purpose."

"I'm mortified! And what's worse is that I trusted you, Knox. I trusted you with my business, and more importantly, with my heart."

"Baby, please…"

He took another step closer, and she turned her back to him, needing the distance because she hurt so much she couldn't stand it.

"Aubrey, Landon said what he did because I pushed him to the limit, not because he thought it was true. When he realized you heard him, he apologized. I could see the shame in his eyes for saying it."

"He should be ashamed." She turned around, breathing hard, and said, "But you're good at pushing until you get what you want, aren't you? I told you I didn't want drama in my life and you're fighting with your family? Lying to me?"

"*Not* lying."

She glowered.

"Please just let me explain. It's true that Landon told me he wouldn't let you use the inn, but I really thought I could change his mind, and not just because I'm pushy. Aubrey, Landon had a relationship with Carlos Ruiz. All that media hype you heard about was because the press got wind of their relationship."

"Nice try, but Carlos isn't gay. Please don't try to make this okay by telling more lies."

"I'd never do that! Just let me finish. Hear me out." He told her everything—how Landon had broken down in his office, about the pictures and Carlos paying off the media, and how he'd known Landon was still in love with Carlos.

"Great." She threw her hands up in the air and leaned back against the wall. "Your brother's life was falling apart and you pushed him to the edge. No wonder he was so upset."

"I wanted to *help* him, and yes, I wanted to get this inn for your movie. There's nothing I wouldn't do for you. I never pull favors from my family, but don't you see? For you I'd risk everything. I want to give you the world, and you can hate me for the way I tried to show that, but at least hear what I'm telling you. Know that I never outright lied to you. I fully believed with all my heart that Landon would come around. And this week? When I went to California? I went to talk to Carlos."

Her brows knitted, and she shook her head. "Did Landon know?"

"No. I was so torn, wanting the inn for you but not wanting to screw him over. He loves Carlos. That much was clear. And when I realized he'd been ignoring all those calls at dinner, I put two and two together and knew Carlos was still reaching out. So I took a risk. I headed to California to see if I could make some sense of things. It turns out that Carlos had not only reached out, but he'd been leaving Landon messages pleading for a reconciliation for weeks. Carlos confirmed everything Landon had told me, but he said he'd been calling Landon ever since the engagement article was published. He *knew* he'd done the wrong thing. He's here. Downstairs. He's ready to come out to the world for Landon, if Landon will take him back."

"That's great for them, but it doesn't help me trust you."

"I know. I fucked up, Aubrey. I didn't lie, but I should have told you what we were up against. At the time I didn't think it was my story to tell. Landon said he didn't want anyone to know about him and Carlos. I didn't know how to handle it, except that I wanted him to stop hurting. I love *you*, Aubrey, and I want a life with *you*. I know now that my allegiance should have been to you. I should have protected you by telling you the truth, and instead I was protecting my brother, who will probably never appreciate that I tried to help. I wanted to tell you the inn wasn't an option before the party. When we were in the bathroom getting ready and you were looking at me like I was everything you ever wanted…"

His apologetic eyes tore at her heart. "You were," she said shakily.

"I *am*, Wattsy. I still am."

"I have to be able to trust you."

"You can, baby. Everyone messes up sometimes. When you were looking at me like that, I realized I had to let you down and let go of the hope of securing the inn for the movie. I wanted to tell you right that second, to explain everything that had gone on, but then you rushed out, and I didn't have a chance."

"That's why you offered to come with me and said you wanted to talk to me before the party." She'd been in such a hurry, she hadn't even given a thought to what he wanted to talk about.

He nodded. "I went looking for you so I could explain all of this, but Paige said she hadn't seen you. Then I thought you went to see Landon, so I found him, and it all came to a head."

She looked down, remembering the little white lie she'd told, and felt herself softening toward him. "I went to the kitchen, not to find Paige."

"I saw a shattered dish…?"

She pressed her lips together, struggling as she processed all that he'd said. Her eyes filled with tears. She looked up at the ceiling, blinking them away, and said, "I made you cookies."

"Cook—" His lips curved up in a tentative smile. "*Love* cookies?"

She rolled her eyes and then swiped at them.

He stepped closer again, and she said, "I'm still mad."

"I know," he said, taking her hands in his. "You have every right to be. I'm new at all of this, but I'll never do something stupid like that again."

"Yes, you will. You can't help it."

"I *can* help it," he said too quickly.

She shook her head. "You can't. You're a fixer, and you don't care about drama. You just follow your stupid heart."

"I do. You're right. But that doesn't mean I won't try harder."

"If this is going to work, we need ground rules," she said as firmly as she could.

"You name them. I'll try to follow them."

"No more mixing business and pleasure."

"No more mixing business and pleasure." He pulled her close, his lips a whisper from hers, and said, "Which is a shame, because I really enjoyed mixing the two in your dressing room yesterday."

She felt herself smiling and tried unsuccessfully to school her expression. "Okay, that kind of pleasure is fine."

"What else?"

"Up-front honesty, all the time, even if you think you can finesse something to change it. And I don't want to argue about what constitutes a lie. Just be straight with me."

"Done. What if I want to surprise you with something?"

"Obviously that's fine, but, Knox, we have to be careful not to hurt each other. Relationships are new for both of us."

"Speak for yourself. I've been in a monogamous relationship with you for two years. That's not new."

She laughed softly. "You know what I mean. Things like this will come up, and we have to be able to navigate them together. To count on each other to do the right thing."

"I agree. Starting now." He brushed his lips over hers and said, "Aubrey, my love, I can't lie, I won't omit, so I have to say what's on my mind. I love you with all my heart, Aubrey Stewart, and I'm not perfect. I'm stubborn, and Landon isn't wrong when he says I bully my way through life, even though I see it differently. If you give me a chance, I give you my word that I will try to do everything I can to be the man you deserve."

"Do you need a deadline?" she teased, feeling the knots in her chest loosen.

He kissed her smiling lips and said, "Not this time. It's going to be my goal every day for the rest of my life."

"You really hurt me," she said again. "If I were a guy, I would have decked you."

"If you were a guy, you'd probably be dating Landon, not me."

She laughed.

"Can we talk about the cookies that are spread all over the hallway downstairs?" He kissed the edge of her mouth and whispered, "The *love* cookies?" He pressed a kiss to the other side of her mouth and said, "The ones you said you'd only make for your one true love?" He brushed his lips over hers and said, "You love me, Wattsy."

"*God...*" she said in one long breath, her love for him filling her up inside. "I must be crazy..."

"I can't hear you." He cupped his hand around his ear.

Tears sprang to her eyes as she said, "I wanted this moment to be perfect."

He gazed into her eyes and whispered, "This is perfect, sweetheart. We just survived our first real fight, and it was a doozy. It took us two years to get to this point. The way I figure it, we've got another two years to learn how to deal with things better. Who knows, hundreds of cookies and lots of effort and maybe we can avoid another one of these heart-wrenching blowouts."

"For a minute there I thought you were building up to something about makeup sex."

He waggled his brows, and she shook her head.

"We have to attend the ball. I promised your family." She put her arms around his neck, searching the eyes of the man she couldn't help but love, and said, "Thank you for trying to get the inn for me and for trying to help Landon. I appreciate you explaining what happened even though I was so upset. But most of all, I'm really glad you're willing to work together to learn how to keep these misunderstandings from happening, because I don't want anyone but you, Knox, and I haven't for a very long time."

"That's good, because you already gave me the key to your heart. Finders keepers."

"God, I love you," she said. "I really do, so kiss me like you have all the time in the world and you never want to let me go."

As he lowered his lips to hers, he said, "I will, and I won't, and we're *definitely* going to be late for the ball."

Epilogue

THERE WAS NO place quite as beautiful as the Colorado Mountains in June, and with the recent renovations Beau had done, the Sterling House had never looked prettier. Standing regally against the backdrop of mountain peaks, flowering meadows, and tall, stately trees, Charlotte's family inn was the perfect setting for her fairy-tale wedding. Beau had gone all out, hanging hundreds of fancy candle lanterns from trees and building a wedding tent that brought the enchanted forest indoors for his beautiful bride. Miles of white silk were draped over an artfully built frame of tangled branches and decorated with tiny white lights and strings of faux pearls. In the center, hanging from an ornate iron tree, was a crystal chandelier with pink lights. It was an intimate setting for a large, close-knit crowd, with tables draped in white, flowers spilling out of lush centerpieces, and their family and friends arriving to celebrate their big day.

If only Charlotte would stop crying.

"You're my maid of honor," Charlotte cried to Aubrey. She sat in the dressing tent, her knees together, the skirt of her gorgeous gown puffing up around her. Her dark hair was loose and wavy, the way Beau loved it, with a simple headpiece made of flowers around the crown. She looked tiny surrounded by so much tulle, her big wet eyes blinking away tears. "Shouldn't you have told me to have a *fake* wedding first, so I could get all these tears out?" Before Aubrey could respond, she looked at Libby, Presley, and Beau's sister, Jillian, who was one of her bridesmaids, and said, "Couldn't *anyone* have warned me how I'd feel today?"

The girls all answered at once.

"These are happy tears, Char," Aubrey reminded her. "It's totally fine to be happy!"

Libby knelt beside her. "Every bride cries. It's to be expected."

Presley handed her a homemade candy bar from a silver tray. "Eat this. It'll help."

One of Beau and Charlotte's friends who owned a chocolate shop in Allure, Colorado, had made an array of chocolates for the wedding, including homemade Twix bars, Charlotte's favorites.

"I love you!" Charlotte tore open the candy and chomped into it. "I can't stumble down the aisle with a *red* nose."

"You *won't*," Jillian reassured her. "We'll fix your makeup, and you'll look like a princess. The truth is, even if your nose was red and your eyes were puffy, Beau is so head over heels in love with you, he'd still lose his mind. But if you get chocolate on that gown, I might give you a black eye."

Jillian and her twin brother, Jax, both fashion designers, had taken elements from Charlotte's mother's and grandmother's wedding gowns and created an ice-blue Cinderella-type gown for Charlotte. The corset was sheer with embroidered ivory appliqués, shimmering light-blue sparkles, and off-the-shoulder lace. The multilayered tulle skirt had embroidered French lace trim along the hemline. She really did look like a princess.

Charlotte saluted and then shoved the rest of the bar into her mouth.

"Look at me," Aubrey said, trying to gain control and refocus Charlotte's emotions. When Charlotte lifted her chin, Aubrey dabbed at her tears with a tissue. "I know all your dreams are finally coming true, and yes, you're going to cry from sheer happiness. But isn't that what fairy tales are made of? Emotions that are bigger than life?"

Charlotte nodded with a mouthful of chocolate. She put her hand out, and Presley handed her another homemade Twix bar.

Jillian groaned. "I'm going to die if you walk down the aisle with splotches of brown on your dress."

Charlotte smiled, and a piece of chocolate fell from her lips right onto the skirt. All the girls yelled, "No!"

"Nobody move," Jillian said, arms outstretched, guarding the skirt. "Get me tweezers from the makeup bag."

Libby hurried away and returned with tweezers.

Jillian pointed the tiny metal prongs at Charlotte and said, "Don't even breathe."

"This is serious shit," Presley whispered.

"Shh!" Jillian carefully plucked the offending candy from the skirt. Then she leaned closer, her deep burgundy hair curtaining her face as she inspected the dress for evidence of their mishap. Her hand shot out to the side and she said, "Towel, please."

Presley pressed a towel into her hand, and Jillian spread it over Charlotte's lap. Then she rose to her full height of *petite pixie* and said, "Swallow what's in your mouth, and then no more food for you until after you say *I do*. Got it?"

Charlotte nodded, her amused eyes swept over them, and

they all burst into hysterics. Charlotte popped up to her feet and said, "Okay, I think I'm done with happy tears."

"Seriously? Who are you?" Presley said. "*Sybil?*"

Charlotte twirled and said, "I'm the bride of the gorgeous, loving, incredibly-talented-in-bed Beau Braden!"

"Ew! He's my *brother*!" Jillian snapped, making them all laugh again.

"Remind me never to get married," Aubrey said as she sank into a chair. "This is way too much drama for me."

"Oh, please." Charlotte waved her hand. "You're living with Mr. Drama."

"Yeah," she said dreamily. "I can't deny that."

She and Knox had been living together for months, although it hadn't happened with a decision of moving in together. After the night of the ball, their lives simply blended together a little more each week, until they realized they'd been staying in Aubrey's house during the week and in Knox's loft on the weekends, which they usually spent knocking around the city. They had dinners with his family every few weeks and saw hers often. Things weren't perfect with Knox's parents, but they'd found a happy medium between socialite and parenthood, and their newfound warmth had bled into Landon and Knox's relationship, easing them all onto solid ground. Carlos had proposed to Landon and had come out to the public the weekend of the ball. Much to his surprise, most of his fans had embraced and supported them. There were a few loud-mouthed assholes that Knox had wanted to hunt down and kill, but Landon had talked some sense into him.

"You denied it for weeks," Presley reminded her. "'We're not shacking up. He's just staying over.'"

Aubrey grinned, unable to deny that, either.

Libby smoothed her dress and said, "I'm just glad you didn't end up moving to the city full-time. I would have missed you."

Knox and Aubrey spent a few evenings a month with Libby, Presley, and Nolan, and quite often Paige, Becca, and Taylor would join them. Paige had wrangled Becca and Taylor into joining her book club, and once a month they all took off to talk books, which Aubrey believed was code for girls-gone-wild time. She was glad Paige had found more close friends.

Grace Montgomery sauntered into the tent, looking gorgeous in a short navy dress, with her long dark hair pinned up in a pretty twist. "It's like an LWW reunion in here. I would grab Amber so you guys could do an LWW cheer, but she's too busy hogging Emma." Emily "Emma" Louise was Brindle and Trace's baby girl. Everyone called her Emma, except Trace, who insisted on calling her Emma Lou. "Are you ready? Beau said almost everyone is here, but guests are still arriving. I swear the Bradens have more cousins than I've ever seen in one place."

"I know!" Charlotte exclaimed. "And I love every single one of them. I'm so glad Hal Braden agreed to walk me down the aisle. He was so close to my parents, they'd want him to do it."

"If Beau lets him," Grace said. "Beau's brothers keep giving us looks like *hurry up before he bursts*! I'm afraid if you don't get started soon, the next screenplay I'll be writing will be about a groom who loses his mind waiting for his bride."

"I'd make that movie," Aubrey said. The details for Charlotte's movie had finally come together. Once the dust had settled, Landon had graciously offered for Aubrey to use the inn, but since they'd secured the replica of Snow White's cottage that Knox had found in Seattle she'd decided to go with the Brookstone and film everything on one coast. Besides, since

Carlos and Landon were going to be married at the Monroe House, she figured that would cause enough of a media ruckus.

Aubrey looked around the tent at the women who had been part of her life for so long, had helped her build an empire, and had loved her despite all her failings. As they gathered around Charlotte, fussing with her dress, hair, and makeup, Aubrey pushed open the flap of the tent, her eyes quickly finding her man, who stood at the far end of the yard with Beau and his brothers. Her heart beat faster, and she absently touched the bracelet he'd given her. She knew he had the key necklace beneath his dress shirt. He never took it off. She had never realized she wasn't living a full life, but her drama-prone man had changed all of that, and she couldn't imagine a life without Knox in it, drama and all...

"DUDE," GRAHAM SAID to Knox. "You haven't taken your eyes off that tent since the girls went in there to get ready."

Knox winked at his beautiful Aubrey, who was peeking out of the tent, and said, "Don't even pretend you and Morgyn didn't disappear into the inn supposedly in search of a bathroom and return looking like you'd been to heaven and back a *half hour* later."

"I don't think we were supposed to notice that," Beau said as he fidgeted with his jacket.

Knox and his brothers had been trying to distract him in an effort to take the edge off, but he was still looking at his watch every few minutes like an expectant father.

Or a husband-to-be.

That'll be me one day.

Graham looked at Morgyn, sitting with her sisters, who were all fawning over Brindle's baby. "Look at my beautiful wife. Do you blame me for stealing her away?"

"Not at all." Knox couldn't blame him any more than he could stop himself from imagining what his and Aubrey's babies would look like one day, as he'd been doing ever since he'd held little Emma.

Graham shook his head and said, "My Sunshine is the sweetest woman to walk this earth."

"Have you *met* my girl?" Beau laughed. "Char's the sweetest—"

"I'll let you two hash that one out. My Aubrey's got more spice than sugar," Knox admitted. "And I *like* her that way."

"Christ, are you fools mooning again?" Zev stepped between Beau and Knox. "What is it about dudes in relationships? They turn into chicks, looking all dreamy and shit."

Zev was the nomad of the Braden family, a long-haired— and from what Graham had said, emotionally tortured— treasure hunter. After the tragic death of Tory Raznick, Beau's girlfriend of a decade earlier, Zev had broken up with his long-term girlfriend, Carly Dylan, left town, and had never looked back.

"Hey, don't knock a happily ever after," Beau said.

Zev scoffed. "Not everyone's into fairy tales, right, Nick? Jax?"

"I'm definitely not into *fairy* tails," Nick said with a cocky grin. He was the biggest, gruffest of the Bradens, with bulbous muscles earned from years of ranching.

Jax laughed and ran his hand down the front of his suit coat. He was lean and fit, and though he designed wedding gowns for the rich and famous, he was as down to earth as the rest of the Bradens. "If you could look as good in a suit as I do, maybe you'd get more women."

"Hope we didn't miss the ceremony. This one got stuck in her shop," Cutter Long, a handsome, black-haired cowboy, and one of Charlotte's closest friends, said as he came around the corner with Carly Dylan, another of their friends. Both of them carried trays of chocolate desserts.

Carly stopped cold, eyes locked on Zev. "Zevy…"

"Carls…?" Zev looked like he'd seen a ghost. He glanced at the tray, and then his gaze slid to Cutter and his eyes narrowed.

Knox saw Graham's mother hurrying over to the tent where the girls were filing out and said, "Looks like it's time, Beau."

Cutter nudged Carly. "Come on, let's set these down."

Carly followed him toward a table, glancing over her shoulder at Zev, who looked like he was chewing on nails.

Graham leaned closer to Knox and said, "Looks like my brother's going to have a tough evening. Better get the alcohol ready."

"Uh-huh," Knox said absently, watching Aubrey walk across the lawn with the girls.

The guys were lining up to walk the girls down the aisle, and Beau was on his way to the altar. Knox should be finding a seat, but his legs were carrying him toward Aubrey. He didn't want to be the guy looking in from the outside, wishing he had what someone else did. He knew what he wanted, and she was standing right in front of him.

"Knox," Aubrey whispered. "You need to sit down. The wedding is starting."

"I will." He dropped to one knee, causing everyone to gasp.

"Knox! Get up," Aubrey whispered. "Please," she said, tears

welling in her eyes. "This is Beau and Char's wedding."

"I'm sorry, Char," he said with an unstoppable smile.

"Don't be," Charlotte said. "It's the magic of the inn!"

He was vaguely aware of the happy murmurs and *Oh my goshe*s sounding around them, but he was so in love with Aubrey, so wrapped up in the emotions glistening in her eyes, she was all he saw.

"I planned on doing this tonight, but we promised to clue each other in when something was going on. Here's your clue, baby." He took the gorgeous diamond ring from his pocket and said, "You came into my life like a dream, and I *never* want to wake up from it. I love you, Aubrey. Will you marry me?"

Tears streaked her cheeks as she nodded vehemently. He slipped the ring onto her finger, and as he rose to his feet she leaped into his arms and kissed him. Cheers rang out around them, and when their lips finally parted, she beamed at him from within his arms and said, "You have the worst timing, drama boy."

"You're going to be my wife, Wattsy. I'd say my timing is perfect."

Ready for more Bradens & Montgomerys?

I hope you have enjoyed getting to know the Bradens and Montgomerys. If you want to read more about Knox and Aubrey's friends, pick up EMBRACING HER HEART, the first book in the Bradens & Montgomerys series. If you've already read the previous books in the series, get ready to fall in love with Zev Braden and Carly Dylan in *Searching for Love*.

Zev Braden and Carly Dylan have known each other their whole lives. Their close-knit families were sure they were destined to marry—until a devastating tragedy struck, breaking the two lovers apart. Over the next decade Zev, a nomadic treasure hunter, rarely returned to his hometown, and Carly became a chocolatier, building a whole new life across the country. When a chance encounter brings them back into each other's lives, can they find the true love that once existed, or will shattered dreams and broken hearts prevail? Find out in Searching for Love, a deliciously sexy, funny, and emotional second-chance romance.

Have you met our Bayside Summers friends?

Fall in love at Bayside, where sandy beaches, good friends, and true love come together in the sweet small towns of Cape Cod.

Desiree is tricked into spending the summer on the Cape with her badass half sister and a misbehaving dog. What could possibly go wrong? Oh, and sparks fly every time Desiree sees her hunky, pushy neighbor, Rick Savage. Yeah, there's that…

New to the Love in Bloom series?

I hope you have enjoyed getting to know the Bradens and Montgomerys. If this is your first Love in Bloom book, you have many more love stories featuring loyal, sassy, and sexy heroes and heroines waiting for you. The Bradens & Montgomerys (Pleasant Hill – Oak Falls) is just one of the series in the Love in Bloom big-family romance collection. Each Love in Bloom book is written to be enjoyed as a stand-alone novel or as part of the larger series. There are no cliffhangers and no unresolved issues. Characters from each series make appearances in future books, so you never miss an engagement, wedding, or birth. You might enjoy my other series within the Love in Bloom big-family romance collection, starting with the very first Braden book, LOVERS AT HEART, REIMAGINED.

More Books By Melissa Foster

LOVE IN BLOOM SERIES

SNOW SISTERS
Sisters in Love
Sisters in Bloom
Sisters in White

THE BRADENS at Weston
Lovers at Heart, Reimagined
Destined for Love
Friendship on Fire
Sea of Love
Bursting with Love
Hearts at Play

THE BRADENS at Trusty
Taken by Love
Fated for Love
Romancing My Love
Flirting with Love
Dreaming of Love
Crashing into Love

THE BRADENS at Peaceful Harbor
Healed by Love
Surrender My Love
River of Love
Crushing on Love
Whisper of Love
Thrill of Love

THE BRADENS & MONTGOMERYS at Pleasant Hill – Oak Falls
Embracing Her Heart
Anything For Love
Trails of Love

Wild, Crazy Hearts
Making You Mine
Searching For Love

THE BRADEN NOVELLAS
Promise My Love
Our New Love
Daring Her Love
Story of Love
Love at Last
A Very Braden Christmas

THE REMINGTONS
Game of Love
Stroke of Love
Flames of Love
Slope of Love
Read, Write, Love
Touched by Love

SEASIDE SUMMERS
Seaside Dreams
Seaside Hearts
Seaside Sunsets
Seaside Secrets
Seaside Nights
Seaside Embrace
Seaside Lovers
Seaside Whispers
Seaside Serenade

BAYSIDE SUMMERS
Bayside Desires
Bayside Passions
Bayside Heat
Bayside Escape
Bayside Romance
Bayside Fantasies

THE RYDERS
Seized by Love
Claimed by Love
Chased by Love
Rescued by Love
Swept Into Love

THE WHISKEYS: DARK KNIGHTS AT PEACEFUL HARBOR
Tru Blue
Truly, Madly, Whiskey
Driving Whiskey Wild
Wicked Whiskey Love
Mad About Moon
Taming My Whiskey
The Gritty Truth

SUGAR LAKE
The Real Thing
Only for You
Love Like Ours
Finding My Girl

HARMONY POINTE
Call Her Mine
This is Love
She Loves Me

THE WICKEDS: DARK KNIGHTS AT BAYSIDE
A Little Bit Wicked
Wicked Aftermath

WILD BOYS AFTER DARK (Billionaires After Dark)
Logan
Heath
Jackson
Cooper

BAD BOYS AFTER DARK (Billionaires After Dark)
Mick
Dylan
Carson
Brett

HARBORSIDE NIGHTS SERIES
Includes characters from the Love in Bloom series
Catching Cassidy
Discovering Delilah
Tempting Tristan

More Books by Melissa
Chasing Amanda (mystery/suspense)
Come Back to Me (mystery/suspense)
Have No Shame (historical fiction/romance)
Love, Lies & Mystery (3-book bundle)
Megan's Way (literary fiction)
Traces of Kara (psychological thriller)
Where Petals Fall (suspense)

Acknowledgments

I had so much fun writing Knox and Aubrey's story and meeting their families. I fell hard for each and every one of them, and I am excited to write their siblings' love stories! No book is ever written in a vacuum. I am forever grateful to my behind-the-scenes team who keep me afloat and grounded at the same time. And I am inspired on a daily basis by my fans, many of whom are in my fan club on Facebook. If you haven't yet joined my fan club on Facebook, please do. We have a great time chatting about our hunky heroes and sassy heroines. You never know when you'll inspire a story or a character and end up in one of my books, as several fan club members have already discovered.

www.Facebook.com/groups/MelissaFosterFans

Remember to like and follow my Facebook fan page to stay abreast of what's going on in our fictional boyfriends' worlds.
www.Facebook.com/MelissaFosterAuthor

Sign up for my newsletter to keep up to date with new releases and special promotions and events and to receive an exclusive short story featuring Jack Remington and Savannah Braden.
www.MelissaFoster.com/Newsletter

And don't forget to download your free reader goodies! For free ebooks, family trees, publication schedules, series checklists, and more, please visit the special Reader Goodies page that I've set

up for you!
www.MelissaFoster.com/Reader-Goodies

As always, loads of gratitude to my amazing team of editors and proofreaders: Kristen Weber, Penina Lopez, Elaini Caruso, Juliette Hill, Marlene Engel, Lynn Mullan, and Justinn Harrison. And, of course, I am forever grateful to my family, who allow me to talk about my fictional worlds as if we live in them.

Meet Melissa

www.MelissaFoster.com

Melissa Foster is a *New York Times* and *USA Today* bestselling and award-winning author. Her books have been recommended by *USA Today's* book blog, *Hagerstown* magazine, *The Patriot*, and several other print venues. Melissa has painted and donated several murals to the Hospital for Sick Children in Washington, DC.

Visit Melissa on her website or chat with her on social media. Melissa enjoys discussing her books with book clubs and reader groups and welcomes an invitation to your event. Melissa's books are available through most online retailers in paperback, digital, and audio formats.